WINTER'S HARBOR

Visit us at www.boldstrokesbooks.com

WINTER'S HARBOR

by

Aurora Rey

2015

WINTER'S HARBOR
© 2015 BY AURORA REY. ALL RIGHTS RESERVED.

ISBN 13: 978-1-62639-498-8

THIS TRADE PAPERBACK ORIGINAL IS PUBLISHED BY
BOLD STROKES BOOKS, INC.
P.O. BOX 249
VALLEY FALLS, NY 12185

FIRST EDITION: NOVEMBER 2015

CREDITS
EDITOR: ASHLEY TILLMAN
PRODUCTION DESIGN: SUSAN RAMUNDO
COVER DESIGN BY G. S. PENDERGRAST

Acknowledgments

I am so grateful to everyone at Bold Strokes Books. It's an honor to be part of a company and collection of writers who nurture both the art and business of books. A thousand thanks to my editor, Ashley Bartlett, who manages to humor me and whip me into shape simultaneously. Finally, thank you to the friends and family who cheered, listened, and encouraged. I'm a lucky girl to have you in my life.

Dedication

For AMH, who makes everything seem possible.

Chapter One

Traffic was light on the Sagamore Bridge. As Lia made her way along Route 6, the flow of cars continued to thin. It was a far cry from the tangle of traffic that gripped Cape Cod for most of the summer. It was the sixth of November and she was on her way to Provincetown.

At first, the highway was nondescript. She drove past exit signs and through small towns. There were gas stations and self-storage facilities and grocery stores and housing developments. Once she hit Orleans, however, it began to change. Businesses for locals were replaced with gift shops and cafés advertising boxed lunches. Although they were all tucked away now, Lia could imagine the massive inner tubes and boogie boards piled against the buildings and affixed to the roofs. In addition to houses, clusters of cabins and cottages were visible from the road. A few had vacancy signs hung, but most announced that they were closed for the season.

The landscape itself also changed. The vegetation thinned and was dominated by what she thought of as scrub pines. They looked hardy, like they were accustomed to harsh winds and salt air. Along the shoulder of the road, sand replaced dirt and gravel. Although she couldn't yet see the ocean, she could sense it. Even with the windows up, it was in the air.

Lia crested the part of the highway that revealed the entire tip of the Cape spread out below. To her right were the rolling dunes of the National Seashore. To her left, Cape Cod Bay. The water was a steely gray, several shades darker than the overcast sky. The little beach cottages that lined the shore were still. Despite the handful of cars parked in driveways, there was no sign of human movement. In the far distance, the Pilgrim Monument marked the center of town.

Since traffic was virtually nonexistent, Lia opted to drive through town instead of around it. She didn't even take the split for Bradford Street, wanting instead to see what it was like to drive straight down Commercial. There were a few people walking along the sidewalks and a pair of middle aged men jogging in spandex pants and knit hats. Most of the galleries appeared closed, but the little East End gourmet market was open. A young guy was walking out with a canvas bag. She liked to think he was headed home with the makings of a romantic dinner.

The real estate agency she'd worked with to arrange the rental of her apartment was just a few blocks down. Lia pulled into a vacant parking spot directly in front of the office. She glanced in the mirror, decided she looked okay for having spent the last six hours in the car, then climbed out.

When she walked in, a set of bells on the door jingled cheerfully. It seemed a little early for Christmas decorations, then she realized it was less a festive statement and more a way to announce her presence. The reception desk was unoccupied. Just as she was about to call out a "hello," a woman emerged from one of the offices.

Lia guessed that she was middle aged, maybe a little older. Her silver hair was cut short and spiky. She wore a dark blue shirt, a pair of light khaki pants, and penny loafers polished to a high shine. Lia sighed. Gay people seemed to be the rule rather than the exception—one more reason to love Provincetown.

"Good afternoon. How can I help you?"

Lia found herself smiling. "I'm Lia—Cecilia—Brooks. I'm here to pick up the keys to an apartment I'm renting."

"Yes, hello. I'm Jan Stein, the one you've been emailing. I've got the keys and the paperwork in my office. Come on back."

There was a slight hesitation before Jan turned and led the way. Lia was pretty sure she was being sized up by the older woman. Did she look more frightful than she thought? Or was this woman trying to figure out what she was doing arriving in Provincetown after everyone else had gone? Or why she was alone?

She followed Jan into a small office decorated with photos of the monument taken at different times of day and from different angles. "Those are beautiful." Lia gestured to the wall.

Jan beamed. "Thank you. My son, Damien, took them. He's fifteen."

Lia smiled. Getting someone talking about their kids was the perfect way to divert attention from herself. "Wow. He's quite a talent. Does he sell them?"

The apartment she was renting came furnished, but it would be nice to add a few of her own touches. And since the majority of her possessions were in an apartment she no longer considered hers, she'd have to find some as she went.

"He did for the first time this summer. A friend of mine owns one of the galleries and took several dozen on consignment. Damien was beside himself."

"Very impressive. I'd love to buy a couple if there are any left."

"Oh, he's already started building inventory for next season. If you want to stop by tomorrow, I'll bring some in and you can take your pick. He does the lighthouse, too, and the harbor."

There was an openness, an ease of conversation, that made Lia feel at home. It helped her relax and made her feel like less of a curiosity. "That would be great. I'll come back in the morning."

"He'll be so excited. Now, your apartment. First month and security deposit are all set. Your lease is for six months. Rent is due by the third and you can drop off a check here or mail it to the office." Jan handed her a printed copy of the lease. "Any questions?"

Lia looked it over. It was the same document she'd signed and emailed to the agency the week before. "I don't think so. It all looks good to me."

"Excellent. So what brings you to Provincetown for the least touristy time of year?"

And there it was. In truth, she didn't mind questions. Part of what had soured her on New York was how detached she felt from any sense of community. She was open by nature and liked interacting with people on a more human level.

"I was looking to get away. Since I do my work remotely, I had my pick of places to go. Provincetown is always near the top of my list, and I'm looking forward to experiencing its quieter side."

Maybe her explanation sounded a little scripted, but it was true. She was looking to get away. Things with Dani had finally reached the breaking point and she was desperate for a change of scenery. There was no need to add the part about her being the dupe. Her friends told her she was crazy to move somewhere that essentially closed in on itself for winter, but that fact made it all the more enticing.

"I'm not sure 'quiet' does it justice, but we're happy to have you one way or the other. You'll need these."

Lia took the keys that Jan handed her. "Thank you so much."

If Jan wanted to ask more questions, she resisted, and Lia was grateful.

"It's a pleasure. Now, your entrance is on the left-hand side of the house, down the sidewalk. Your parking spot is the one on the far left. No one is in the other units now, but people will occasionally come and go."

"Perfect. I'm so looking forward to it."

Jan extended a hand and gave her a reassuring smile. "We're glad to have you. I do hope I see you tomorrow."

She shook Jan's hand and returned the smile. "Absolutely."

Lia walked out of the office and back to her car. It was only four in the afternoon, but the sun was already beginning to dip low in the sky. It would be dark within the hour. Although she didn't want to think of the next six months as a hibernation, there was something appealing about the idea of cocooning herself here. She could work and rest and revel in the quiet. She wouldn't think about traffic or subways or her ex getting frisky with some twenty-something coed. To the extent it was possible at this point in her life, Lia decided she would be happy in this tiny town completely out of the way to anywhere but itself.

She started her car and continued to make her way down Commercial Street. Since there was no one behind her, she drove slowly. She passed the Lobster Pot and Spiritus Pizza, the Marine Specialty and the town hall. It was reassuringly familiar, yet she had never seen the town so still. It could have been eerie, but she found it peaceful.

There were a few people on the street and most of them waved. She saw two older women in matching windbreakers, a younger guy who looked like he was on his way to a hot date. As she left the main commercial stretch, storefronts gave way to cedar-shingled houses with tidy yards and picket fences. Lia approached a woman jogging with a golden retriever. As she got closer, Lia couldn't stifle a small sigh of appreciation. She had short hair and broad shoulders. The dog matched her pace perfectly with no sign of a leash.

The woman lifted a hand in a friendly wave, which Lia returned with a smile. She glanced in her rearview mirror and watched as they turned a corner and disappeared from view. Although she couldn't imagine being with someone—physically or emotionally—anytime soon, it was reassuring to know that she still noticed, and enjoyed, a good-looking woman.

When Commercial Street turned sharply to the left, she continued straight onto Tremont. At Vine Street, she turned right and drove slowly until she found the house number for her unit. She turned into the parking spot assigned to her, cut the engine, and sat for a moment. For better or worse, and for at least the next six months, she was home.

CHAPTER TWO

In the winter, Alex closed the bakery at three. If she had one other person working, they could zip through the cleaning in under an hour. Today was one of those days. And since there was little more than a chill in the air, she got Murphy and they headed out for a run. In the off season, she didn't even bother with a leash.

They went a block up to Bradford Street and headed toward the West End. She preferred to run on the beach, but she only did so barefoot, so when the weather turned, she kept to the streets. She'd take Murphy down at some point so he could chase sticks, but that didn't make for much of a workout.

When they hit Vine, Alex turned to make the loop back up Commercial. There weren't many people out and about, so it was easy to wave to everyone she passed, most of whom were familiar faces. She loved that Provincetown became just another small New England town after Labor Day, and the feel of fall put her in a good mood. She looked down at Murphy, who was loping along happily with his tongue out. "Ready to go home? It's dinner time."

Mention of dinner seemed to quicken Murphy's pace. They ran the rest of the way at a near sprint, arriving home breathless and sweating. As promised, she put down his dinner before stripping off her running clothes. He crunched enthusiastically while she showered and was lounging contentedly by the time she was dressed and ready to leave.

"I won't be long. I'll tell your buddy Stuart you said hi."

Alex jogged down the stairs, double checked that the back door into the bakery was locked, and walked the short distance to the Squealing Pig. Once there, she found Stuart already at the bar. She sat down on one of the empty stools next to him. "I'm not that late, am I?"

"I haven't been here long." He gestured to the beer in front of him. "And I didn't bother waiting."

Alex nodded to the glass. "What are you having?"

"It's a red ale, not half bad."

Sam, the bartender, finished mixing a martini. He handed it to someone further down the bar, then walked to where they were sitting. "Hey, Alex. What's your pleasure?"

She tilted her head toward Stuart. "I'll have what he's having."

"Coming right up." Sam filled a glass from the draft and handed it to her. "Tab?"

Before she could respond, Stuart raised a hand. "Just put it on mine."

Sam nodded and moved away to take another order.

"Thanks, pal. I'll get the next round."

"It's on me. It's good to see you."

"Likewise." She lifted her glass. "To the off season."

Stuart tapped his glass to hers. "To the off season."

"How're Connie and the girls? I feel like I haven't seen them since school started." Stuart was the harbormaster in Provincetown, but he and his family lived in Truro.

"Maddie has decided she wants to play hockey, which of course means Beth wants to play hockey." Stuart's daughters were eleven and eight. With few exceptions, Beth wanted to be just like her older sister. Both looked like miniature versions of their mother, who had the striking dark features of her Portuguese ancestors. Stuart often joked that his blond hair and blue eyes didn't stand a chance in that gene pool.

Alex chuckled. "That sounds awesome and a little bit dangerous. How does Connie feel about it?"

"She's thrilled. I think her worst fear was having prissy little girls. I, on the other hand, think it's a terrible idea."

"Aw, come on, Stu. It'll be good for them."

"I know, but I can already see the broken arm or, worse, broken nose."

"Think of it this way. If they stick with it, you won't have to worry about any boys thinking they can mess with them."

"I suppose that's a silver lining."

"That's the spirit." She gestured to Sam for another round of beers, handing him a credit card to open a tab.

"So, what about you?"

"What about me?"

"Are you officially in a dry spell? No more flavors of the month until spring?" Stuart poked her with his elbow.

Alex made a face. "Well, I don't like to think of it as a dry spell, necessarily..."

"Who was the last one? She was a looker."

Alex scratched the back of her head. "Her name was Sabrina and she was a looker. She left in September when school started."

"She was a student?" Stuart's voice went up an octave, the way it always did when he was overly excited about something. It was obvious that he was both scandalized and intrigued by the idea.

"She was going back to school to get her teacher's certification. I'm not a cradle robber, you perv."

Stuart lifted his hands defensively. "I'm just saying she seemed young."

"She was my age." Alex huffed. "She just had the body of a twenty-two-year-old."

Stuart nodded appreciatively. He was madly in love with his wife, but his rapport with Alex included admiring beautiful women, including the ones she dated.

"Really, though, no one on the horizon?" Stuart asked.

Alex shrugged. Although she didn't like to think of it that way, winter was often a dry spell. Most of the women she dated came to town for the summer, or part of it. Most of them also sought her out. She enjoyed the company, among other things, but she rarely pursued women. Since she wasn't looking for anything serious, it seemed like the responsible thing to do. Usually, it worked. "No one on the horizon."

Stuart frowned. "Do you ever think about something more serious?"

They'd been friends for going on six years. In that time, he'd teased her plenty about dating vicariously through her, but every now and then he got earnest. He was big on family, and deep down, wanted her to find a nice girl and settle down. Alex found it endearing, mostly.

"Sure, of course I do. That doesn't mean it's going to just land in my lap."

"You mean the way your flings usually fall into your lap."

Alex considered. It was sort of how things worked in P-town. Much like the tourists, many of the residents were seasonal. Although gay men had the reputation for cruising, it wasn't uncommon for a pretty woman to appear for the season and indulge in a no-strings-attached summer tryst. "Well, yeah. It's not like I crave one-night stands, but that's what a lot of the women around here are after. I'm not going to force something just for the sake of having someone around."

He sighed. "There's probably something between forcing it and not even trying."

"At best, serious relationships suck all your energy. At worst, they practically kill you."

She thought that might earn a chuckle, but Stuart's frown only intensified. "I know you've had your heart broken, but I hate to think you'd miss out on the real thing because you weren't willing to take a risk."

Stuart was probably the only person, besides her sister maybe, who she felt comfortable confiding in. "You're right. I know you're right. But still. I'm not into long-distance relationships, and there aren't any local women I'm interested in. I'm not sure where that leaves me."

She looked over at Stuart. He was looking at her with a combination of affection and concern. Wanting to lighten the mood, she said, "Cut it out. You look like my dad."

Stuart smiled slightly. "Hey, now, I'm barely old enough to be your big brother."

They spent the next hour talking about the rookies for the New England Patriots, and agreed to get together on Sunday to watch the game. "Come to the house. Connie will make chili and the girls will be thrilled to show off their new hockey gear."

Alex agreed, and decided she was very much looking forward to a family kind of day. As they walked out of the bar, she found herself thinking that she was lucky to have Stuart. Although it was a somewhat unlikely friendship—straight family man and commitment-shy lesbian—it worked. "I'll see you this weekend. Four o'clock."

"Four o'clock. If you bring one of those chocolate torte thingies, I'll provide dinner and beer."

"Deal."

CHAPTER THREE

Lia looked through the windshield at her new home. The house was built in the late 1800s and had, at some point along the way, been divided into three condos. Before getting out of the car, she studied the front of the house. It looked just as it did in the photos she saw online—cedar shingles grayed from the salt air, white trim and shutters, postage stamp front porch.

She hauled one of her suitcases out of the back seat and made her way down the pea gravel path to the side entrance. Bracing the screen door open with her hip, she unlocked the main door and pushed it open. She stepped inside and put her suitcase down, felt along the wall for a light switch and flipped it on.

She found herself in the main living space of her apartment. The kitchen and living room were one open space. Open shelves in the kitchen revealed a pretty assortment of glassware and serving dishes, along with white plates, bowls, and mugs. Polished concrete counters flanked a gorgeous old farmhouse sink. In the living area, an oversized red sofa sat in front of a large window that overlooked the backyard. There was a flat-screen television sitting atop a shabby-chic dresser. Every other wall was lined with bookcases that were overflowing with books, which were old, new, and everything in between. At the far end of the room, an open staircase led to the single bedroom and bath.

Lia sighed. It was perfect.

She'd lucked out, considering how quickly she chose it. Although the decision to leave had been brewing for the better part of two months, deciding where to go, finding a place, and leaving came together in under forty-eight hours. She could admit that was her general way of doing things. She would mull over her options, weigh the pros and cons, and obsess about making the wrong decision for weeks, if not months. When she'd settled on something, though, she wasted no time putting it in motion.

When Lia discovered that Dani was having an affair—with her administrative assistant of all people—it was no different. At first, she was devastated, heartbroken. She'd never have said things between them were perfect, but Lia always felt like there were more good times than bad. She'd thought the feeling was mutual.

The more she thought about the affair, however, Lia found she was more mortified than heartbroken. She was embarrassed that she'd been duped, humiliated that the whole thing was such a cliché. It was paired with the nagging feeling that she'd been Dani's loyal lapdog. She'd followed Danielle and Danielle's career to New York. Danielle wanted an apartment on the Upper West Side and friends with weekend homes in the Hamptons, so that's what they had. Lia had convinced herself that she wanted those things as well, that their lifestyle was a big adventure compared to her small town upbringing.

She'd also considered herself to be intelligent and independent. In the end, she felt like a weak willed fool. She hated that most of all.

At first, she'd moved into the guest room. She told Dani she needed space, some time to sort out her feelings. Dani, ever reasonable and sure of herself, respected that choice. It was only after several weeks that she began to suspect Dani was merely waiting her out, waiting for her to see that their life together was more important than some indiscretion that had come between them. The realization made her angry, perhaps even angrier than the affair itself, and pushed her over the edge.

Lia went online and started researching her options. She wanted out of the city, that much she knew. Without much direction, she typed "short term lease gay" into the search engine and landed on a website called Home Away From Home, and an advertisement for vacation rentals in Provincetown. It was both different and familiar, and it was near the ocean. When she saw the price of a one-bedroom condo—a month for less than the price of a week in July—she looked no further.

She contacted the real estate company that managed the property, negotiating an additional ten percent off by signing a six-month lease. She sent the paperwork and paid her security deposit and first month's rent via PayPal before she told another soul about her plan. When Dani had come home that evening, she'd already started packing. She explained her plan, expecting Dani to put up a fight. Instead, Dani nodded soberly and agreed that, if Lia felt she needed a break, she would respect it. Lia was very explicit that her leaving was neither impulsive nor temporary, but she got the sense that Dani didn't entirely believe her. At that point, the last thing she wanted was another argument, so she didn't press the matter.

The next morning, Dani wished her safe travels and went to work. Lia stood in the living room for a good twenty minutes, wondering if she should try to get a storage space for her books and the other things from the apartment that were officially hers. Overwhelmed by the idea, she filled two boxes with her favorite books and photographs of her family. She loaded them, along with three suitcases and several duffel bags, into the trunk and back seat of her car. She pulled out of her overpriced parking spot in the building's basement garage, turned into traffic, and didn't look back.

Now here she was. The manic feeling that had buoyed her through the packing and the leaving, the driving and the arriving, was gone. She couldn't decide if she was unsure of her decision or, perhaps more likely, unsure of herself.

Lia hefted her suitcase up the narrow staircase to the bedroom on the second floor. For some reason, the fact that the apartment had two levels appealed to her. It was one of those things that she'd fixated on as a child, living in a sprawling 1950s ranch style house. It was a fixation that had not been alleviated by the two-thousand-square-foot Manhattan apartment Danielle had chosen for them. At the top of the stairs, the bedroom opened up through a door to her right and the bathroom, she surmised based on the tile floor, was to the left. She pulled the suitcase into the bedroom.

Lia nudged it into a corner, then flopped on the bed and looked around. Like the living room and kitchen, the bedroom had a definite Cape Cod feel without being overtly beachy. The walls were a bluish gray that was a shade darker than she would have been bold enough to choose. The quilt on the bed was mostly blues and grays, the curtains and the furniture white.

It felt homey and comfortable, neat without being spare. She could imagine herself in the bed with only the small lamp on the nightstand to illuminate the pages of her book. She could imagine waking up slowly, stretching and rolling around before starting the day. Although she had no sense of direction and couldn't begin to fathom whether the wide double window faced east or west or south or north, she imagined a certain amount of light would filter in when day broke. It was, in every way possible, exactly what she wanted—needed—right now.

Lia was surprised to realize that she'd begun to cry. For a moment, she sniffed, determined to pull herself together and focus on the positive. It occurred to her, though, that there was no one to see whether or not she put on a brave face. There was no one to feel sorry for her or to try and convince her that everything would work itself out in the end. There was no one, even, to tell her that tears were a waste of time.

So she let them fall. She curled up in the middle of the bed, hugged her knees to her chest, and sobbed. She sobbed until her eyes were puffy and she'd given herself a headache. When she stopped, the pale light of late afternoon had disappeared and she was completely in the dark. She stayed where she was and, for a moment, thought about not moving until morning.

Instead, she sat up and willed her eyes to adjust to the lack of light. Eventually, she could make out the outline of the furniture and the door. She made it to the light switch without tripping on anything and flipped on the overhead light. She winced at its brightness, then took a deep breath. She blew it out and took another. She realized just how long it had been since she'd really filled her lungs.

Whether it was the increased oxygen flow or the good long cry, she felt considerably better. Her eyes still burned, though, and her head throbbed. She unzipped the suitcase and dug around for her travel bag of toiletries. She stripped off her clothes and walked to the bathroom. When she flipped on the light, she let out an audible "ohhh."

Centered under a window was a gorgeous claw-foot tub. She set down her things and opened the door to the tiny linen closet. In addition to a big stack of towels, she found a nearly-full bottle of almond oil bubble bath. She lifted her eyes in a silent prayer of gratitude and began the process of drawing herself a bath.

An hour later, Lia pulled herself from the now tepid water. She toweled off and studied herself in the full-length mirror on the back of the bathroom door. Unlike a lot of her straight friends, she had never been terribly obsessed with her body. It wasn't perfect by any means, but she'd always thought the proportions were good. Now, however, knowing Danielle had chosen a petite and perfectly tanned twenty-four year old instead of her, she looked at herself with a more critical eye.

Her full breasts weren't as perky as they'd been when she was in her twenties. There were stretch marks on her abdomen and she had what her mama called chicken skin on her upper arms. Her thighs rubbed together when she walked. Lia lifted her breasts and let them fall, then poked her midsection. She flexed her biceps, did a couple of yoga poses. She frowned at the mirror, then smiled.

Fuck it. I already hate her. I'm not going to start hating myself on top of it.

She walked into the bedroom and checked the clock. It was 7:48. She contemplated putting on clothes and going in search of dinner, but decided the bed was far more appealing. She pulled on a pair of sweatpants and an old Smith T-shirt and crawled under the covers. She was asleep almost immediately.

Chapter Four

Alex hoisted the twenty-quart mixing bowl onto the table. She tipped it onto its side and coaxed the massive blob of dough onto the work surface. With a wide, stainless steel bench scraper, she began portioning off pieces of dough that would become loaves of seven grain bread. She didn't bother weighing them individually, but a scale would have shown each to be within an ounce of two pounds. Making bread for ten years had that effect on a person.

Once the dough was divided, she shaped each ball into a fat log and plopped them into the loaf pans she'd greased earlier. She slid the pans into the proof box and set the timer for ninety minutes. Her other timer buzzed, announcing that the sourdough bread in the oven was done. She pulled the pans and moved them to a cooling rack.

Production in the off season was very different. During the summer months, Alex kept a staff of fifteen, mostly culinary students looking to build their resumes while enjoying as much of summer as possible. Alex taught them a lot and paid them enough to enjoy their off hours. It was a win-win arrangement, and she'd developed relationships with some of the schools so that the quality of the interns outweighed the high turnover.

Winter, however, was a different story. She had Jeff, her full-time manager, and a part-time cook named Darcy. They both lived in town year-round and didn't mind transitioning to a wider variety of responsibilities when customer traffic dwindled. Between the three of them, they covered breakfast and lunch six days a week with no trouble. Alex also changed her baking routines. She experimented with recipes, with refrigerating and freezing dough, so that she could offer freshly-baked breads and pastries every day without the impractical task of making small batches of everything from scratch every day.

Today's schedule included multi-grain and sourdough, muffins, and brownies. She'd bake croissants that had been shaped earlier in the week and frozen, along with cookies. She would also whip up some individual bread puddings with the day-old bread. She'd be done by eleven and ready to assemble salads and sandwiches for the lunch crowd.

While she worked, Alex listened with one ear to the goings-on in the front of the bakery. Jeff was chatting with the regulars, flirting where flirting was welcome. She poked her head out now and again, once to give Jeff a break, but mostly to check the cases and say hello to some of her favorite customers. It was work she loved and she took pride in it.

When Darcy, her lunch cook, walked in at nine, Alex was surprised by how quickly the morning was passing. She raised a flour-covered hand in greeting and then repositioned herself in the small kitchen so that Darcy would have room to work. "Good morning, sunshine."

"Good morning, boss. How goes it?"

"It goes, it goes. What magic do you have in store for us today?" Hiring Darcy was one of her best decisions. Alex had given her some recipes as a starting point, but handed over most of the control over the lunch menu within a month of her starting.

"Well, it's Tuesday. That means French onion soup and crab and corn chowder. I thought I'd get crazy with the mac and cheese and do a pancetta and portobello mushroom."

"God, just hearing you say that makes my stomach growl. I look forward to conducting some quality control."

"I'll be sure you get first taste." She tucked her bag and coat into the cubby in the corner and donned an apron and the ball cap she wore to keep her hair back.

"Best perk of being in charge, for sure. How's Liam?" Alex had a soft spot for Darcy's son. He was a serious, intellectual sort—a particularly endearing personality for a six-year-old. He also had his mother's striking blue eyes and dark hair. Even if he stayed nerdy,

Alex was sure that the girls, and maybe the boys, would have a hard time resisting him.

"Oh, he's loving life. He comes home from school every day and insists on going right to his desk to do his homework." After washing her hands, she started pulling ingredients out of the refrigerator. She piled them on the work table and took out a large cutting board.

"They give that much homework in first grade?"

Darcy shook her head. "I think he invents more than half of it."

Alex laughed. "Sounds like a good problem to have. I hope the habit sticks."

"Ha. You and me both. I just signed him up for karate so he doesn't spend all of his time reading. I think I won him over by calling it the study and practice of an ancient martial art."

"You're hilarious. Let me get these in the oven and I'll clear out to let you work." Alex slid two pans of shortbread cookies into the oven and went to the sink to wash up. "I'm going to go check things out front. Will you pull those in twenty?"

Darcy glanced up from slicing onions to double check that the timer was on. "No problem."

Alex left the kitchen and walked out to the front of the shop. Jeff was handing change to Kyu, the manager of the SeaSpray hotel next door. "Hey, Kyu," Alex said jovially.

"Hey, Alex. Keeping warm over here?"

"We're trying. How're things across the way?"

"Sleepy enough for me to wander over here for a pick-me-up. You guys take care, now."

He left and Alex turned to Jeff. "I'm good to cover here if you want to go do your ordering."

"Oh, that would be great. I was hoping to sneak out a little early today."

"Hot date?" She enjoyed teasing him and he made it easy. Jeff had a hot date more nights of the week than not.

"You know it."

"What's his name?"

"Edwin. He's here on a writing fellowship. I think he's looking for some inspiration."

Alex rolled her eyes. "Well, then, you better inspire."

"Don't I always?"

"Always."

"Thanks, Chef."

As Jeff scooted away, Alex called after him, "Don't call me Chef." It was a habit he'd picked up from watching Gordon Ramsey's *Kitchen Nightmares*. When he discovered the formality irritated Alex, he resolutely refused to stop.

Once he was out of sight, Alex poured herself a cup of coffee and picked up the Sunday *Times* crossword puzzle. She didn't get very far before the door opened. She looked up to see Jan Stein from Provincetown Realty. Jan had helped her sort through the contract and other legal issues when she bought the bakery. She'd also grown up in the same Boston neighborhood as Alex, only about twenty years prior. Between that and a shared love of the Red Sox, they'd become friends.

"Hey there, sexy."

Jan grunted. She didn't like to speak before she'd had at least one cup of coffee. Alex, in turn, gave her a hard time by being as perky as possible. She handed Jan her usual, a large coffee, black.

After taking a long sip, Jan sighed. "G'morning. How's things?"

"Can't complain. You?"

"Not bad. Office is quiet. New tenant at the Harrison place, but no one else so far this week. This new tenant…quite a looker, and she came to town solo. Definitely your type."

Alex rolled her eyes. "You say that about every seemingly single woman under the age of fifty."

Jan made a puzzled face. "Is that not accurate?"

"You're an ass."

"Just one of the many reasons you love me."

"Somehow I keep forgetting that." Alex was about to say something off-color when Stuart walked in.

Jan turned to leave. "Thanks for the coffee, hot stuff. Bruins-Rangers tonight, remember."

"You bet, sunshine. Hopefully Kimble won't suck."

With Jan on her way out the door, Alex turned her attention to Stuart. "Good morning, Mr. Harbormaster. Your usual?"

"Please. But let's not get on Kimble this early in the season, eh? It's not like we've got anyone else to play between the pipes."

Alex poured coffee into the travel mug he handed her. "Muffin?"

"Yes, darling?"

Alex rolled her eyes. Even if she thought it was funny, she refused to encourage him.

He shrugged. "Sure. Surprise me."

She took a crumb-topped muffin from the case and put it into a small paper bag.

"Connie wants to know what she would have to do to get the recipe for that chocolate thing you brought the other night."

Alex grinned. It was deceptively easy, as well as one of her best-kept secrets. "Tell her it was given to me by an old French master and I'm sworn to take it to my grave. However, I'd happily trade her one for a pot of her chili any day of the week."

"I think she'll take that."

"Anything exciting on the agenda today?"

"We're replacing some of the support beams under the pier before the weather really turns. We've got a crane coming in from Wellfleet."

"I'd love to see that. How about I stop down later with coffee for the crew?"

"If you come bearing coffee, they might even let you operate the crane."

"In that case, I'll bring some pastries, too." She moved her hands back and forth as though she was working a pair of joysticks.

"Great," Stuart said, picking up his coffee and muffin. "I'll see you later."

Alex waved as he left. With no one else waiting to be served, she picked up her crossword and tried to remember the name of Jimmy Carter's Secretary of State.

CHAPTER FIVE

When Lia woke, she had no idea where she was. She panicked for a moment, then realized she was in her new apartment. Light was filtering in through the white curtains on the windows, just as she'd imagined it would. She rolled over and blinked at the small clock on the bedside table. It was just after eight.

Lia couldn't remember the last time she'd slept for twelve hours straight. Even when she'd had the flu, and walking from one end of the apartment to the other had exhausted her, she grew restless quickly and struggled to stay in bed for more than a few hours at a time. She rolled around for a moment, stretching and enjoying the weight of the duvet covering her. As she climbed out of bed, she realized she also couldn't remember the last time she felt so rested.

She ambled into the bathroom, regretting that she hadn't bothered to brush her teeth the night before. She glanced in the mirror and let out a guffaw. Her hair, dampened in the bathtub, but neither washed nor dried, was standing completely on end. Knowing that taming it would be a lesson in futility, she stripped off her sweats and stepped into the tub. After carefully pulling the shower curtain around the inside, she turned on the water and stood beneath the hot spray.

She gave her scalp a good scrub and the rest of her a quick wash. She brushed her teeth with extra vigor. Feeling significantly more human, she went back into the bedroom and realized that most of her clothes were still in the car. She settled for jeans and a sweater, figuring she'd do little more with her day than unpack and shop for groceries. She twisted her hair into a bun and headed downstairs. In the kitchen, she found a coffee pot and filters, but no coffee.

Lia drummed her fingers on the counter. She should probably accomplish something before rewarding herself. Of course, she'd be much more productive after a nice cup of coffee. Besides, she had skipped dinner, and Mama always said that you should never go grocery shopping on an empty stomach. Perhaps she'd wander into town for coffee and breakfast before starting the work of settling in.

The sun was shining, so she grabbed her sunglasses and a jacket from the car. She slipped them both on, then stepped out into the street. Other than some gulls screeching overhead, there was no sound. She tucked her hands into her pockets and started the short walk into town with a smile on her face.

As she meandered down Commercial Street, Lia realized just how many of the shops and restaurants were closed up for winter. She saw sign after sign promising passersby "we'll see you in April!" She passed a few people on the street. Since a couple of them were carrying cups of coffee, she figured she was heading in the right direction and kept walking. When she got to The Flour Pot Café, an "open" sign and the faint aroma of coffee made her sigh. If her memory was correct, this place had amazing coffee and baked goods.

When the door opened, Alex was scowling over twenty-eight across, a seven-letter Norse god. She looked up, expecting one of her usual customers. She was surprised to see a pretty, yet unfamiliar, woman smiling at her. She set down her cup and stood.

"Good morning."

"Hello, good morning."

The woman's cheeks were pink from the chill in the air and her eyes were bright. She had a slightly rumpled look about her that Alex found incredibly sexy, along with dark hair, dark eyes, and killer curves. Since Alex had never seen her before, she was intrigued. "What can I get for you today?"

"Coffee, please, the bigger the better. And I'll definitely have to pick out one of these lovely treats." She looked over to the case where the muffins and croissants were displayed.

"I'm afraid the selection isn't huge. We pare down quite a bit in the off season." Alex always felt the need to explain when there weren't at least a dozen things to choose from. "Cream and sugar?"

"Just cream, please. Yes, if I remember correctly, your offerings in the summer would rival a French patisserie. I see, however, that y'all have chocolate croissants, so I needn't look any further."

The more she spoke, the more Alex picked up on what she was certain was a Southern drawl. It wasn't very pronounced, but faded in and out like maybe she'd lived there once and didn't anymore. "You got it. For here or to go?"

"Here, please."

Alex assessed the woman who was smiling at her again. It was a pretty smile, warm and reassuring. A rare smile, as Nick Carraway would say. She poured coffee into a thick white mug, stirred in some half-and-half, and set it on the counter. She then took a chocolate croissant from the case and set it down on a saucer next to the coffee. "Always a good choice. And since I make croissants every day for some of our lunch sandwiches, we are never without them."

"That's very good to know, about the sandwiches and the chocolate croissants." She pulled money from her wallet and handed it to Alex. "You make them yourself?"

"I do. I own the place. I bring in quite a bit of help in the busy season, but I do most of the baking myself in the winter." She handed the woman her change, which was promptly dropped into the tip jar.

"Wow. I'm very impressed."

"Flattery will get you everywhere. I'm Alex, by the way."

"Lia." She extended her hand. "It's nice to meet you."

Alex shook Lia's hand and smiled. "Likewise. Enjoy your breakfast."

"Thanks, I will."

Before Lia could walk away, Alex stopped her. "Where are you from? You sound sort of Southern, but I can't quite pinpoint it."

"You're good. Louisiana. Cajun country by way of Massachusetts and then New York for the last ten or so years."

She took her mug and saucer and headed over to a small table by the window. Alex was admiring her curves as she walked away when the door to the café opened and Tom French walked in. "Morning, Alex."

Alex grudgingly turned her attention. "Good morning, Tom. The usual?"

"Yes, please."

Alex poured coffee into a large paper cup. She stirred in cream, lots of sugar, and topped it with a plastic lid. "How are you this fine autumn day?"

"No snow, yet, so I suppose that makes it a good one."

"You're going to leave me, aren't you? You're going to take Charlie and head south and I'm never going to see you again."

"Your face is the reason I stay. I couldn't bear to live without it."

Alex snorted. "That might be true about my baked goods."

She took a banana-nut muffin from the case and put it into a paper bag. She handed both to him and said, "I'll put it on your tab."

"Thanks, honey." Tom winked at her—he winked at everyone—and turned to leave. He caught sight of the newcomer and, winking at her as well, wished them both a good day.

When he was gone, Alex returned her attention to Lia. Lia looked up and seemed surprised to find Alex looking at her. Rather than glancing away, Alex offered a slow smile.

"That," Lia gestured to her plate, "was exquisite."

"Thank you." She loved a woman who enjoyed food.

"Just how quiet is it around here at this time of year?"

That was a strange question. Alex considered for a moment. "I'd say we revert to your average sleepy small town. Not a ghost town by any means, but definitely quiet. A number of the restaurants and galleries close, but the fishermen are still working and most of the non-touristy businesses stay open."

"That's reassuring." Lia, done with her coffee and croissant, stood and walked to the counter with her mug and saucer.

"Can I get you another cup of coffee?"

"Yes, please." She handed Alex her mug. "You are now officially my favorite place in town."

"Glad to hear it." She refilled Lia's mug and handed it back to her. She took that as her opening. "And what, if you don't mind my asking, brings you to Provincetown in the middle of November?"

Something passed through Lia's eyes that made Alex immediately regret asking the question. "I'm sorry. I don't mean to pry."

Lia stopped sipping her coffee and shook her head. "No, no, it's fine. I've actually just moved into an apartment in the West End. I was looking for a change of scenery and found a very reasonable six-month lease."

So she was the new tenant. Jan was right about one thing—Lia was definitely a looker. She had gorgeous brown eyes and rich chestnut-colored hair that escaped the bun she wore and curled around her face in the most alluring way. She was tall, too, probably less than an inch shorter than her own five-eight. Alex, who had an eye for such things, also sensed that, beneath the jeans and sweater, was a luscious hourglass figure. And it appeared she was sticking around for a while. Nice. She offered Lia her most winning smile. "Well, then, welcome to the neighborhood."

Lia visibly relaxed. "Thanks. And since you're rolling out the welcome wagon, let me ask you a question."

"Of course."

"I saw a sign as I walked in that you have Wi-Fi."

"We do."

"Do y'all mind hangers-around?"

"Hangers-around?"

"Would it be a bother if I came in some mornings and camped out at one of your tables to do some work?"

"Oh, I see." Alex thought about this pretty woman sitting in her shop for hours on end. Perhaps she wasn't in for a dry spell after all. "You are most welcome anytime. I'll even promise not to distract you too much."

Lia beamed at her. Alex made an internal note to do whatever it took to get her to do that on a regular basis.

"Thank you, and, you know, it would be nice to have some distraction now and again."

"Ditto."

"Well, then, as much as I'd like to hang around for the rest of the day, I didn't bring my laptop with me. There's also the matter of needing to unpack and not having a stitch of food in my apartment." Lia set down her now empty mug. She stepped over to the table where she'd been sitting and slipped on her jacket. "I will, however, be back tomorrow."

"I'll look forward to it. Oh, and if you need anything or have any questions as you're getting settled, let me know." For some reason, that seemed to make Lia get shy all of a sudden. If Alex wasn't mistaken, Lia even blushed.

"Thanks. I really appreciate it."

With that, Lia left, turning to offer a wave as the door closed behind her. A woman who could, and would, plop herself into a new place for six months. Alex wondered what exactly this Lia did for a living that would allow her to run off on a whim. Why was she there?

A dozen questions swirled in her mind and she'd resisted asking any of them. It was none of her business. And if Lia's initial reaction was anything to go on, she had no interest in sharing. That was fine by Alex. She'd rather flirt than play confidante anyway.

CHAPTER SIX

L ia left the café and stood for a moment on the curb. She contemplated walking down to the real estate office to look at the photographs Jan promised to show her, but it made more sense to run all of her errands in the car. She headed back the way she came, turning her face to the sunshine that still held a hint of warmth. Whether it was the sugar and caffeine in her system or the prospect of being able to do her work in a café with an insanely attractive proprietor, Lia found there was a bit of pep in her step.

Back at her apartment, she carried the boxes and bags from her car inside. She piled everything in the living room, unsure of what needed to be upstairs and what would stay down. With her car empty, she drove the block up to Bradford Street and headed back toward the East End.

When she walked into the real estate office, an older woman was sitting at the reception desk that had been empty the afternoon before. "Good morning," she said cheerfully. "How can I help you today?"

Lia returned the smile. "Hi. My name is Lia Brooks and I'm here to see Jan."

"Sure, just a moment." She pressed a couple of buttons on her phone. "Hi, Jan. I have a Lia Brooks here to see you."

The woman hung up the phone and then squinted at her. "Wait, are you Cecilia Brooks who is renting the Harrison place?"

"One and the same."

Lia watched the woman's eyes light up as she threw her hands in the air. "Oh, it's nice to meet you. I was gone yesterday before you picked up your keys, but I wanted to welcome you to town. I'm Stacia."

"Thanks," she replied, trying to match Stacia's enthusiasm. It was like she was in some gay parallel universe to her hometown. "And it's nice to meet you, too."

"Now, I don't want to come across as pushy, but I know you're planning to stay through April and life can be pretty dull around here this time of year. If you're looking for something to do, or to make friends, I organize a book club and a poker group. There's always room for another at either."

She couldn't stifle a laugh. This Stacia was beginning to sound an awful lot like her Great Aunt Mae. It was completely random and utterly charming. "You know, both of those sound like a lot of fun."

Stacia winked at her. "You sound like my kind of gal. I can email you the details if you'd like."

Lia was pretty sure she'd been winked at more times in the last twenty-four hours than she had been in the last year. There was not a lot of winking on the Upper West Side, at least not directed at her. The fact that the most recent was coming from a woman who had to be pushing seventy was icing on the cake. "I would love that. You can use the one you have on file here."

At that moment, Jan appeared from down the hall. "She didn't sign you up for her bowling league, did she? Don't be fooled by that sweet smile. She's a hustler."

Stacia scoffed in mock outrage and Lia tried to swallow the giggle that was threatening to come out. "Not at all. I asked if there were any book clubs in town and she offered to let me into hers." Now it was her turn to wink.

Jan chuckled. "If you say so. It's good to see you again. How are you settling in?"

Lia shrugged. "Getting there. I'm heading to the grocery store now, but wanted to stop here first and take a look at the photos."

Twenty minutes later, she left with two photos for herself and one for her parents. She also had an invitation to play poker with half a dozen lesbians on Sunday, and she was pretty sure most of them were twice her age. Amused and rather pleased with herself, she headed to the store.

Despite having the best intentions, she spent over three hundred dollars at the market. On the drive home, she convinced herself it wasn't really all that unreasonable, considering she was stocking a kitchen from scratch. She needed everything. Once home, however, and she had to unload it all, she wondered what the hell she'd been thinking. It felt as though she had bought at least one of everything.

She spent a couple of hours putting things away, filling the fridge and organizing the tiny closet pantry that was still bigger than any pantry she'd had in New York. When that was done, she made a turkey sandwich, then spent the rest of the afternoon unpacking. The closet and dresser provided plenty of room for her clothes. She arranged her jewelry and makeup, placed some of her books and family photographs in the bedroom and living room. She'd need to get frames for the new photographs, but there was a perfect spot for them on the wall that connected the living room to the kitchen.

By the time Lia was satisfied that her new home felt sufficiently homey, the sun had set and it was once again dark outside. She flipped on a couple of lamps and headed to the kitchen to pour herself a glass of wine. She considered cooking something, but opted for cheese and crackers instead. Dani, the health nut, always chided her for eating too much cheese, too many carbs. With that in mind, she cut an extra-generous amount of Brie from the wedge she'd bought, putting it on a saucer with a stack of cracked wheat crackers and a bunch of grapes.

Lia picked up her dinner and wandered into the living room, setting the plate down on the coffee table. She browsed the bookcases as she sipped, glad to have so many books at her disposal, even if they weren't her own. There were a couple of rows of classics, a few oversized art books stacked on their sides. Other than that, Lia realized, every other shelf was packed with books about lesbians.

Biographies sat next to anthologies of erotica; there were photo books and books about gender theory and sexual identity and lesbian history. And romances. There was an entire shelf of them. She had never seen such a collection in one place, excepting perhaps the gay bookstore she'd discovered in Greenwich Village. She'd never even heard of many of the titles now lined up neatly before her.

Intrigued by the title, Lia pulled *The Persistent Desire* from the shelf. On the cover, there was a photo of two people from the hip down, lying on the ground with legs entwined. One was clad in trousers and boots, the other in a short skirt that rode up to reveal the tops of stockings and pale thighs. The subtitle announced it was a femme-butch reader.

Lia took the book and her glass of wine over to the couch. She turned on the table lamp and sat down, tucking her feet underneath her. Two hours later, her glass was empty and her cheese and crackers long gone. She'd plowed through nearly half of the stories and essays. She looked around, blinking and pulling herself back to reality. She stood to stretch her now stiff limbs, feeling aroused and restless and unsettled.

It wasn't as though she'd never heard the phrase butch-femme before. A girl couldn't attend Smith College and identify as a lesbian without learning the lexicon. In truth, lots of people had asked her if she was femme when they learned that she was gay. According to Dani, it was because she wore skirts, liked makeup and jewelry. Dani had a personal disdain for the intricate layers some people used to explain their sexual preferences. She brushed it aside, calling it outdated and anti-feminist. Since, at the time, she considered being Dani's girlfriend her primary identity, she never questioned her or bothered looking into it on her own.

It was, Lia realized irately, just one more instance where doing things Dani's way had come back to bite her in the ass. She paced back and forth between the kitchen and living room areas. Femme. She turned the word over in her head a few times. She tried saying it out loud. It felt...obvious. Dani wasn't especially masculine in how she dressed, especially for work, but she did have a powerful, at times aggressive, personality. Lia thought of the other women she found attractive, women like k.d. lang and Rachel Maddow. She also thought about her newest acquaintance, the incredibly sexy owner of the Flour Pot Café—the way her jeans hung low on her hips and the dark gray chef coat pulled slightly over broad shoulders and arms. Now that she wasn't with Dani, Lia could explore, and maybe even embrace it.

She imagined talking with Alex, casually working it into the conversation. "I'm femme," she could say. Or, maybe, "It must be a femme thing." She wondered if Alex identified as butch. She suddenly had an image in her head of Alex wearing trousers and boots, lying in the grass next to Lia's stockinged legs and exposed thighs. Although slightly embarrassed by her thoughts, she found herself aroused. Very aroused.

She walked into the kitchen and refilled her wine. She tucked the book under her arm and headed upstairs to continue reading in a nice hot bath.

CHAPTER SEVEN

Although she was officially giving herself a break from alarm clocks, Lia was wide awake at 6:45. It seemed that ten years of routine had given her a pretty reliable internal alarm clock. Still, she felt rested. Since she'd stayed up past midnight reading, she attributed it to getting a good night's sleep. Well, that and the fact that she'd slept twelve hours the night before. Given the restlessness and insomnia of the past few months, it was refreshing.

She tossed back the covers and got out of bed. She looked around, still trying to absorb the details of the space so that they would become familiar, so that the room would feel more like home and less like someone's guest room. She then proceeded with what she called her token yoga. It was less a formal meditation or workout and more a series of poses and stretches that made her feel limber. She should probably find a studio and start with classes again. Like so many things in life, she needed structure to accomplish anything beyond her comfort zone.

When she was done, she plodded into the bathroom. Once again, her hair stood out at odd angles, flat on one side and an oversized mess of curls on the other. Perhaps she should invest in a shower cap like the one her grandmother used to wear. She smiled at the memory, as well as the thought of how ridiculous she'd look in a shower cap, and stepped into the shower.

Lia washed her hair and loofahed all over. She shaved her legs. It made her tights feel good on her skin and now was certainly not the time to let herself go. She toweled off and took the time for full-body moisturizer. As she rubbed lotion into her skin, she realized just how much her pampering and grooming had become tied to whether or not she thought Dani would be in the mood. She huffed at the thought.

Since she'd been so thorough in her unpacking and organizing, she was able to walk over to the closet to find something to wear. She found herself thinking about Alex, about wanting to look nice, about feeling sexy. Although her first instinct was to rein herself in, she shoved the thought aside and pulled out one of her favorite fall skirts and a matching sweater. There was no harm in feeling good about herself. Being put together didn't mean she was on the prowl.

The fact that she'd even thought the phrase "on the prowl" made her chuckle. She decided to go for it, putting on just a hint of makeup, earrings, and her favorite knee-high brown boots. When she was done, she assessed herself in the mirror, making sure it didn't look like she'd put in too much effort. Chuckling to herself again, she headed downstairs. She stuck her head out to check the temperature then put on a light coat and her favorite scarf. She grabbed her bag and keys and headed out the door.

When she arrived at The Flour Pot, it was significantly busier than it had been the morning before. Checking her watch, Lia realized it was just a little after eight, a full hour earlier than she'd ventured out yesterday. It made sense that there would be a rush before the start of the average workday. As she stood in line, she watched people place their orders for coffee and muffins and croissants. Everyone in front of her took their order to go.

Alex worked the register and wrapped up pastries while a guy who appeared to be in his twenties made espressos, cappuccinos, and lattes. When it was Lia's turn, she stepped in front of the register and smiled. "Good morning."

There was a flicker of recognition in Alex's eyes and then she flashed a smile of her own.

"Good morning, Lia. What can I get for you today?"

Alex remembered her name and it gave Lia a flutter. And that smile. It was a dangerous smile, she decided. She had no doubt that many hearts beat a little faster when it was bestowed. She gave little thought to her heart racing these days, but she could at least appreciate it. "Chocolate croissant and a latte, please, and I'll have them here."

"Coming right up." Alex called Lia's coffee order over to Jeff. She took Lia's money gave her change, then handed her a saucer with the croissant on it.

"Thanks." Lia glanced at the plate. Again, it was a beautiful croissant.

"My pleasure. Jeff will have your coffee at the end of the counter."

Lia stepped aside so the next person could order. Her latte appeared in what felt like thirty seconds. She took her cup and plate to the same table she'd sat at the day before. While she ate and sipped her coffee, she watched the people come and go. Alex greeted most of them by name and about half of them had a "usual."

It reminded Lia of Boudreaux's, the bakery in the town where she grew up. Boudreaux's was more donuts and apple fritters than croissants, though, and the only coffee choices were Community brand regular or decaf. Still, it was one of her favorite places as a child. And while the clientele here was far more gay, there was the same small town, close-knit feel. It made Lia feel, if not homesick, nostalgic. She nodded and smiled and said good morning to the customers who caught her eye as they left. She imagined she was recognized as an outsider, a curiosity. She wondered if that would fade. She hoped it would.

When she was done with her breakfast, Lia pulled out her laptop and powered it on. She opened the report of findings she'd been sent the day before and read through the forty-three pages of hypotheses, experimental parameters, control groups, and results. She read the hypotheses and the results again, then opened a fresh Word document.

After drafting the first few paragraphs, Lia glanced up and realized the pre-work crowd had cleared out. Jeff was nowhere to be seen and Alex was rearranging the things that were left in the display case. She stood up and caught Lia watching her.

"I'm glad to see you again," Alex said.

"Likewise. I tend to get antsy when I work at home. Besides, y'all have pastries."

Alex shrugged. "We do what we can. So, if you don't mind my asking, what is it you do that you can so readily do anywhere?"

"I'm a science writer."

"Science writer? What do you write, textbooks?"

Lia shook her head. Alex had the same puzzled look that most people got when she told them what she did for a living. "Journal articles, mostly. Scientists send me their research findings and I write them up for publication in scientific journals or for mainstream media."

"That's interesting. I don't think I ever thought about science that way."

Alex sounded genuinely curious. Lia decided to give her the benefit of the doubt. "I didn't either, always. I majored in Biochemistry and English. I wanted to be a writer more than a doctor or someone who lived in a lab. My advisor in college encouraged me to look into scientific publishing. I did and it seemed like the perfect fit for me."

"That makes sense." Alex leaned on the counter. "Do you do it freelance or do you work for a specific group or company?"

"I started as an editorial assistant at *The Journal of Cellular Biochemistry*." When Alex raised an eyebrow, she added, "Yes, that's a real thing and, yes, there are people who read it."

"I'm not doubting." The look Alex gave her seemed playfully defensive.

Lia crossed her arms in mock annoyance. "Anyway. A few of the researchers I worked with asked if I could do writing for them on the side. I did that for a couple of years and then started my own company. It turns out that a lot of scientists hate to write."

"I bet."

"And I love research, but I hate actually having to do the experiments. Since I've got more science background than most writers, I don't ask a lot of questions or need a lot of explanation to do the work. A few of the people I work with are social, but I think most appreciate that they hardly have to speak to me at all."

It was Alex's turn to laugh. "I can imagine. Plus, you get to work anywhere."

"Exactly."

"Well, then, I'll let you work. You've got about two and a half hours before lunch rush. And we're open until three."

"Thanks, and thanks for the hospitality."

Alex looked at her quizzically. "That is such a Southern thing to say."

"Why, thank you," Lia drawled.

Alex chuckled. "I have no idea why or how you managed to find your way here, but I'm glad that you did. Good luck with your work." With that, Alex disappeared into what Lia figured was the kitchen. She sat for a moment. Was that flirting? Did she just flirt with the sexy butch baker? Maybe it was just friendly conversation. It felt more than friendly though. She was probably imagining things. After about a minute and a half, Lia realized she was staring into space. She forced herself off the meandering path of overanalyzing the interaction and got back to work.

As predicted, people started trickling in around 11:30. Jeff reappeared and was manning the register. As with the breakfast crowd, most customers were greeted by name. She watched as he punched orders into the computer screen at the register. He'd put in a couple of orders, then disappear into the kitchen, reappearing with a bag or a plate, handing them off to the people he'd rung out a few moments before. For a two-person operation, it seemed remarkably efficient.

More people sat down to have their lunches than had for breakfast. A few people said hello to her. If she came in more days than not, she wondered if she'd start to get to know some of them. As much as she'd wanted to get away, she felt uncomfortable being completely anonymous. It was one of the things she kept with her from her small town childhood, and one of the things she hated about New York.

By quarter after one, things slowed considerably. She took the opportunity to order her own lunch. As tempting as she found the chicken salad sandwich, she had just enough restraint to resist consuming two croissants in the same day. She opted for a spinach salad with chopped eggs and a shallot-champagne vinaigrette. It was delicious, although not as delicious as the hunk of rosemary and olive oil bread that came on the side. She did have that weakness for carbs.

After having her lunch, Lia worked for another hour, then started packing up her things. She didn't want to have to be politely asked to leave when the café closed. She wanted to say good-bye to Alex, but didn't want to make a show of it. Alex saved her the trouble by coming out of the kitchen and looking right at her.

She felt herself blushing, and then blushing more because she was convinced that Alex had noticed. She slipped on her jacket and picked up her bag. "Thank you for the lovely setting, as well as the delicious food. I can assure you you'll be seeing a lot more of me."

Alex picked up a bit of paper from near the register and scribbled something on it. Oh God, was she giving Lia her number? What was she supposed to do? Lia tried not to panic as Alex walked over to where she was standing.

Alex handed Lia two small cards. One was for a free coffee after she bought ten, the other was for a sandwich or salad. Alex had initialed the first space on each. "You're going to want to have these, then."

Lia looked at them, then at Alex. She was rewarded with her second wink of the day. Lia swallowed. "Thanks. I'll fill these in no time."

"I sure hope so. Enjoy your afternoon."

"You, too." Lia waved and walked out into the pale November sunshine.

She strolled home leisurely, replaying the conversation with Alex in her mind. It was such a relief that Alex wasn't trying to hit on her. She had no desire to get involved with anyone and she was lousy at letting people down. Alex was just being friendly, practicing good customer service. For the life of her, Lia couldn't figure out why she suddenly felt disappointed.

CHAPTER EIGHT

At three, Alex locked the front door and flipped the "open" sign to "closed." Armed with a spray bottle full of sanitizer and a clean towel, she made her way around the small dining area, wiping tables and straightening chairs. About halfway through, she noticed a scarf on the floor.

She immediately recognized the cream colored wool and chunky knit design. It was the scarf Lia had been wearing when she walked into the shop. She picked it up and, without thinking, gave it a sniff. The perfume was subtle—something citrusy and floral—but it sent an arrow of heat straight to her gut. The scent would be stronger on Lia's skin, warmed by the heat of her body.

Alex rolled her eyes and placed the scarf on the counter. Apparently, not having sex for a couple of months had given her a one-track mind. She went about the rest of her routine, trying not to think about Lia's neck or where else she might spritz her perfume.

After finishing the cleaning, she checked that the door was locked, climbed the back stairs, and was home. One of the reasons she fell in love with The Flour Pot was the size of the kitchen. The other was the spacious loft apartment on the second floor. The copper pots she'd found at a flea market and polished back to life hung from a pot rack over the center island. Cupboards she'd sanded and painted showed off glassware and an eclectic mix of serving dishes. The commercial grade stove she bought on discount when buying new appliances for the bakery gleamed.

Although it had been her home for three of the six years she'd lived in Provincetown, Alex was still amazed by the fact that it was hers. Well, hers and the bank's perhaps, but that was a technicality. It was everything she had ever wanted a kitchen to be, and she'd made it that way.

Murphy was waiting with his tongue out and tail wagging. "How's my boy?" she asked him. The dog promptly sat, tongue still out and tail now swishing back and forth across the floor. Alex took his leash from the hook by the door and he stood, doing his happy dance. She slipped on her Carhartt jacket, stuffed the leash in her pocket just in case, and off they went.

Since the sun was still shining, she figured they would walk toward the beach instead of going for a run. First, however, Alex wandered down Commercial Street into the West End of town. She resisted the urge to walk by Lia's place, if for no other reason than she'd left Lia's scarf at home and didn't have a good excuse to drop by. Murphy, thrilled to have so many bushes and lampposts to smell and pee on courtesy of their slowed pace, strolled with her.

Alex loved the neighborhood. The houses were mostly old and close together. Almost all of them were sided with cedar shingles, some recently done, but most the weathered brownish-gray for which Cape Cod was known. Some had front porches, some had neat little gardens pruned back for winter. White picket fences and arbors were covered in vines no longer in bloom. Each was different, but everything felt as though it went together. If she hadn't ended up at the bakery, she would have tried to find a place here in her price range. It would have been a tall order.

They walked down one of the public walkways toward the water. Even with a breeze, the water harborside remained mostly calm. Alex found a piece of driftwood and tossed it. Murphy bounded after it, picked it up, and trotted back. He dropped it at her feet and looked up, clearly asking her to do it again. She obliged, throwing it almost to the water's edge but not quite. In the summer, Murphy loved nothing more than chasing sticks into the water. He'd probably do the same without hesitation now, so she was careful not to tempt him.

After a half hour, she called it quits. Murphy seemed to have had his fill and didn't even cast longing looks back at the water as they walked from the beach and began to loop back toward home. With daylight savings time over, the sun was setting earlier and earlier.

Alex checked her watch; it was barely past five o'clock. The wind was picking up as well, adding to the chill in the air. They didn't dawdle on the way.

Alex left her shoes at the door and walked into the kitchen. She opened a large bin and scooped Murphy's dinner into his bowl. He sat patiently, glancing at his food and then looking to her for the signal. "Go ahead," she said, and he dove in.

While he crunched, Alex headed to the bedroom, stripping off clothes as she went. She dropped her gray chef coat and t-shirt into the hamper, followed by jeans, socks, bra, and boxer briefs. In the bathroom, she cranked the shower nice and hot and stepped under the spray. While she scrubbed away the hours of kneading and chopping and whipping and stirring and slicing and serving, she found her thoughts drifting again to Lia.

The attraction she felt had been immediate. She always had a soft spot for the femme types, especially smart and quirky ones. That fact had proved to be a bit of a blessing and a curse. In her experience, the prettier they were, the harder she fell. Alex had fallen hard twice in her life, once in college and once with her boss a few years later. Both times, she'd had her heart broken. After that, she swore off trying to find "the one," preferring instead to keep her relationships focused on mutual enjoyment.

One of the key reasons she left big city life was to simplify things. That applied to her love life as much as it did to everything else. What she couldn't decide was if Lia would be a nice addition to that, or a giant complication.

For no reason but a strong gut feeling, Alex thought Lia wasn't the type of woman interested in a fling. Nor did she seem to be attached to anyone. She wondered if the change of scenery that Lia was looking for was as much about escaping a person as escaping a place. Alex respected that, but it definitely set off warning bells. The question was whether or not she intended to heed them.

Shaking off her curiosity, she turned off the water and toweled off. She padded into the bedroom naked and pulled out a pair of sweatpants and an old, gray, Bruins T-shirt from the bottom drawer of her dresser. Content in her lounge wear and slippers, she wandered back to the kitchen for a beer and to flip through her mail.

There wasn't much of note, except for the new issue of *Esquire*. Her sister, Meg, had gotten her a subscription after Alex teased her about reading *Cosmo*. That had been while they were still in college, but Alex had enjoyed reading it so much that she renewed it over and over again. This month's issue included a feature on the rise of small-batch bourbon distilleries.

She flopped on the couch and invited Murphy to join her, happy to have a relaxing evening at home. After a while, she dug around in the refrigerator for some soup. She warmed it up with some of the day's leftover bread.

She sat at her dining room table to eat, turning on the television and looking for a football game worth watching. Not finding one, she turned the channel to catch the second half of Jeopardy. When it was over and her dishes were loaded into the dishwasher, Alex picked up her magazine and flopped back on the couch. She found herself restless, however, after flipping through just a few pages. It was unlike her, and more than a little irritating.

Her thoughts turned again to the scarf and its owner. Lia would likely come back to the bakery in the next few days and she could get it then. But maybe she wouldn't. The idea of not seeing Lia again, or at least of not knowing when, started to gnaw at her. She'd just return it. The bakery was closed tomorrow anyway. She'd walk over to Lia's place and return the scarf and be done with it. No big deal.

Feeling only slightly more settled, she rubbed Murphy's ears for a while, then picked up her phone. She had no interesting email, so she switched over to the Twitter feed she rarely read. She used it mostly to follow sports news and a few bands she liked, some celebrities, a few chefs and bloggers. Alex perused with tepid interest until she happened upon a link from her favorite queer culture blogger entitled "Sexy Librarians: NSFW."

Alex clicked on it and landed at a photo gallery of women of all shapes and sizes, each one posing somewhere in a library. There were butches in tweed and andros in argyle sweaters; they stood in the stacks and sat at circulation desks. Femme-types in prim skirts and blouses offered coy smiles while women in lacy lingerie pored over books studiously. Some of them were silly, but the majority were sexy.

She scrolled until her eyes fell upon a curvy brunette. She was wearing black stockings and killer heels, a lace bra with matching panties, and glasses. It was a side shot and the woman was leaning over a library cart filled with books, ostensibly browsing the titles. She looked just enough like Lia that Alex instantly pictured Lia in the photo. She imagined the swell of Lia's breasts in the black lace bra, Lia's pale stomach and smooth thighs showing over the tops of the stockings. Alex could feel her hand on Lia's skin, in the deep curve of her lower back.

Almost without realizing it, Alex began massaging her breasts. She imagined what it would feel like to have Lia there, straddling her thighs and teasing her. While her left hand pulled and tugged at her nipples, Alex moved her right down her stomach and slid it beneath the waistband of her pants. She was hot and wet. Alex started tracing slow circles over her swollen clit and didn't even try to stifle the moan that escaped her.

With her eyes closed and images of Lia dancing through her mind, she teased herself. When it felt like her clit was going to explode, she moved her hand, sliding her first two fingers deep inside herself. She arched back, pumping and pressing. The pressure built and she let it take her.

The orgasm left her panting and shaky. She couldn't remember coming so hard from touching herself. She told herself that it was the result of not having sex for the last three months. But as she got up and walked to her bedroom, her thoughts were still very much focused on the woman who'd appeared in her coffee shop and clouded her brain for the last two days.

Alex was unaccustomed to being infatuated. It wasn't her personality and it wasn't her style. Infatuated, however, was exactly what she seemed to be.

CHAPTER NINE

S ince she worked for herself and set her own schedule, Lia always did her cleaning on Mondays. It reminded her of Grand-mère's tradition of using Monday as a wash day. She would put a pot of beans on the stove early, throw in the ham bone from Sunday supper or some smoked turkey necks, and do the week's laundry while scrubbing the house from top to bottom.

Lia remembered going there after school to help her with the housework, and the house would smell of simmering red beans and lemon oil. There'd be no work left, but always a freshly baked cake. She'd cut them each a big piece and let Lia have a café au lait that was mostly lait. It was their little secret, and Lia grew to treasure the time with her grandmother far more than getting first dibs on the dessert that would be devoured by her brothers later.

Lia didn't pretend to inherit the meticulousness with housework, but she did like to keep the tradition. Most Mondays, that consisted of changing the sheets, running the vacuum and mopping floors, and doing a quick clean of the bathroom. In theory, Lia added other chores on a rotating basis, things like dusting baseboards and cleaning kitchen appliances, but she was rarely so ambitious. So about once per month, she set aside the entire morning to give the things she missed a thorough cleaning.

Her Provincetown apartment was no different and, even though she'd been there for only a week, today was the day. She put on a pair of old shorts and a tank top and piled her hair on top of her head. She set the coffee on to brew, then pulled out the ingredients for red beans and rice. The only pot in her apartment large enough to use was the lobster pot, so she set it on the stove and dumped in the drippings from the bacon she'd indulged in over the weekend. She sautéed onions, bell peppers, celery, and garlic in the bacon grease. Once they were soft, she added the beans she'd soaked overnight, water, and some andouille sausage she'd been lucky enough to find at the little gourmet grocery on the other end of town.

With the beans cooking, Lia poured herself a cup of coffee and pulled out the cleaning supplies. Before she got to work, she brought her phone over to the docking station for the stereo so she could queue up the appropriate mood music. She browsed her collection, selecting soundtracks, then Broadway, then *Evita*. All of her friends, in addition to Dani, teased her about the choice of show tunes to accompany housework, but she was unswayed.

Now that she didn't have to worry about neighbors sharing her walls, she could crank it up and sing to her heart's content. With Ché lamenting the circus of Eva's funeral, Lia picked up a bottle of Windex and got to work. An hour and a half later, she was covered in sweat and pleading with Argentina not to cry for her.

Although she'd decided to return the scarf, Alex continued to hem and haw before making the short walk to Lia's apartment. She really didn't want to seem like a stalker. She was just being nice. She didn't want to presume Lia would be a regular, and the café was closed on Mondays. She wanted to go for a long walk with Murphy anyway. Showing up with a dog would seem less stalkerish, right?

Alex and Murphy strolled toward the West End. Since she came that way often, and had a general fascination with houses, she knew that author Melissa Harrison's place was on Vine Street. When she saw the car with New York plates, she knew she was in the right place.

She was halfway up the driveway when she heard the music. Although it took her a few more steps to make out the words, she quickly recognized the iconic song from *Evita*. By the time she got to Lia's door, the orchestra was swelling and Alex could make out two voices—the one in the recording and an off-key, but heartfelt, accompaniment. She peeked in the window and saw Lia, a dust rag in one hand and a bottle of furniture polish in the other. Her arms were outstretched, beseeching the invisible crowds beneath her nonexistent balcony. It was ridiculous, and it nudged Alex's attraction to her up yet another notch.

She knocked on the door to no avail. She looked down at Murphy, who was tilting his head from side to side in an attempt to figure out what the noise was. She decided to enjoy the show until the song ended. As the music faded, she tried again.

The brisk knock on the door nearly gave Lia a heart attack. She yelped, dropped the bottle of furniture polish she was holding, then spun around in the direction of the noise. Alex was at her door, smiling through the glass. *Oh, God.*

Lia hurried over to the speaker to cut the music and then to the door. She opened it, feeling flushed from both the work and the embarrassment of being caught channeling her inner Eva Perón. She offered Alex a sheepish smile. "Hi." She then noticed the dog sitting obediently at Alex's feet. "And hello to you, too. What's your name?"

"Hi," Alex said, ruffling the dog's ears. "This is Murphy."

She bent so the dog could sniff her hand. "You're a very handsome boy, Murphy."

"Sorry to startle you."

Lia tried not to think of how frightful she must look. That quickly morphed into wondering what Alex was doing at her house, and how Alex knew where she lived. "It's…it's fine. It doesn't take much to scare the living daylights out of me."

"Well, I'm sorry just the same. It was quite a performance."

Was Alex flirting with her, or making fun of her? It was hard to tell. "How much of that did you see?"

"Only a minute or two. It was very moving."

Flirtatious teasing, was that a thing? It was a little weird. But nice. Sort of? Should she flirt back? She cocked her hip and gave a dramatic head toss. "Thank you," she said, trying to make her voice sound playful. "I do pour my heart into every role."

"Tony-worthy, truly."

Ha! It was flirtation. They were flirting. Alex the sexy baker was flirting with her. But that still didn't explain what Alex was doing at her house.

"I, uh, I have your scarf."

"Oh." So that's what she was doing there. That was weird. Nice, but weird. Not that she would say that. "That's so nice. You really didn't have to go to the trouble."

"Murphy and I walk out this way anyway. It was no trouble at all. Besides, it's going to be wicked cold tomorrow. I figured you'd want it." Alex spoke quickly, as though she were nervous. "Jan, from the real estate office, is a regular customer and happened to mention there was a new person at the Harrison place. I figured she must have been talking about you."

Well, that explained how Alex knew where she lived. If she were in New York, she'd be tempted to call the police. In her hometown, everyone in town would know where the new girl was living. P-town was probably more like Vacherie than New York, at least in terms of how gossip traveled. She could deal with that. Thinking of home made her remember her manners. Even if it freaked her out a little, Alex had done something nice and she was keeping her in the doorway like someone selling vacuums.

"I appreciate it. Come in, come in, both of you."

"I don't want to intrude."

"You aren't, not at all. Please." Lia waved them in with her hand. She wondered if Alex always went out of her way to do nice things. Then she wondered what she was supposed to do with her. Again, manners kicked in. "Can I offer you a cup of coffee to warm your bones?"

Alex stepped inside and motioned Murphy to follow. She decided that she had passed the test—the one about whether or not she was being creepy. Relieved, and happy to be invited in, she said, "That would be nice, if you're sure it's not any trouble."

Lia took a sweatshirt from a hook by the door and slipped it on. Alex was both disappointed and thankful. On one hand, the tank top showed off Lia's breasts beautifully and she was enjoying the view. On the other, the last thing she wanted was to be caught staring at Lia's cleavage. That would definitely tip the scales back toward creepy.

Lia grabbed a mug from one of the open shelves in the kitchen. "How do you take it?"

Alex pulled her attention back to the conversation. "Just a little milk or cream if you have it."

"Coming right up." She filled both mugs and added a splash of half-and-half to each. "Will you sit for a little while? I'm more than ready for a break."

"Sure." Alex followed her into the living room area and took a seat on the sofa. Murphy immediately stretched out in front of her, placing his head on his paws. This ploy was working even better than she'd hoped. Not that it was a ploy.

Lia, who'd taken a seat at the other end, set down her cup and pointed at the dog. "Would he mind some attention?"

Alex laughed at the question. "He loves attention. My only warning is that you might have a hard time getting him to leave."

Lia laughed as well, then got on her hands and knees and crawled the short distance to where Murphy was lying. Alex, who was watching her, was immediately struck with a vision of Lia, clad in the sexy librarian getup, crawling toward her. *Get a grip, McKinnon. You are going to start drooling if you aren't careful.*

Lia only petted Murphy's head a few times before he rolled over and flashed his belly. Lia buried her fingers in the thick fur on his chest. "You're a good boy."

His tail thumped and Alex rolled her eyes. "He has no shame."

"And why should he?" She turned to Murphy. "Why should you? There's nothing to be ashamed of. You just like getting your loves, don't you?"

"So I take it you're a dog person."

Lia, now sprawled on the floor so she could pet Murphy with both hands, sighed. "Yes. We always had at least two in the house when I was growing up. When I left for college, I swear I missed them more than my family because I could at least talk to my family on the phone."

Alex frowned. "You haven't had one since?"

Lia sat up. "My ex did not like dogs."

Alex sniffed her disapproval.

"I know, right? Should have been a sign that it was ill-fated from the start."

Alex knew it was important to tread carefully. She never wanted to be one of those women who is always bad-mouthing other people's exes. She said diplomatically, "I'm sure that was hard. I was without a dog during college, too, and I swore when I graduated I would never be again."

Lia smiled faintly and Alex feared she was going to clam up. It was time to change the subject. "What is it that smells so good?"

"Red beans."

"Beans? I've never encountered beans that smell like that."

"It's my Grand-mère's recipe, with a little bit of improvisation. I didn't have a ham bone laying around."

"Well, she must have been a phenomenal cook, and she must have passed it down to you." She hoped she wasn't laying it on too thick. Lia didn't seem put off, so that was good.

"She was, and she taught me most of what I know, including the tradition of red beans and rice on Mondays."

"Why Mondays?"

"It was something the women could leave on the stove while they did the wash."

"Really?"

"Yep. The funny thing is that you can go to a fancy restaurant in the French Quarter and, without fail, Monday's special is red beans and rice."

"That's cool. I love the stories behind food traditions." She also loved that Lia seemed to relax and open up when she talked about food. She made a mental note to remember that for future conversations.

Lia smiled. "It was also a way to get another meal out of Sunday's ham bone."

"Of course."

Lia glanced at the clock. "They should actually be ready just about now. I need to cook a pot of rice still, but I'd love for you to stay."

Things were going even better than Alex had hoped. Still, she didn't want to press her luck. "I'd be lying if I said I wasn't hungry. You sure?"

"I'd love the company, and it's the least I can do to repay you. Besides, as much as I love them, I do not need to eat an entire pot of beans."

Alex followed Lia into the kitchen, watching as she measured water and rice. It was obvious from the way she moved around the space, handled utensils, that she cooked a lot. She tried to focus on Lia's hands so that she didn't get caught staring at the way Lia's shorts accentuated both her long legs and her exceptionally nice rear end. They chatted while the rice cooked, about dogs and music and grandmothers' cooking. Lia set napkins and spoons at one end of the small dining table, poured two glasses of iced tea. When the rice was done, Lia spooned some into two bowls, then ladled over some of the beans. She lifted a bottle of hot sauce and, at Alex's nod, dashed some onto each serving.

Lia carried the bowls to the table, motioned for Alex to sit. "Normally I'd make cornbread to go with them, but I've been eating so much of your bread, I opted to refrain."

"We never do cornbread at the bakery. I should rectify that." Alex sampled the beans. They were creamy and savory with a flavor far more complex than she expected. "Wow. These are amazing."

"Thanks. That's high praise coming from a chef."

"Pastry chef. That's not the same thing. I cook some savory dishes, but nothing to write home about."

"I find that highly unlikely, but I'll take the compliment nonetheless. How long have you owned The Flour Pot?"

Alex thought for a moment. "Just over three years. I worked there for three before that."

"Was that always your goal? Did you know this was where you wanted to end up?"

Alex chuckled. "Not in the least. I went to the Culinary Institute in Hyde Park and we were crazy competitive with each other. My plan was to work my way up to a Michelin-starred restaurant in Boston."

"But?"

Alex thought about the time she spent climbing that ladder, spending months at a time making nothing but tarts or truffles or sponge cakes. She toiled her way into chocolate work, creating artful flourishes for plated desserts and exotic bonbons for exclusive events. She even did a few showpieces—towering sculptures of perfectly tempered chocolate in elaborate and whimsical designs. "There was this constant pressure to do something new and exotic, things like molecular gastronomy. It started to feel more like one-upmanship than craftsmanship."

"So everything you see on the Food Network is true."

"Only less glamorous and with ridiculous hours."

Lia shook her head. "I can't imagine keeping that up."

"Exactly. I decided that wasn't the life I wanted."

"And Provincetown was the antidote?"

Alex considered. The decision to move to Provincetown had been an impulsive one, fueled by her restlessness and a blossoming relationship that had taken an unfortunate turn. "Sort of. I came out for the summer, figuring I'd work for the season and then figure out what to do next. I landed at the bakery."

"And then what happened?"

Alex wasn't big on talking about herself so much, but Lia looked sincerely interested in her story. "The Flour Pot is one of the places that stays open year-round. I stayed, too, for the next year and the year after that. I got to know Doreen, the owner, and her wife Syd. They were ready to retire to somewhere that was warm more than three months of the year. I think they decided I would take care of the business, run it like they did."

"And now it's yours."

Alex smiled. "And now it's mine. I honestly don't think I could have dreamed up such an opportunity if I'd tried."

"What a great story."

"Thanks. And now that I've talked your ear off, I'll do the dishes."

"Oh, you don't have to—"

"It's a rule. When I cook you a meal, you can do the dishes."

Lia looked at the woman now standing at the sink, filling it with hot, soapy water. Lia put her hands on her hips, wondering how things had gotten so cozy all of a sudden. "You cook me a meal nearly every day."

"That doesn't count. You pay for your meals at the bakery."

"How about I wash and you dry?" It occurred to Lia that she was negotiating dish duty with a virtual stranger. It should have been weird, but somehow wasn't.

Alex stepped aside. "Deal."

When they were done, she handed Lia the dish towel. "Thank you again for the amazing lunch. I hope I didn't put too much of a wrinkle in your day."

"It was great to have some company." Although she would have said so no matter what—her mama taught her well—she meant it. As disconcerting as it had been to have Alex show up on her doorstep, the company had been nice.

"Well, I won't keep you any longer." Alex picked up her jacket and Murphy immediately joined her. "I'll see you at the bakery soon, I hope."

"You most certainly will."

After they left, Lia sat down in the kitchen and looked around. Her eye caught the scarf that had prompted Alex's visit and she started drumming her fingers on the table. Was it a friendly gesture or was there more to it?

Alex seemed to have everything going for her—looks, brains, personality. Lia replayed their conversation in her mind. It was definitely flirtatious. What she couldn't decide was if Alex was one of those women who flirted with everyone. That was probably the case. That had to be the case.

Yet, each time they spent any amount of time together, Lia found herself more and more taken. A not-so-small voice in the back of her mind warned her she was being too open, too easy, that she was dancing on the edge of something more than just friendliness. She needed to rein herself in. It was one thing to enjoy a little banter. It was another thing entirely to be genuinely attracted to someone.

Alex was a blip, a passing distraction. She allowed Lia to forget for a moment the reason she came to Provincetown in the first place. Emphasis on moment. She needed to remember that forgetting could be a very dangerous thing.

Chapter Ten

A lex stole a glance at Lia, who was sitting at a table near the window typing away. It was the table she'd claimed as her own and sat at more days than not for the better part of two weeks. Lia was oblivious to the observation, so she indulged in a longer look.

She was nice to look at. She had a way of wearing clothes that, without being revealing, showed off her curves. Her hair was this mass of dark curls that always looked a little sex tossed. She had a way of biting her lip when she was concentrating on her work. It made her look both studious and sexy, much like a librarian. She suddenly wanted nothing more than to start nibbling on those lips.

Under normal circumstances, she wouldn't give a second thought to asking Lia out, to finding out whether the attraction was mutual, to seeing where things might lead. There was that nagging feeling in the back of her mind, though. She couldn't decide what it meant and she couldn't quite shake it. Alex admitted to herself that she was fretting. She did not fret, nor did she stand around and do nothing.

She'd ask Lia to go out for a drink. It would be casual, neighborly even. Arriving in Provincetown in November was not conducive to a robust social life. Although some people chose to come at that time for just that reason, Lia didn't give off the hermit vibe. She had, after all, become a regular at the bakery. She also seemed more than happy to chat, not only with Alex but with a few of the regulars who'd taken it upon themselves to make introductions.

Alex nodded to herself. She'd ask Lia to go out for a drink. It didn't have to mean anything. So what if she found herself consumed by a need to kiss her, to see if her lips were as soft as they looked? She'd cross that bridge when she came to it.

At around 2:00, before Lia had a chance to sneak away, she walked over to the table with two cups of coffee. "Care for a little break?"

Lia, who'd been completely absorbed in her work, was clearly startled by the sound of Alex's voice. She jumped, banged her knee on the underside of the table, blushed. She glanced at Alex with a look that was half smile, half grimace. "Sorry?"

Smooth move, McKinnon. "No, I'm sorry. I didn't mean to startle you. I seem to have an unfortunate habit of doing that."

Lia chuckled and made a serious face. "It's not you, it's me."

"Funny. You're funny."

"I have my moments. What was the question again?"

"I asked if you wanted a little break." She gestured with the two cups.

"Oh, that's so nice of you. I would love a break."

Alex set down the cups and pulled out the chair across from her. "Do you mind if I join you?"

"That would be lovely."

It was a full smile Lia flashed her this time. Alex tried to ignore the warmth that moved through her. "So, is work going well?"

"It is. I've got a couple of things in the works. Coming here is perfect. I always get antsy if I don't leave the house at least once every day or two."

"Well, we're happy to have you. And I don't just mean here at the bakery. It's always nice to have another soul around in the winter." It helped that she was a gorgeous, smart, funny soul, but Alex didn't mention that part.

Lia nodded. "I can imagine. I've been here a few times, but only in the summer. I knew it would be quiet, but I underestimated exactly what that meant."

She chuckled. "Well, it doesn't help that most of the people still around are heading into hibernation mode. It'll get worse when the weather really turns."

"Really turns?"

"After December, the Nor'easters start to blow in. There's something about when it's five below and snowing sideways that makes people want to hunker down."

Lia swallowed. "That would do it."

Alex studied the woman across from her. Her eyes were as big as saucers. It was hard not to laugh. She wondered what on earth Lia Brooks was doing here. "Well, before that happens, a lot of the locals take advantage of their free evenings by having drinks and getting cozy down at the Crown & Anchor. If you're going to winter here, you should make an appearance sooner rather than later."

"That's very friendly advice. Thanks."

She couldn't tell if Lia was shutting her down or looking for an invitation. "Always happy to help out a newbie in town."

"So when does one go? What's the attire? I don't want to look like some intrusive tourist." Lia sounded so earnest, like she was trying to understand some foreign culture.

"Weeknight crowd tends to be a little on the early side, and it's definitely casual. If you're not busy tonight, we could head over together around five. I'll know just about everyone there and I'd be happy to introduce you to some of the usual suspects."

Lia went from smiling to looking like a deer in the headlights. Clearly, the invitation was a surprise. From the looks of it, it was an unwelcome one. "Um…"

Alex's brain kicked into high gear, trying to find a way to backpedal that would give them both a graceful exit. "Or some other time. It's no big deal."

Lia seemed to regain a little of her composure. "Thanks. That's really nice of you. Tonight's not good, but yes, maybe some other time."

Alex shrugged, trying to keep her tone super casual. "Sure. Whenever. Open invitation, no pressure."

"Great. Thanks. Really. I, um, should actually be going. Thanks for the coffee."

"Of course. It was nice to take a break with some company."

Lia nodded. "Yeah. Absolutely. Have a good afternoon."

Alex watched as Lia picked up her things and scurried out of the café. For the life of her, she couldn't figure out why there'd been such an abrupt shift. It was just a casual, friendly invitation, right?

She got up and started her end-of-shift cleaning. As she went about her routine, Alex found herself mildly irritated. What she couldn't decide was whether she was irritated with Lia or with herself.

❖

Lia walked home, berating herself for being such a flake. Alex had done nothing more than invite her to the neighborhood bar. Friends, even casual acquaintances, did that sort of thing all the time. Even in the context of their semi-flirtatious chatting, it wasn't a big deal. Why did she freak out?

There was no reason to think Alex was trying to make anything of it. She might have even done it out of pity. Oh, God. What if Alex had invited her out of pity? Okay, now she was just being dramatic. She needed to calm herself down. A little perspective wouldn't hurt either.

Lia walked in the door of her apartment and set down her bag. After checking the time, she picked up her phone and dialed her best friend.

"Hey!" Sally drawled the greeting in a way that was unique to Southerners; it managed to be both languid and enthusiastic at the same time.

"Hey, Sal. Am I interrupting anything?"

"Not at all, sugar. I was in court all morning and am just finishing a late lunch."

"Oh good." Lia hesitated. How should she frame this?

Sally had been her best friend since they were five. They'd been in the same preschool class and, within days of knowing one another, were inseparable. That continued throughout elementary, middle, and high school. Both the only girl in a family of boys, they became the sister neither of them had.

Sally was the first person she came out to. With sweaty palms and a knot in her stomach, she told Sally about her crush on the captain of the girls' basketball team, about liking girls in general. She was convinced Sally would no longer be her friend, that hugs and sleepovers and confidences would become suspicious or, worse, repugnant.

To the contrary, Sally found the entire thing delightful. It was, by her estimation, one of the more exciting things to happen in their quiet, small town existence. She cheered Lia on in coming out to her parents and brothers; she consoled her through her first heartbreak. Going to college nearly a thousand miles apart had been a difficult decision for them both. Armed with email, instant messages, and weekly phone calls, they managed to remain one another's cheerleaders, confidantes, and more. Lia was the maid of honor in Sally's wedding and godmother to her sons.

"I get the feeling you aren't just calling to chew the cud."

"Well…" Lia paced back and forth across the kitchen.

"Spill." As a lawyer and a mother of two little boys, Sally was an expert at getting people to do just that.

"A woman invited me to have a drink with her and I freaked out."

"I'm going to need a little more than that."

Lia took a deep breath. "Almost every day since I got here, I've been going to this café to work. The woman who owns it has been really nice and welcoming and today she invited me for a drink at the bar where all the locals hang out."

"I gather this woman is a lesbian?"

Lia thought about Alex—her looks, her casual confidence, the unmistakably flirtatious banter. "Oh, yeah."

"I see. So, did you freak out because she asked you to join her for a drink or because you're attracted to her and you don't know what to do about it?"

In addition to being highly persuasive, Sally also had a laser-sharp intuition. Occasionally, it caused Lia serious vexation, but mostly, it was really nice. She stopped pacing. "I suppose it's the latter."

"That's good. If you'd lost pleasure in a friendly cocktail and the local bar, I'm not sure what I'd do with you."

"You're so right." Lia told her about Alex showing up with her scarf, how the initial awkwardness gave way to easy conversation.

"It definitely sounds like flirtation. But, Lia, you know what? That's not a bad thing. Flirting with someone doesn't mean you have to jump into a relationship. Or even sleep with them, for that matter."

"Right."

"Of course, I think sleeping with someone might be just what you need right now."

"Sally." Lia tried to sound exasperated, but it came out more scandalized.

"Okay, okay. Too much. We don't have to talk about that right now. Right now, I think you should accept the invitation, go out for drinks, and have a little fun. Can you do that?"

Sally had a way of making it sound so uncomplicated. "I can do that."

"Good. I have to meet with a client in ten minutes. Call me this weekend?"

"I will. Thanks, Sal."

"My pleasure. Just remember, don't do anything I wouldn't do."

Lia rolled her eyes. Sally had definitely been the wild one in their friendship. "That doesn't leave much off the list."

"Exactly."

CHAPTER ELEVEN

Lia sat at the table she'd already come to think of as hers. The lunch crowd had thinned, but Alex was nowhere in sight. Alex had been friendly, but definitely cooler toward her when she arrived that morning. Lia hoped that meant the ball was in her court, not that she'd blown her chance to spend time with Alex.

As if on cue, Alex emerged from the kitchen with a bottle of glass cleaner and a roll of paper towels. Without making eye contact, she walked around the counter and started cleaning the front of the display case. Lia took a deep breath. This was her shot. She got up and walked about halfway to where Alex was standing.

"Hey, Alex?"

Alex stood and turned. She offered a smile. "Hey. Did you want something?" She gestured to the case.

"No. I mean, yes." Why was this so difficult?

Alex looked confused but didn't say anything.

"I mean, I don't want anything to eat, but I wanted to talk to you."

"Oh. All right."

"I'm sorry I left so quickly yesterday. I'd completely forgotten I was supposed to be somewhere." It was a lie, and probably not very convincing, but that was okay. "I'd love to get a drink with you."

Alex smiled and it seemed genuine. "It's fine. Yeah, that would be great."

"Tonight is good or, really, any night this week but Thursday. I've joined a poker group."

Alex chuckled and Lia couldn't tell if Alex was amused by her change of heart or the fact that she was in a poker group and felt the need to share it. She was nodding, though, so that had to be a good sign.

"Tonight would be great. Is five good for you?"

Lia felt her shoulders relax. She hadn't blown it. "Five is perfect."

"You're welcome to stay here and work if you don't want to go home and come back. I'll run up and shower after closing and we can walk over."

"You live upstairs?"

"I do. There's an apartment on the second floor. It's one of the main reasons I fell in love with the place."

"I bet." Lia hesitated, then decided she could do this friendly-flirty thing. "I'd love to see it sometime."

Alex searched Lia's face for meaning. The woman had gone from practically running out the door to inviting herself to Alex's apartment. It felt like a game of cat and mouse, but Lia didn't really seem like the type to be coy. Alex was usually able to read women with ease. Not being able to tell was driving her nuts.

"Sure." She didn't know what else to say.

"Thanks for letting me stay. I promise I won't be in the way."

"I've no doubt. I'll let you get back to work." Alex returned to the kitchen, feeling even more unsure about what she was getting herself into than she had before.

At four, she went up to her apartment to shower and change. She stood in her bedroom, naked and damp, obsessing about what to wear. More irritated by the fact that she was obsessing than her choices, she yanked a pair of gray pants and a dark blue sweater from the closet. She dried her hair with just a touch of pomade and assessed herself in the mirror. Satisfied, she pulled on a nicely worn pair of brown boots and grabbed her North Face jacket from its hook by the door. She let Murphy out to do his business, indulged him in an early dinner, and promised she wouldn't be home too late.

As she entered the kitchen through the back door, Alex made a point of making a fair amount of noise. The last thing she wanted to do was scare Lia out of her skin again.

"You ready?"

Lia looked up and, for a second, Alex was pretty sure she was being checked out. Lia seemed to remember herself, though, and it passed. "That was quick," she said.

Alex shrugged and smiled. "Shall we?"

With the sun down, the temperature was falling quickly. Lia tucked her hands into her coat pockets and said, "I'm trying really hard not to think about Nor'easters."

Alex couldn't help but laugh. "Power of positive thinking."

In fewer than ten minutes, they were at the Crown & Anchor.

"The Central House is where the locals hang out," Alex said as they went inside. While the restaurant opened to a fairly large dining room, the bar was small and intimate, with warm lighting and a roaring fire. At this time of night, it had a relaxed, local happy hour feel. She congratulated herself on choosing it.

"I'll get the first round," Lia offered. "What's your pleasure?"

It was unlikely Lia was being a tease, but she couldn't help but think of an entirely different kind of pleasure. Although tempted to say as much, Alex thought it might be a little soon to test those waters. She got the distinct impression that Lia was less brazen than her banter implied, even if she was wearing high boots and a tight sweater.

"No, no. I insist. What will you have?"

"I'll have a beer. Whatever you recommend that isn't a stout."

"You got it."

Lia looked around. "Table by the fire okay?"

"Absolutely."

Lia headed to a small vacant table near the fireplace. She shrugged off her coat and willed herself to relax. She tried to silence that little voice in the back of her head that said Alex felt sorry for her. Then she tried to silence the other little voice that said Alex just wanted to sleep with her. She shook her head. Only she would be obsessing at both ends of the spectrum.

The crowd was light and it didn't take long for Alex to get their drinks. As she returned to the table, Lia squared her shoulders, determined to be good company.

"I got a winter ale and an IPA. Preference?" Alex asked as she set down the glasses.

"Both sound good. You?"

"Start with the winter, then," Alex said, sliding one glass across the table and picking up the other. "It's a local brew."

Lia picked up the glass, raised it. "To new friends."

"To new friends."

As they drank, Alex pointed out several people in the bar, sharing tidbits of information and town gossip.

"I wonder what they're saying about me." Lia hadn't meant to say it out loud. Now Alex probably thought she was a total dork.

Alex made a point of looking around, as though spies might be attempting to infiltrate their conversation. "They want to know who the hot new woman is who's been hanging around my bakery."

"They are not." Not the answer she was expecting. Hot? Surely, Alex was poking fun at her.

"I swear."

Not seeing a graceful exit, she raised a brow. "And what's the verdict?"

"That her name is Lia. She's gorgeous and she's here for the winter."

"Get out." Lia tried to stifle the flutter she got when Alex referred to her as gorgeous. She felt like a silly high schooler, and worried Alex thought as much.

"Yes, they're also dying to know two very important things."

"What two things?" This was absurd, but maybe a little fun, too.

"Is she gay and is she single?"

"I see. And what do you say to that?"

Alex shrugged. "After telling them that it's none of my business or theirs, I tell them I'm just getting to know her."

"A very diplomatic answer." Lia considered. She could cloak herself in privacy, but she didn't see the point. She wanted to feel connected to this little town she called home, for however long that was. Being antisocial wasn't going to get her anywhere. "Well, I'll give it to you straight from the source."

"An official statement?"

She nodded. "On the record. To the first question: most definitely. To the second: recently." Lia picked up her glass and drank. She watched Alex lean back and mull over the information.

"I'm happy to hear the former, and sorry about the latter."

"Don't be. It was my choice and it was the right one." She was not going to spend her evening rehashing her broken heart. She also didn't want to spend the whole evening talking about herself. "What about you?"

"What about me?"

"Are you? Gay, single?" She put on her best inquiring-minds-want-to-know, talk-show-host face. It was more about changing the subject than being flirtatious, but that was okay.

"Most definitely," Alex said, borrowing her phrase. "On both counts."

She couldn't decide if Alex was indicating that she was available, or that she wasn't interested. She hated herself for being completely out of practice when it came to this kind of banter. Even if she wasn't looking to get involved, Sally was right. A little casual flirtation was good for the ego. Now she couldn't even do that well. That wasn't entirely true. She managed to do just fine with other people. It was Alex. Whether or not she wanted to admit it, Alex stirred up things, made her feel things. It brought out every nervous and awkward tendency she had.

"Good to know." Their glasses were empty, and Lia pounced on the distraction. "May I get the second round?"

"How about you fetch them? I already have a tab open." When she frowned, Alex added quickly, "I promise you can buy next time."

"Deal." Lia stood and picked up their empty glasses.

Alex congratulated herself on planting the seed for another date and watched Lia walk to the bar. She took a moment to appreciate the sexy boots Lia was wearing, the way her hips swayed slightly when she walked. While Lia waited for the bartender to pull their beers, Alex noted that Anita, the local accountant, leaned over and said something that made Lia laugh. It was rich and uninhibited, the kind of laugh that could warm a person from the inside out. It was clear that Anita enjoyed it as well, a fact that hit her with a small ping of jealousy. It was an unfamiliar and unpleasant feeling. Alex pushed it aside as Lia made her way to the table with a pair of pint glasses.

"I don't mean to pry, but what are you doing for Thanksgiving?" Alex didn't know what possessed her to ask, but it was out of her mouth before she could stop herself.

Lia looked away. She answered without making eye contact. "I'll just make a small dinner here. My family tried to convince me to come home, but I'm not a huge fan of flying. Trying to do it during the busiest travel week of the year isn't worth the toll on my psyche."

"You'll come for dinner at my place." It wasn't phrased as a question. Alex couldn't stand the thought of Lia being alone on the holiday.

"Please don't feel sorry for me. I'll be fine."

The sharpness in her voice caught Alex off guard. She'd clearly hit a nerve. "I don't feel sorry for you at all. I'm already having a mishmash of people over. It'll be casual. And fun."

Afraid she was starting to oversell, Alex shut her mouth. She watched Lia mull over the invitation, probably formulating a polite excuse.

Lia looked her in the eye. "Only if you swear it doesn't interfere with your plans at all."

"The more the merrier. I really do swear. It will be a few people you recognize from the bakery. My sister Meg and her husband will come out from Boston. A new face will liven things up a bit."

"Okay. It sounds really nice. Thanks for the invitation. What can I bring?"

Well, that was easy. Alex mentally patted herself on the back. "Got any Southern specialties up your sleeve?"

"I do make some mean praline sweet potatoes."

"Speak no further."

About two hours, and three beers, after they'd arrived, Lia and Alex emerged from the bar. There were snowflakes falling around them and everything in sight was covered with a light dusting of snow.

"Oh." Lia threw her arms out and turned in a slow circle.

Alex couldn't tell whether Lia's enthusiasm was genuine or more the result of the drinking. Either way, it was charming, and sexy. Lia had a way of being at once a deeply complicated woman and a disarmingly simple one. It made her want to test the taste of her, the feel of her skin, the response of her body to kiss and touch. Alex readily embraced the desire she felt, but remained unsettled by the additional stirring that seemed both exciting and a little dangerous.

"Can I walk you home?"

Lia turned toward her. She seemed to remember where she was, walked the two steps back to where Alex was standing. "I don't want to put you out."

"You're not, I promise. And it would make me feel better knowing you were home safely."

Lia poked her lightly on the chest. "You're one of those chivalrous types."

Alex had been called a lot of things by a lot of women, but she was pretty sure that chivalrous had never been one of them. "Neighborly. You're still new to town, and I fear I've gotten you a little drunk."

"I'm not drunk. Tipsy, but not drunk. I will, however, accept your offer, because it's nice, and I'm usually bad at letting people do nice things for me."

Alex wanted to ask for an explanation, but didn't. Instead, she bowed dramatically and gestured for Lia to lead the way. Lia laughed and tucked her hand into the crook of Alex's arm and the two of them started walking toward the West End. It was hard not to like tipsy Lia. They walked in companionable silence. Lia leaned into her slightly and the proximity allowed her to just catch the scent of Lia's perfume, the same one she discovered on Lia's forgotten scarf.

When they arrived at Lia's, Alex flipped on the flashlight function of her phone while Lia dug out her keys and unlocked the door.

"Thank you so much. I feel more like a local already."

"It was my pleasure, both to introduce you to a neighborhood hangout and to spend the evening with you."

Lia turned to Alex. Through the light haze clouding her brain, she had a flash of Alex's hands in her hair, her mouth taking hers. Lia had to shake off the wave of desire that washed over her. "The, ah, the feeling is mutual."

Unbeknownst to Lia, Alex was having the exact same thoughts. Her brain, however, was clear. And as much as she wanted to pull Lia against her and kiss her senseless, Alex sensed it was too soon. And if Lia's judgment was impaired, it could ruin everything. She settled for keeping it light. "Will I see you tomorrow, then?"

Lia smiled. "Absolutely."

Alex walked the short distance back to her place. She mulled over the decision not to kiss Lia. It was unlike her to be hesitant. Of course, Lia wasn't like the women she was used to—women who knew what they wanted and had no qualms expressing it. That said, Lia might be exactly the kind of woman who waited for the other person to make the first move.

When she got home, Murphy was curled up on the couch. He got up and stretched, trotted over to the door when Alex motioned for him to go outside to do his nightly business. "Should I have kissed her? I keep thinking I should have kissed her." Murphy looked at her intently, then lifted his paw. He placed it on her thigh at the exact place her phone sat in her pocket. Alex pulled out the phone, then scratched the dog's ears. "Genius, my friend. Genius."

Lia was about to climb into the tub when her phone buzzed. She picked it up and read the text from Alex.

I really wanted to kiss you. Just saying.

Lia felt a flutter in her stomach that then migrated decidedly south. Whether it was from the beer or Sally's pep talk, she felt suddenly brave. She bit her lip and thought for a moment before replying.

I really wanted you to. Just saying.

She slid into the hot, sudsy water and thought again about what it would be like to have Alex's lips on hers. Her phone buzzed again almost instantly.

Duly noted.

CHAPTER TWELVE

Meg and Rob arrived late Wednesday night. Alex could tell that Meg was dying to grill her about the addition to the guest list, but it was after midnight, so she reluctantly went to bed. There would, of course, be plenty of time for questions in the morning.

When Alex woke at six, she made a point of moving around quietly. She let Murphy out and gave him his breakfast, put coffee on, then started organizing the massive pile of ingredients that would become Thanksgiving dinner. Although she was disappointed that her father was already at his winter condo in South Carolina, it remained Alex's favorite holiday. She didn't begrudge him the holiday with his girlfriend, a Charleston native, but she did miss him. Since he promised he would be in Boston for Christmas, Alex hadn't given him a hard time, or at least not a very hard time.

A little before seven, Meg padded out to the kitchen in leggings and a frayed NYU sweatshirt. She poured herself a cup of coffee and sat on one of the stools at the kitchen island while Alex chopped vegetables.

"So tell me about this Lia."

Alex knew it was coming. It wasn't just that Meg was nosy, which she was, but also that she knew when Alex was withholding something. Meg called it her twin sense. "Good morning to you, too."

Meg set her cup down, straightened her posture, and placed a hand delicately on her chest. "Oh, I'm sorry. I didn't realize we were standing on ceremony. Good morning, sister. Happy Thanksgiving."

"Have I told you lately that you aren't funny?" Alex resisted the urge to throw some onion at her, but only because she didn't want Murphy to eat any that fell on the floor.

"Not lately. So tell me about this Lia." She took a bite of cheese Danish. "This is delicious, by the way."

"Thank you. She's spending the winter in town, by herself. I hated the idea of her having Thanksgiving dinner for one in her little apartment."

"What a noble gesture. Are you planning on getting in her pants? Or have you already?"

She considered a flippant response, but Meg could always tell when she was lying and it would make her all the more suspicious. "She's gorgeous, and there's definitely chemistry."

"But?"

"But she's just getting out of a relationship. And it was enough to make her leave New York City and come all the way to Provincetown at the start of winter."

"So she's damaged. And damaged means messy."

Alex put her knife down. "That's just it. I'm sure she's hurt, but she doesn't give off a wounded vibe. I haven't been able to figure her out."

Meg nodded. "But you want to."

"Yeah." She picked up her knife and resumed chopping. "I do."

"Just remember she's a person and not a puzzle."

Before Alex could reply, Rob emerged from the bedroom.

"I smell coffee. Please tell me there's coffee."

Meg hopped down from her stool to pour Rob a cup. She passed Alex and poked her in the ribs. "I'm just saying."

Aside from not having a stand mixer, the kitchen of Lia's apartment was well-equipped. There was a decent set of pots, baking dishes and cookie sheets, utensils, measuring cups and spoons, and more. After realizing that she wouldn't need to buy any equipment, she decided to pick up ingredients for a couple of her other typical Thanksgiving dishes. She was accustomed to preparing the whole meal; she was worried she wouldn't know what to do with herself if she only had to make one thing.

She unloaded the ingredients she'd picked up the day before and turned the oven on to preheat. She gave the sweet potatoes a good scrub, poked them with a fork, and set them on a baking sheet. She slid them into the oven and got to work on her pie crust. It was a risky move to bring a pie to dinner at a pastry chef's house. Still, her bourbon-pecan was always a hit and it wouldn't feel like Thanksgiving without it.

With the crust chilling, Lia grated a mixture of cheddar and Gruyère. Technically, her grandmother's cheese straw recipe only called for cheddar, but Lia had taken a number of liberties over the years. She also added crushed garlic and cayenne pepper. She liked to think that Grand-mère would have approved of the additions. Lia worked the dough slowly by hand to ensure that the butter and cheese were completely kneaded into the flour. When it came together, she wrapped it in plastic and put it into the fridge.

She rolled out her crust, laid it gently in the pie plate she found. She trimmed and crimped the edges, added two heaping cups of pecans, then poured in the mixture of eggs, corn syrup, vanilla, and bourbon. She took the sweet potatoes out, put the pie in. She spent the next couple of hours whipping up the sweet potatoes, topping them with brown sugar and pecans, and rolling out and baking her cheese straws.

When everything was done, Lia still had a leisurely hour and a half to get ready. She chose a tweed skirt and scooped-neck black sweater, along with her favorite tall boots. With time still to spare, she decided to go ahead and call her parents. As usual, they were happy to hear from her. They were glad to hear she had plans, since her holidays had for so long revolved around Danielle. They said they missed her and hoped she'd come home for a visit soon. After she hung up, she texted her brothers and Sally.

She thought about calling Dani. They hadn't spoken since she'd left, but given how many years—how many holidays—they'd spent together, it felt weird to have no contact at all. It wasn't like she wanted to be friends or anything, but Lia wasn't one to hold onto anger. She hesitated for a moment, then settled on a text.

Happy Thanksgiving. Hope your day is filled with good food and good friends.

Lia read over the message. She decided it wasn't too personal or too impersonal, then hit send.

She loaded her things into the front seat of her car and headed over, parking around back the way Alex had instructed. Lia managed to carry everything at once, but she had to ring Alex's doorbell with her knee. While she waited, she wiggled until her skirt fell back into place and blew a stray curl out of her eyes. When the door opened, it wasn't Alex standing on the other side, but a lankier and more feminine version of her.

"You must be Lia. I'm Alex's sister, Meg. Let me help you with that." Meg took the pie Lia was holding as well as the bottle of wine tucked under her arm.

"Thank you so much, and it's nice to meet you."

"Likewise. Have you been here before?"

"I haven't."

"Okay, follow me."

Lia did as she was instructed, following Meg up a narrow set of stairs. At the top, she found herself in a bright, open kitchen. Alex, who was stirring something at the stove, looked over and called a greeting. Her smile quickly became a furrowed brow. "I thought you were bringing sweet potatoes."

"I did." Lia lifted the canvas shopping bag holding the casserole dish. "They're right here."

Alex turned and put her hands on her hips. "I thought you were bringing only sweet potatoes."

Lia shrugged. "I'm Southern. This is how we roll."

Alex laughed, then tucked her tongue in her cheek and nodded. "I see. Well, I suppose the more-the-merrier philosophy applies to food as much as people. Come unload and then I'll introduce you around."

Lia set down her bags. She pulled out the casserole dish and handed it to Alex. "This needs to be warmed if you have room in the oven."

"Got it." Alex took the dish and slid it into the oven next to one of the most beautifully browned turkeys Lia had ever seen.

"That looks amazing." She gestured toward the turkey while pulling the little silver serving tray she'd found out of her other bag.

Alex came over to study it. "So what else did you bring?"

"Cheese straws, old family recipe. They're a great little snack with wine before dinner. And, perhaps against my better judgment, a pie."

Alex carefully removed the plastic wrap from the cheese straws and sampled one. "These are delicious. If I'd known they existed, I would have demanded that you bring them. Why would a pie be against your better judgment?"

Lia blushed. "Bringing a pie to a CIA-trained pastry chef is like asking—"

Alex interrupted. "One, you're adorable. Two, you'll be pleased to know that I hate making pies. For some reason, I had a harder time making a decent pie crust than just about anything else I learned in culinary school. I've avoided them ever since."

"That's hilarious. Thank you, for the compliment and for making me feel better."

Alex winked at her. "Anytime. Now, let's get you to the living room before the natives start to get restless."

In addition to Meg and her husband Rob, Jeff was there with a bookish guy named Edwin. Shortly after, Tom and Charlie, who she recognized from the café, arrived. Wine was poured and Lia's cheese straws, along with some olives and baguette with caramelized onions and Brie, were devoured. By the time dinner was served, Lia felt more at ease than she did during most of the Thanksgivings she spent in New York.

At the table, expanded with leaves until it was halfway into the living room, she was seated between Alex and Meg. Although they shared similar looks and mannerisms, it was clear that they had very different personalities. Meg was a complete extrovert and peppered Lia with questions about her childhood and decision to move north. Lia really wanted to ask similar questions about her and Alex's childhood, but she was afraid of making her interest seem too obvious.

Whatever nervousness she'd felt about crashing a family holiday dissolved. And although she stole plenty of glances at Alex throughout the meal, she was kept distracted enough not to think about whether or not Alex still wanted to kiss her. Which was for the best, really, since the moment had likely passed and nothing was going to happen.

After everyone had eaten their way through seconds, if not thirds, she was allowed to help wrap up leftovers, then was banished to the living room while the non-cooking types did the dishes. The football game on television reminded her of home—home-home, not the years she'd spent with Danielle. This group was boisterous and silly and loud; it reminded her of family Thanksgivings when she was little.

Once everything from dinner was cleaned up and put away, talk turned toward dessert. There were a couple of protests of being too full, but bring-it-on won by a slim margin. Meg got up to put on a pot of coffee, and Alex got out dessert plates and forks. Lia went with them. "Is there anything I can do to help?"

"Actually, I need to get the other desserts from the bakery fridge. Will you give me a hand?"

"At your service."

Alex headed downstairs and she followed. The bakery kitchen was dimly lit. When Alex opened the door to one of the large, stainless steel coolers, it cast a pool of light between them. She handed Lia a pumpkin cheesecake and then took out what looked like an elaborate chocolate torte. She nudged the door closed with a hip. Lia turned to go back upstairs, but Alex stopped her.

"Wait." Alex set the chocolate cake on the table behind them. She took the cheesecake from Lia and set it down as well.

"What is it? What's wrong?"

Alex took a step and closed the space between them. "Nothing is wrong. I just don't think I can make it through the rest of the evening without doing this."

Alex placed one hand in the curve of Lia's lower back, the other in Lia's hair. She paused for only a second, as if searching for any sign of hesitation. Lia parted her lips to say something, but there were no words. It must have been all the encouragement Alex needed.

Maybe the kiss wasn't entirely unexpected, but Lia was unprepared for the onslaught to her senses. Alex's lips were warm, teasing at first. Quickly, however, the soft brush of her mouth became more demanding. Lia's head began to swim. Suddenly unsteady on her feet, she leaned into the heat of Alex's body.

Lia couldn't remember ever being kissed like this. To be fair, she couldn't actually think about much of anything, but she was pretty certain this was unlike any kiss she'd ever experienced. Her body was tight with yearning and she could feel herself become wet. The wanting bordered on desperate.

As if she could sense that wanting, that desperation, Alex turned slightly so that Lia's back was pressed against the cooler door. She pulled her lips away from Lia's mouth, tracing tongue and teeth down her neck to the low, scooped neckline of her sweater. Lia felt her skin flush; she wanted nothing more than to give herself over to this sudden explosion of desire.

She was on the verge of saying as much when a voice called down to them.

"Is everything all right down there?"

Lia jumped, but Alex kept her arm tight around Lia's waist. "Yep, we're good. Be right up."

Although the blood was still pumping hot under her skin, Lia was able to regain a small amount of composure. She looked at Alex, who was now grinning at her.

"Oh. My. God." That was all she could manage.

Alex gave her a squeeze, then released her. "Sorry. I didn't mean to ravage you. I mean, I did, but not in the bakery with people milling around upstairs."

"Don't apologize. Please, don't ever apologize for doing that."

Lia could see Alex swallow hard, but she didn't know what it meant. Alex picked up the cheesecake and handed it to her for the second time.

"Then I will simply promise to do it again soon, under slightly different circumstances." She picked up the cake and motioned for Lia to lead the way upstairs.

Meg was waiting for them in the kitchen. Lia watched them exchange glances, after which Meg smiled. "Lia, I cannot wait to try your pie."

❖

It was after ten when the party started to break apart. Alex walked Lia to her car. "I'm really glad you came."

"I'm really glad you invited me."

"I'll see you again very soon?"

"I'll be at my usual table on Saturday."

Alex nodded. "I'll be counting on it."

Lia didn't trust herself to keep any physical contact casual at that point, so she climbed into her car. As she backed onto the street, Alex didn't move. She lifted her hand in a wave, and Alex did the same.

On the short drive home, Lia touched her fingers to her lips. They felt warm and slightly swollen. Her mind drifted to the heat, the hunger of Alex's kiss and Lia felt another wave of arousal course through her. Apparently, the moment hadn't passed. Alex was attracted to her, wanted her. It was both exciting and unsettling. She was going to have to decide what to do, and fast.

When she got home, Lia felt far too wound up, and far too full, for sleep. She changed into sweats and turned on the second half of the late football game. Dani did not enjoy football, so Lia had drifted away from following anything more than the win-loss record of her New Orleans Saints. Tuning in was like rediscovering an old friend.

She picked up her phone and found texts from all of her brothers, Sally, and a couple of her nieces and nephews who were old enough to have cell phones of their own. There was no text from Dani. Lia couldn't decide whether or not she should be surprised. Instead, she decided it didn't really matter. She snuggled under her blanket and watched Detroit wallop Green Bay.

CHAPTER THIRTEEN

A lex had never been timid when it came to asking women out. Even in high school, before she'd come out to herself or anyone else, she'd initiated kisses during study sessions with her friends. When she decided she was interested in girls, she cajoled the only other lesbian she knew, a girl who'd graduated a year ahead of her and was home on Christmas break, to take her to the dyke bar near her house in Boston. With "X" marks on her hands, she flirted and danced and made out with a woman who must have been at least ten years her senior.

Truth be told, it wasn't the asking Lia out that gave her pause. The ease of spending time together combined with the jolt of electricity from their stolen kiss made Alex crave to discover what else was there. Rather, it seemed to Alex that, if she were to get involved with Lia, there would be more at stake. When it came to relationships, she wasn't one for having a lot at stake.

As she'd told Meg, Lia didn't radiate "wounded bird" the way some women did. She could spot that a mile away. She knew how to flirt casually and give compliments while keeping that type of woman safely at bay. Lia, on the other hand, seemed grounded—content if not entirely happy. She had a quick wit and an even quicker laugh, but if Alex got too flirtatious, she'd get quiet, stop making eye contact. She had an almost detached way of talking about her ex, more like she'd shut the door on those feelings rather than worked through them.

It all made Alex want to respect her privacy and press for details simultaneously. That is what gave her pause. If they became involved,

Alex had no idea if Lia would keep that emotional detachment, or get weird and clingy, or what. Having no idea what might come next left her uneasy.

She looked over to where Lia was typing away. Alex knew from their conversation earlier that morning that she was working on the findings of a study that had something to do with making red blood cells replicate at an accelerated pace. Lia's eyes sparkled as she talked about it. Alex knew enough about medicine to know that anything that could minimize the need for transfusions and bolster the blood supply would indeed be huge news. Lia was giddy as a schoolgirl to be writing about it and Alex found the whole thing ridiculously charming.

Alex sighed. It was useless to deny that what she felt toward Lia was a passing attraction. The lightning hot kiss they'd shared in the bakery on Thanksgiving was not something that she could, or even wanted to, ignore. The matter at hand was deciding how far to take it.

"How goes it?" Alex walked over to Lia's table with two cups of coffee.

It had become a bit of a ritual. Around two, after the lunch rush and before she started cleaning up for the day, she brought Lia a cup of coffee and they chatted for a bit. That first day, Lia had seemed annoyed by her work and Alex wanted to distract her for a while. The next day, she found herself craving a break before cleaning out the refrigerators. In the weeks since, they'd hardly missed a day.

Lia looked up and was all smiles. "It's going really well. I almost can't believe what I'm reading, but they've reproduced the results a dozen times. Once this is published, other labs will try to do the same. If they do, it could completely change the face of hematology research in this country, and beyond."

She had a thing for a woman who got excited about hematology research. That was a first. "It sounds exciting. We might have to get a plaque to commemorate the work done at this very table."

Lia lightly kicked her. "Don't make fun."

Alex raised her hands. "No making fun, I swear. It's very satisfying that such meaningful work is being done in my shop."

Lia smiled. "That's very sweet. Really. How about you? Seemed extra busy today."

"The Holly Folly is this weekend. The shop and gallery owners are getting ready, bringing in some temporary help."

"Oh, that's right. You know, I know my way around a kitchen. If you don't have someone lined up to help out and need an extra pair of hands, I'd be happy to jump in."

It was the last thing Alex expected her to say. "Really?"

"Absolutely. You wouldn't even have to put me on payroll. I'd work for store credit."

Lia winked and Alex felt her pulse quicken. This woman was full of surprises and growing more irresistible by the minute. It took only seconds for her to decide to throw caution to the wind.

"I think we could arrange something. I'll be here starting at four in the morning both Saturday and Sunday. We'll be open until eight in the evening both days. Let me know what hours you want and I'll put you on the schedule."

There was a glint in Lia's eye. "If I come in at four, do I get to help you make croissants?"

Alex was struck by a vivid image of herself standing in the kitchen behind Lia, guiding her hands over a big rectangle of dough. She could almost feel Lia's backside pressing against her as she worked the rolling pin. She had to look away to regain her composure. "I'd certainly never turn down that offer."

"It's a deal, then."

"It's a deal. And while I plan to compensate you for your time, I'd love to take you to dinner as a token of thanks." Again, she was asking her out with a pretense other than a straightforward date. Why did she keep doing that?

Lia looked at Alex, wondering if the invitation was an offer of obligation, one of gratitude, or something altogether different. Like a date. It had been so long since she'd been asked out on a real date, she wouldn't even know how to tell. There was that kiss. Even if she was otherwise ready to dismiss the idea that Alex found her attractive, the kiss was intense. If it had half the effect on Alex as it had on her, maybe it was a date.

She'd been doing plenty of thinking about whether or not she wanted Alex to kiss her again. At this point, her brain said no, her body said yes, and her heart was abstaining. One thing was for sure—

the sparks that flew between them during the all-too-brief kiss in the bakery were greater than any she could remember feeling, for Dani or anyone else. If for no other reason than that, she wanted to see what would happen if they kissed again. "I'd love to."

"Well, the week is going to get busier and busier. Tomorrow night would be great if you're free."

"Tomorrow night would be perfect."

Alex picked up their now-empty coffee cups. "Perfect. It's a date."

Lia swallowed hard, but her smile didn't falter. Although her brain contended that the phrase was one with multiple meanings, she forced herself to shove aside the doubt. It was a date. There would be dinner, just the two of them. There would, without a doubt, be kissing. Would there be more? Lia was pretty sure that Alex would be up for more, whether or not she pressed it. She would need a game plan, and fast.

When she got home from the café, Lia did some more work. She grilled some chicken and made a big salad for her dinner. When she was sure that Sally had made it home from work and finished dinner with her family, Lia picked up her phone.

"Hey, girl." Sally always seemed happy to hear from her, a fact that always warmed Lia's heart.

"Hey, yourself. What are you up to?"

"Will's on bath duty, so I'm flopped on the couch folding laundry."

"Oh, good. How was your Thanksgiving?"

"Will's folks came in from South Carolina, which was great. Logan had a stomach bug, which was less than great."

"Sorry to hear that."

"He's over it now. Fortunately, it was just a twenty-four-hour thing."

"That's good. Poor guy."

"How about you? How was dinner at the sexy baker's?"

Sally knew about the near-kiss when Lia and Alex went for drinks. Lia filled her in on Thanksgiving, the steamy kiss in the kitchen, and Lia's offer to help during the upcoming busy weekend. When she was done, she said, "I think I'm going on a date."

"I see. And you're trying to decide if it is, in fact, a date? Or are you trying to decide whether or not it's a good idea?"

Lia rolled her eyes heavenward. The girl was good. She took a deep breath. "Both. I think it's a date. It's dinner, so I'm pretty sure it's a date. If it is a date, then what do I do about it?"

Sally, who'd refrained from inserting commentary while Lia told the story, launched in. "Yes, it's a date. This woman clearly thinks that you are smart and sexy and fun to be around. I like her already. As for what you should do, I've said before I think you'd benefit from a hot roll in the hay and I still do. How long has it been since you've had sex?"

Lia chuckled. Sally was never one to mince words. "Almost a year."

"Cripes. I knew things with Dani had gotten bad, but I didn't realize you weren't sleeping together at all."

Lia sighed. The last time she and Dani slept together was New Year's Eve. For a while, she'd bought Dani's story about being stressed at work, about it being a phase that would pass. Of course, Dani had been wetting her whistle just fine with her assistant. Although the deep hurt was starting to fade, the sting of the insult remained. "Yeah, I know."

"Okay, tell me what's holding you back?"

Sally had a way of getting her to say things she hadn't even said to herself. She wondered if it had anything to do with the fact that Sally got people to confess things for a living. Persuasion was practically her middle name.

"I'm afraid of getting hurt. I don't want to be made a fool of again. I think I might be a bad lover."

The first two were expected. The third was something she hadn't even admitted to herself. Lia cringed at the thought.

"Just because Dani is a fucker, it doesn't mean you are lacking in any way."

"I know, but—"

"No but. Her midlife-esque crisis has nothing to do with you."

Lia sighed.

"I think you should do it."

"Do what?" Lia asked, even though she knew what Sally meant.

"I think you should date, have fun, put yourself out there, have a fling. All of it. It will be good for you."

"Yeah, I just—"

"Lia, you are the girl who came out to her parents, her very Catholic parents, at sixteen. You're the girl who went to college a thousand miles from home. You are the girl who knows what she wants and is fearless. Where is that girl? Where is that woman?"

Like so many other times in her life, Sally managed to say what Lia had wanted her mother to say, to value the parts of her that her mother never quite understood. Lia found herself wondering if she would have been brave enough to be that girl if she and Sally had not been friends. She didn't want to consider how different a person she might be.

"Lia?"

"Sorry." She brought her focus back to the conversation. "You're right. You are absolutely right. I'm going to do it."

"Thatta girl. I can't wait to hear all about it."

CHAPTER FOURTEEN

Alex rang the bell at Lia's apartment at 7:00 on the dot. To her surprise, she found herself nervous. Alex couldn't remember the last time a date made her nervous. She rolled her shoulders a couple of times and tried to shake it off.

When Lia opened the door, her nerves were promptly replaced with a shot of pure lust. Lia's hair was swept up into some sort of twist, but there were bits that had escaped to curl softly around her face. She wore a black dress that revealed a tantalizing hint of cleavage. It was a deceptively simple cut, seemingly to simultaneously hug every single one of her curves while flowing and falling almost modestly to a hem right above her knees.

Alex swallowed and tried not to be obvious. "You look fabulous."

"Thank you, and likewise."

"Thanks. We're going to drive since we're heading to the East End, but you'll want a coat anyway. It'll be in the twenties by the time we're done with dinner."

The last thing Alex wanted Lia to do was cover up, but it would only be for a little while. She wanted Lia to shiver, but not from cold.

"I've got one right here." Lia took a coat from a hook by the door and slipped it on. "So, where is it we're going?"

"A surprise. It's a little out of the way place, a favorite of P-town's old literary set."

Lia picked up her purse. "You had me at 'out of the way.'"

Ciro and Sal's was indeed out of the way, at least from Lia's daily routine of walking between her apartment and the café. The sign on the street was small and unobtrusive, the entrance down a narrow gravel driveway. The inside was warm and dimly lit. Exposed brick walls and wine barrels made the entire restaurant feel like an old wine cellar. Candles and Chianti bottles sat on every table.

They were shown to a small table against one of the walls. The dining room was by no means full, but there were couples and small groups at more than a few tables. Lia took her seat and looked around.

"How is it I never knew this place existed?"

Alex smiled at her. "How many times have you been to Provincetown?"

Lia thought for a moment. "Four or five. My ex and I came here for a few days every other summer or so."

"Well, it's not completely hidden from tourists, but it is past most of the galleries, so you aren't likely to happen upon it. And it's definitely not one of the hot spots, if you know what I mean."

Lia nodded. Dani leaned toward the trendy, the exclusive. She'd never pick something so old school. "I do."

They shared an order of bruschetta and an arugula salad with capers and lemon. When their main courses arrived, Alex glanced over at Lia's capellini with tomatoes and mussels.

"I have entree envy."

Lia laughed, feeling ridiculously charmed. "I'll share. As long as I can try yours, too."

Alex cut off a bite of her chicken and held the fork out. "As a gesture of good faith, you get the first bite."

In Alex's car, there was jazz playing. Low and languid, the saxophone and trumpet made Lia think of the hot, humid nights she spent lying outside looking at the stars and thinking about the girls she wanted to kiss. Despite the chill outside, the air in the car felt warm and thick.

Lia indulged herself in a long, slow look at Alex while she drove. She was wearing black pants and a French blue button-down, a charcoal gray pea coat, black boots. Lia tried to study the cuff links she'd noticed at the restaurant, but it was too dim. She thought you could learn a lot about a person based on the cuff links they wore, not to mention the fact that they wore cuff links in the first place. It seemed like the more she learned, the more she liked.

There was no denying the physical attraction. Lia felt it the day they met. She felt it the next day and the day after; she felt it when she was near Alex and when she was alone. More than once, Lia had skimmed her hands over her skin when she was in bed, or the bath. She touched herself while imagining Alex's hands, Alex's mouth, on her body. Thinking of that now, Lia couldn't help but to squirm, relishing the sexual tension that had eluded her for so many months. She wondered if the feeling was mutual.

She tried to conjure Sally's words of encouragement. That dinner had most definitely been a date. There was nothing wrong with letting the attraction play out. She didn't have to throw herself at Alex. She just had to make it clear the door was open. Doing so had never been a decision she'd made consciously. It felt both empowering and terrifying.

The drive was, once again, a short one. Alex pulled her car up behind Lia's and put it into park. Before she could stop herself, Lia heard herself inviting Alex in. "Can I interest you in a nightcap?"

If she was surprised by the invitation, Alex showed no sign of it. Lia tried to tamp down the flutter of anxiety that appeared in her belly. It was fine. People did this all the time.

"You most certainly can."

See? All the time. Lia unlocked the door and stepped inside, holding it open for Alex to follow her. She flipped on the lights in the kitchen and set down her purse. She draped both of their coats over the wingback chair heading into the living room.

"I haven't stocked a full bar, but I have a Cabernet, a Chardonnay, and bourbon."

"Bourbon?" Alex raised an eyebrow. "A woman after my own heart. I'd love a nip of bourbon."

"On the rocks or neat?"

"When it's cold, always neat."

"Now you're a woman after my own heart." Alex made the conversation easy, but still, Lia was grateful to have something to do. She poured a couple fingers of Maker's into each of a pair of highball glasses. She walked over to Alex, handed her one, and motioned to the couch. "Shall we?"

They sat and sipped. Alex looked around. "This really is a great place. It has a lot of character for a rental."

Lia couldn't decide if Alex was nervous or just trying to help Lia relax. Or maybe this was the kind of conversation two people had before having sex. She willed herself to calm down and play along, see where things went. "Right? It's funny, but when I saw this room with all the bookshelves, I was hooked. I figured it's always good to be surrounded by books, even if they aren't mine."

Alex laughed. "Spoken like a true English major."

Lia caught herself fidgeting and made a point of keeping her hands still. She fought the urge to think about what she should do, what signals she should try to send. The bourbon, after the wine with dinner, made it a little bit easier for her to quiet that usually overactive part of her mind. Of course, Alex seemed perfectly at ease. She'd probably done this before. Lia reminded herself that was exactly what she wanted—not a relationship, not a negotiation, just a night with an attractive, engaging, unattached woman.

She put her hand on Alex's arm when she talked. She curled one foot under her and leaned in to listen. She tucked a stray piece of hair behind her ear and made eye contact. Although she couldn't bring herself to make the first move, she sent all the signals she could.

Lia looked down and realized that Alex's hand was on her leg. It was a really great hand, strong from all the hours of kneading and shaping dough. It was a little rough, but impeccably clean. She had a thing for hands, and it was so easy for her to imagine how Alex's would feel on her, inside of her. She drained the last of her bourbon and set the glass on the coffee table.

It must have been the opening Alex was waiting for. She set aside her own glass and leaned in very close. About six inches away from her, Alex paused, as though waiting for permission to proceed. Lia swallowed in anticipation.

Alex's lips were on hers. They were firm and soft at the same time; they were warm and tasted faintly of bourbon. Lia's body, like a slingshot pulled as tight as it could go, snapped alive. Her blood raced through her veins and her skin grew hot. She felt herself grow wet.

There was an immediacy, an intensity, in her desire that she'd never experienced before. It was scary and exhilarating at the same time and she wanted more of it.

Lia slipped her hand to the back of Alex's neck and into her hair. Her other hand went around Alex's waist, trying to bring her closer. She felt Alex grasp at the clip holding her hair and then felt it fall loose. Alex's hands were tugging at it gently, tilting Lia's head back and exposing her neck. Alex's lips moved to her jawline, down her neck.

Lia arched her back. Her breasts were throbbing, desperate to be touched. Alex obliged, tracing her lips down the neckline of Lia's dress and running her hand up Lia's side to cup her breast. Alex bit at her nipple through the fabric. Lia, growing desperate, heard herself saying Alex's name, along with "yes" and "please," over and over.

In one swift, skilled move, Alex shifted and Lia found herself lying on the couch with Alex over her. She felt Alex's belt buckle press into her hip, Alex's thigh nestled between her own. The reality of what she was doing hit Lia suddenly. It felt like she'd just gone screaming past the point of no return.

Alex's body tensed, as though she sensed Lia's hesitation. She pulled back and looked at Lia. "You okay?"

Lia struggled to find words. "I…uh…mmm hmm."

Alex continued to look at her intently. "Are you sure? Because we can stop. I don't want you to feel pressured."

She didn't have to do it. Alex had given her an out. Knowing that made Lia realize just how much she didn't want Alex to stop. "I don't. Feel pressured, I mean. I don't want you to stop. Please don't stop."

Alex smiled and kissed her again, more slowly than before. She moved her free hand to Lia's leg, starting at her ankle and running it up to her knee and under the hem of her dress. As her hand slid higher, Lia felt her fingertips graze the top of her stockings, the clasp of her garter belt.

The hand froze and Lia felt a stab of panic. Was it too much? Too girly? Too straight? When Alex leaned away, she feared she'd managed to turn Alex completely off.

Alex slid the hem of her dress up, exposing Lia's leg. After what felt like an eternity, she tore her gaze away and locked eyes with Lia. "You are gorgeous."

The relief was palpable, and the hunger she saw in Alex's eyes made her suddenly glad she'd opted for the garters. She blushed and resisted the desire to cover herself. Instead, she smiled, ready to let herself be devoured.

Alex untied her dress and spread it open. After trailing kisses across her breasts and down her belly, Alex ran her tongue up and under each garter while her hands kneaded Lia's buttocks. Lia's hips continued to move, lifting and pressing against Alex's touch. Lia felt Alex's fingers slide up the seam of her panties. She'd soaked them through and Alex knew it.

With tortuously slow deliberation, Alex unhooked each of the garters. When Alex leaned back, Lia whimpered. Alex removed her shoes, then slowly slid the stockings down her legs. Her skin felt so hot; she thought she might burst into flames right there on the sofa. Alex trailed her fingers from ankle to thigh. She hooked her fingers into the waist of Lia's panties and inched them down.

Lia lifted her hips, desperate to have Alex on her, inside of her. When she feared she might be on the verge of begging, Alex's tongue found her, pushing her over the edge. Lia thought she called out Alex's name, but she couldn't be sure. The orgasm ripped through her hard and quick. It left her breathless and aching for more.

Lia tried to catch her breath, to bring her vision and her thoughts into some semblance of focus. Alex, who had paused briefly while her muscles shuddered and clenched, resumed making slow circles with her tongue. She traced around and around, avoiding the hypersensitive tip. It was exquisite torture. Lia began to squeeze her muscles, feeling the pressure start to build again.

Alex slid a finger into her, and then a second. It was almost more than Lia could take. She was so wet, Alex's fingers slid in and out of her effortlessly, but she could feel the roughness of Alex's skin with each thrust. Her body clasped around Alex, trying to pull her deeper inside. She could feel Alex's knuckles pushing against the outside of her. All the while, her tongue continued its rhythmic circles.

Lia desperately wanted to come, but was also desperate to hold on to this feeling. She had a fleeting thought that it had never been like this with Dani, or with anyone else. She then found herself unable to think at all. The pleasure became so intense that she was powerless to hold back any longer. She came and the orgasm washed over her again and again. This time, Lia heard herself cry out. Then she felt Alex's body covering the length of her, holding her close.

Although her limbs felt like jelly, Lia needed to touch, to feel, to taste Alex. She untucked Alex's shirt and ran her fingernails lightly up and down her back. Alex moaned softly in her ear, making Lia smile. She nudged herself up and Alex responded, pulling back and letting herself be guided to a sitting position on the couch.

Lia slid her dress the rest of the way off. She straddled Alex and began unbuttoning her shirt. With each button, Lia bent to taste the newly exposed skin. It felt hot against her lips and tasted faintly of salt. Alex's fingers dug into her hips.

When she was done with the buttons, Lia eased her way off of Alex's lap and onto the floor. Kneeling between Alex's thighs, Lia undid her belt and the button of her pants. As she slid the zipper down, Lia looked up. Alex's eyes were dark with desire and fixed on her. Without breaking the gaze, Lia grasped the waistband of Alex's pants and started tugging them down. Alex lifted her hips and Lia quickly worked both Alex's pants and black boxer briefs down her legs.

They seemed to be stuck and she realized Alex was still wearing shoes. She had to lean back to pull them off, causing Alex to chuckle. With the shoes successfully discarded, Lia finished removing Alex's pants. Starting at the knees, she began kissing her way up Alex's thighs, one and then the other, barely skimming her lips across her labia each time.

Alex adjusted herself, opening her legs a little wider. Looking up again, Lia locked eyes with her as she wrapped her lips around Alex's swollen clit. The taste, the feel of her was overwhelming. Lia felt intoxicated. She closed her eyes and allowed herself to revel in it.

Lia teased her with long, slow strokes, up one side and down the other. She dipped her tongue in and felt Alex clench around her. When Alex grabbed her head, Lia began to work Alex up and down, sucking and licking her. Alex bunched Lia's hair in her fists. Lia could feel her getting close, the way the muscles in her thighs began to quiver. She resisted the urge to speed up, keeping her rhythm equal to the thrust of Alex's hips.

When Alex came, Lia felt the heat pour out of her. She felt sexy, powerful. She eased back and looked up at Alex's face. Alex looked slightly drugged, which Lia took as a good sign.

Alex ran her fingers through Lia's hair, cupped her cheek in her hand. "That was amazing."

"Thanks. You, too."

The gnawing feelings of inadequacy that had been plaguing Lia for months evaporated. It was exhilarating, almost as exhilarating as the post-orgasmic glow. She knew it was late, but she desperately didn't want the night to end. Trying to keep her tone light, she asked, "Is it okay if I don't want you to leave?"

Alex flashed a grin. "Not at all. In fact, I was hoping you might ask. Give me one minute."

Lia watched Alex extricate herself from the couch and fish her phone out of her coat pocket. "What are you doing?"

"I just need to text Jeff and ask him to go let Murphy out."

"He won't mind?"

"Let's just say we have a friendly arrangement. And I've taken care of his French bulldogs far more often than he's taken care of Murphy."

"How convenient." Lia laughed, and tried not to think about the fact that such an arrangement had clearly been around for a while.

Alex sent a text, then returned to where Lia was sitting. "Take me to bed?"

This was what mattered. Tonight, at least, there was a gorgeous woman who made her feel amazing and wanted to be with her. It was enough. Lia took Alex's outstretched hand. Leaving their clothes scattered around the room, she led the way upstairs.

Chapter Fifteen

Alex woke just as the sky was beginning to lighten. For her, it was sleeping in. Lia's body was warm and naked against hers. She'd curled up against Alex's chest after they'd made love for the second time and it seemed as though she hadn't moved since. She was snoring softly.

She shifted slightly, wanting to see if she could move without waking Lia. Lia sighed, but didn't stir. She eased herself away, climbing out of bed and pulling the quilt up to cover Lia's bare shoulders. Alex watched her for a long moment before heading downstairs.

She gathered her clothes, which were strewn across the couch and the floor. She pulled them on, then went into the kitchen to hunt for paper and a pen. There was a to-do notepad on the refrigerator and a cup of pens on the counter.

She started a note similar to the dozens of notes she'd left throughout the years. *Last night was amazing. I'll be thinking of you while I knead. Let's do it again soon.* She looked at the words and scowled, ripping the paper from the pad and wadding it up. She huffed out a breath and started again.

Her second attempt was far more personal than her usual approach. It was exactly how she felt, though, and wasn't too mushy, so she didn't over think it. She pulled the door quietly behind her when she left and headed home to take a quick shower and get to work.

Murphy was happy to see her. He never held a grudge. Alex gave him some roast beef with his breakfast and extra attention before heading downstairs. She'd have to hustle to have things in the case by the time they opened. She managed to make it in before Jeff, but just barely. He seemed happy to see her as well. And while he was in no way judgmental, he wasn't one to be appeased with treats and a belly rub.

"So you bedded the Southern belle," he said the moment he walked in. "Whatever would her daddy say if he knew?"

Alex rolled her eyes, but good-naturedly. "You're so crass."

"Oh, really, pot? You're gonna call this kettle black?"

"Touché. Yeah, we spent the night together."

"And?"

"And…" Alex thought for a moment. What could she say? "And it was the best night I've had in a very long time."

Jeff snickered. "It's always the sweet ones that are firecrackers in the sack. I knew she'd be a little minx."

It wasn't as if she and Jeff didn't often trade stories. For some reason, this time felt different. Alex didn't like talking, or thinking, about Lia as a conquest.

"The sex was amazing, but it…" Alex struggled to find the right words. "It was more than that."

She watched Jeff study her. He was probably thinking up some smart-ass comment. Instead, he said, "I'm glad it exceeded your expectations. Feel free to text me anytime to take care of Murph. I still owe you on that front. I'm going to go get ready to open."

Alex watched the kitchen door swing as Jeff went to start his morning routine. She'd expected him to be nosier, and to tease her a lot more than he did. Maybe he wasn't feeling well. Since she wasn't really keen on processing her feelings about the whole thing, she was more relieved than concerned.

She continued her work and allowed her mind to wander to the night before. It had been a surprise when Lia invited her in. Lia did not strike her as a sex-on-the-first-date sort of woman. Well, technically, it was their second, if she counted the night they went out for drinks. Third, if she counted Thanksgiving, although that wasn't really a date in the way she thought about dates.

Lia had been so fucking sexy, though, and eager. It was the eagerness that did Alex in. It felt as though Lia'd been walking through the desert and Alex was a pitcher of cool water. After Lia's moment of hesitation, Alex considered pulling back, suggesting they slow things down. Then she'd discovered the garters. The unexpected feel of Lia's bare skin had sent a jolt of desire right to her core. As far as she was concerned, a woman in a garter belt was enough to tempt a saint, and she was no saint.

When she eased herself back so she could enjoy the view, she found it even more erotic to look at than to touch. Lia's creamy skin stood out in sharp contrast to the black lace and satin ribbons. The bra that matched the panties made her think that Lia could be a lingerie model. An exquisitely curvy and dangerously enticing lingerie model.

Pleasing her had been easy. Alex didn't know if she was coming off of a dry spell or what, but it had taken what felt like a matter of seconds to make Lia come. She'd opened herself and taken whatever Alex gave, and went tumbling over the edge with hardly any effort at all. And then there was Lia's mouth. Alex had had more than a few women go down on her through the years. Never, not once, had it ever felt like that.

Alex cleared her throat. Thinking about it had her turned on again and she didn't want to spend her entire morning aroused, especially since she didn't know when, or even if, she'd be spending the night with Lia again.

When Lia woke, she realized she was alone and felt a flash of regret. She realized quickly that Alex must have left to go to work, which helped the pang to fade to a mild disappointment. She stretched and rolled around, enjoying how loose and limber she felt, but didn't linger in bed too long. She showered, dressed in leggings and a sweater dress.

Downstairs, she felt a moment of hesitation. Would it be awkward to see Alex? Would showing up first thing this morning make her seem like an eager puppy? She didn't have experience with flings. The last thing she wanted was to come across as clingy. She paced in the kitchen, contemplated calling Sally. Then she saw the note stuck on the refrigerator.

Lia,

I can't remember ever enjoying an evening more. It was beyond difficult to pull myself away this morning. I was going to start a pot of coffee for you, but I didn't want to give you a reason not to come to the bakery. I look forward to it. Until then, I'll be thinking of you.

A

With a smile on her face, she gathered her things to work and headed out the door. No longer second-guessing herself, she was anxious to get to the café so she could see Alex, to see how it felt to be around her now that they were lovers. Lovers. It was the first time she'd used that word to describe someone she was involved with, or herself. The very idea of it made her mind flash to the night before. The sex was…mind-blowing. There was no other word for it. Thinking of it turned her on. Lia tried to clear her head while she walked. Even if Alex wanted her, she didn't want to seem too eager.

When she got to the café, the excitement and nervousness combined and left her feeling shy. Jeff knew and would probably tease her with knowing looks and innuendo. Since they'd become friends, he was always ready to share the ups and downs of his love life. While amusing, she was less sure about being the focus of such attention.

She walked in and Jeff was at his usual place behind the counter. As she approached, she watched him nudge the kitchen door with his foot and whistle. Clearly, this was something he and Alex had worked out ahead of time. It was unlikely this alert system was created for her. She shoved the thought aside and focused her attention on Jeff.

"Good morning, Jeff."

Jeff flashed his most charming smile. "Good morning to you, Lia. I must say, you look exceptionally lovely today. You're practically glowing."

Despite her best efforts, Lia blushed. "Thanks. And thank you, too, for taking care of Murphy last night."

He winked at her. "Anytime, honey. Anytime."

Alex emerged from the kitchen. She was wearing her usual gray chef's coat and jeans. If it was possible, she was even more attractive than the first time Lia had seen her. Jeff discreetly disappeared into the kitchen.

"Good morning." Alex offered her a knowing smile that warmed her from the inside. All of the nervousness she felt melted away.

"Good morning. I'm sorry I missed you leave."

Alex stepped around the counter and kissed her. "Not at all. I'm glad I was able to slip out. There is certainly no need for you to be up before six. How are you? Did you sleep well?"

If she was being honest, Lia would have answered that she still felt tingly, and more alive than she had in ages. The kiss Alex planted on her, although brief, only added to the feeling. Not the cool, easy vibe she was going for. "I'm great, and clearly, I slept like a rock."

Alex chuckled. "I'm glad to hear it. Your usual?"

"Yes, please."

"Coming right up." Alex walked back around the counter and took a chocolate croissant from the case and put it on a saucer. She made Lia's coffee herself.

Lia was trying to decide what to say next when the café door opened and several people walked in. She gave a little nod in the direction of her table. "I'll be over there."

As if on cue, Jeff reappeared. Lia headed to her usual table and watched Alex and him work side by side. It was a familiar sight and, in some ways, reassuring. On the other hand, she found herself watching Alex differently. Without any effort, Lia could look over and imagine Alex naked. She could watch Alex's very capable hands and imagine them on her skin, or better, inside her.

Lia felt her skin begin to flush. Afraid that she'd look obvious, she tore her eyes away and focused them determinedly on her computer screen. She managed to be productive, even if only moderately so. After the lunch crowd cleared, Alex appeared as usual with their afternoon coffee.

"I have plans with Stuart after work, but I'll see you in the morning for baking duty, right?"

"Four a.m."

"You know, you really don't have to come in that early."

"Oh, I'll be here."

"I can't wait to bake with you."

When their cups were empty, Lia packed up her bag. Just as she didn't want to seem too eager earlier, she didn't want to come across as a hanger-on now. "I guess I'll see you in a few hours, then."

Alex stood when she did. She leaned in and kissed Lia again. It was more intense than their kiss this morning, more insistent. It made Lia's pulse race. When Alex stepped back, Lia was left unsteady on her feet and wanting. She wondered if that fact was obvious to Alex. She wondered if she wanted it to be.

Alex, in turn, gave nothing away. "I'll see you then."

Chapter Sixteen

I think that I'm having a fling." There was a hint of triumph in Lia's voice. She sat in her bathtub, bubbles all around her and candles lit on the window sill. She rested her head against the pillow she'd made from a hand towel.

On the other end of the line, Sally tsked. "I'll be the judge of that. Tell me everything."

Lia thought back to the conversation earlier in the week, complete with Sally's special blend of pep talk and tough love. Without it, Lia realized, last night might never have happened. She'd have to find a way to thank her for that. In the meantime, she had scoop and Sally wanted it. "Well, we went to dinner and after I invited her in for a drink and we had the best sex I've ever had."

"Shut up."

Lia laughed. In the entire time they'd known each other, Lia had never slept with someone on the first date. "And she stayed over even though she had to be at work before six a.m."

"And?"

"And I'm planning to do it again if given the opportunity."

"I'm so proud."

"Okay, now you're just making fun of me."

It was Sally's turn to laugh. "I'm serious. If you have one fault, it's that you're not impulsive. And you over think everything."

"I think that's two faults."

Sally ignored her. "You deserve this. You deserve to have fun and to feel good, on your terms."

"You always say the nicest things. Thank you."

"I mean it. Now, really, tell me everything. And, more importantly, tell me what you're going to do next."

Lia talked through the details of the evening. She skimmed over the more explicit details, more from her own shyness than any squeamishness on Sally's part.

"So when are you going to see her again?"

"Well…" Lia lifted one of her feet from the tub to examine her toes, "I saw her today briefly when I went to the café to work."

"And how was she?"

"Sweet. She kissed me when I got there. And when I left."

"Nice. And when are you seeing her next?"

"I'll be helping in the bakery over the weekend, so tomorrow."

"Please tell me you're going to get hot and heavy in the walk-in cooler."

Lia snorted. One of Sally's college adventures was making out with her supervisor in the walk-in refrigerator of the campus dining hall. "She doesn't have a walk-in cooler."

"That's too bad. Are you going to, like, date?"

"I don't know." Lia had been trying not to think about that very question herself. "Getting involved with someone seems like the last thing I should be doing right now. I'm trying to take my best friend's advice and not think twenty steps ahead of myself."

"Thatta girl. You should enjoy yourself and see where it goes."

It was doing just that that tended to fill Lia with a certain amount of panic. Still, she was in a bathtub in Provincetown in the middle of winter with no idea where she'd be living six months from now. Clearly, she was building up somewhat of a tolerance.

"I'm trying," Lia said. "I'm also a prune. Let me get out of the bath and dry off. I'll call you in two minutes and I want to hear everything about this Christmas play Charlie is in."

Lia ended the call and sat up. Just as she was leaning over to set the phone on the windowsill, it slipped from her fingers and landed with a plop into her bath.

"Fuck." She fished it out of the water. "Fuck, fuck, fuck." She set the phone aside, climbed out, and dried herself off.

She needed rice and she needed it quickly, but of course she was out. By the time Lia got to the one supermarket in town, it was closed. She sat in the parking lot and thought. Alex would have rice. She'd have to admit to being a klutz, but she'd get to see Alex.

She'd go to Alex's, beg a cup or two, and be on her way. Or... or she could show up on Alex's doorstep, beg a cup of rice, and then seduce her. Lia gulped. She'd never attempted a seduction before, at least not like that. Could she pull it off? Should she even try? Maybe that was a little too ambitious. Maybe she should keep her focus on getting some rice and maybe making out a little. That seemed doable.

When Lia pulled up behind the café, lights were burning in several of the upstairs windows. She was about to climb out of her car when she was struck with the thought that Alex might not be alone. Her stomach turned over and she contemplated driving back to her place and abandoning the whole plan.

"Don't be ridiculous." If Alex was involved with another woman, or women, it was better she know that sooner rather than later.

By the time Lia rang the bell, she was convinced she'd be interrupting either a romantic dinner or an orgy. When Alex answered the door in jeans and a faded Boston Red Sox t-shirt, Lia was, for the briefest of moments, genuinely surprised. Alex, on the other hand, seemed both relaxed and perfectly happy to see her.

"Hi." Lia tried to sound casual.

"Hi. I didn't expect to see you tonight."

Lia blushed. "I'm so sorry to show up on your doorstep unannounced. I dropped my phone in the bathtub and I didn't have any rice and the store is closed, so I was hoping I could borrow some to try to save it."

"You dropped your phone in the bathtub?"

"Yes. I don't usually let myself talk on the phone while in the tub because I have a bit of a clumsy streak, but I did. And, of course, it was when I was done with the call and about to get out that I did it. So. Stupid."

Alex, who'd been nodding intently as Lia related the story, let out a small chuckle. "I'm sorry. I shouldn't laugh. It's kind of adorable, though. Come on up."

She turned and walked up the stairs. Lia shut the door and followed her up, appreciating the vantage point of the way Alex's jeans hugged her ass.

At the top of the stairs, Murphy was waiting and wagging his tail. "Murphy is always happy to have company. He's been an attention hound all evening. Consider yourself warned."

Lia bent to rub his ears. He pressed his head into her hand. When she switched sides, so did he. He was definitely a charmer and reminded Lia of Rhett, a dog her family had when she was little. She stood and, as promised, Murphy started nudging her. Amused, she continued to scratch his head lightly.

"So, you find clumsiness adorable, eh? I should warn you now, you might wind up finding me completely irresistible."

Alex was rooting around in the pantry. She pulled out a clear plastic crock filled with rice and laughed. "Well, it was more the talking on the phone while in the bathtub in the first place. It's such a girly thing to do."

Lia lifted her hands as if she'd been caught at something. "Yes, I'm that sort of femme."

Alex pulled a zip-top bag from a drawer under the counter and poured rice into it. She held it up and Lia dropped in her lifeless phone. Alex zipped it closed and handed it to her. "Sadly, I think you'll have to wait a couple of days to see if it actually works."

"I know, but at least I tried. You're a lifesaver."

"I wouldn't go that far. I am, however, happy to help. I'm also making dinner. Have you eaten?"

"I'd hate to impose."

"Seriously? Did you seriously just say that? I would love for you to stay."

"You're very sweet. Thank you, that would be lovely." Lia sighed. So it wasn't a seduction. Dinner was more her speed anyway.

"I'll even let you do the dishes, as long as you promise not to break any." Alex smirked and winked at her.

Lia bit her lip and shook her head. "I suppose I walked into that one."

"Better that than the furniture. Sorry, sorry, I couldn't resist. I'll act like a grown-up now, I promise."

Lia thought about how often Dani used to lose her patience when Lia had her clumsy moments, as though it was a fundamental laziness of body or mind that caused Lia to knock over glasses or trip over her own feet. Rather than good-natured teasing, the huffs and eye rolls had the effect of making Lia feel like a hippopotamus. It was hard feeling like a hippo when one's partner was a sleek and graceful cheetah. For some reason, Alex's teasing didn't make her feel that way at all.

"I'm making spring rolls. Is that okay with you?"

"I love spring rolls. I've never made them, though."

Alex had all of the ingredients prepped, so she filled a pie plate with hot water and walked Lia through the process of softening the rice paper, filling, then rolling them up.

"The only tricky part is the rice paper. It will stick to itself, which is good for holding them together, but bad if you don't get it to lay flat on the board on the first go."

She stepped aside so Lia could give it a try. It was, as promised, quite easy. Lia was fascinated by the texture of the rice paper, both before and after it was soaked in the water. "It's funny. Sometimes, I have something in a restaurant and all I want to do is go home and try to figure out how to make it. But, for all that I love spring rolls, it never occurred to me to try them at home."

"I know. I feel that way about Indian. I know that if I just buy the right spices, I should be able to make a decent curry, but I've never taken the leap."

"You're right," Lia said. "It really isn't complicated. My roommate from college is Bengali and she introduced me to what she calls 'weeknight Indian,' dishes that you can make in less than an hour. I'd be happy to show you sometime."

"That would be great." Within a few minutes, they'd piled a plate with a dozen rolls. Alex opened the fridge and pulled out a bottle of white wine. "I find the brightness of a Sauvignon Blanc a perfect foil to the sweet and spicy dipping sauce."

"Really?"

"Maybe, but it's more that this is what I have in the fridge. Can I pour you a glass?"

Lia laughed. "Yes, please. I was prepared to be very impressed, you know."

"I did take a wine class at school. I like knowing the different varietals, having a general sense of pairings. The rest of it, though, was way too fussy for me." She poured two glasses and set them on the island. "Okay if we eat in the kitchen?"

Lia accepted the plates Alex handed her, along with a pair of orange linen napkins. She set them at the end of the island where there was a pair of heavy wooden barstools. She picked up her wine and raised the glass. "To not being fussy."

Alex picked up her own glass and clinked it against Lia's. "To not being fussy."

Lia sat and waited for Alex to do the same. Instead, Alex walked up and stood very close to her. "If you don't mind, there is something I've been wanting to do since the second you got here."

Lia raised an eyebrow. It was enough of an invitation for Alex, who proceeded to take Lia's face in her hands and kiss her senseless. It left Lia breathless, aroused, and aching for more. Alex picked up her wine again and sipped. She placed a couple of rolls on each of their plates. "Shall we?"

Lia swallowed. She wondered if Alex was trying to keep her unsteady or if it was merely a side effect. It was true that it had been a while since she'd experienced the flash of a new attraction, but she didn't think that could entirely explain the way Alex made her feel. Deciding she should try to keep the promise she made to herself about not over thinking everything, she picked up one of her spring rolls, dipped it into the bowl of sauce between them, and took a bite.

"Oh. Wow. These are good." She wasn't exaggerating. The flavors and textures played off of one another perfectly, and the sauce was nutty and salty, spicy with just a hint of sweetness.

Alex sampled her own. "Thanks. You did an excellent job rolling."

When they finished eating, they did the few dishes together. Lia dried her hands on a dish towel. "Thank you again for the rice, and for letting me crash your evening."

"Anytime."

Lia didn't want to leave, but she also didn't want to overstay her welcome. She was about to excuse herself when Alex said, "No pressure, but I'd love for you to stay."

Lia's instinct was to say something about not wanting to impose, so she bit her tongue and smiled instead. "Yeah?"

"I mean, you're going to be here in a few hours to start baking anyway. But even without that, yeah, I would."

Lia's heart beat a little faster in her chest. It felt in that moment like things with Alex might be more than a fling, but she didn't pause to think about it. By way of answer, she put a hand around Alex's waist and pulled her close. "Well, by all means, please lead the way."

Alex led Lia to her bedroom, a space of masculine grays and blues that still managed to feel comfortable and inviting. Once it was clear that she was staying, Lia expected—hoped?—to be tossed on the bed and ravished. She hoped to do a bit of ravishing herself.

Instead, Alex kissed her slowly, with a patience and determination that left Lia squirming and aching for more. She removed Lia's clothes as well as her own. She seemed impervious to Lia's roaming hands and insistent whimpers. After what felt like an eternity, Alex pulled the comforter down and laid Lia on the cool sheets. Her pace remained maddeningly slow.

With tongue and teeth, Alex made her way down each of Lia's arms. She kissed the creases of Lia's elbows, the insides of her wrists; she nibbled fingertips and then took the index and middle finger of Lia's right hand into her mouth. When Alex sucked them deep into the back of her mouth, a jolt of heat shot through her. She could almost feel Alex's tongue on her, Alex's fingers working her from the inside. The pleasure was so intense that Lia cried out. It was the closest thing to an orgasm she'd ever experienced without being touched.

Even then, Alex refused to hurry. She began a tortuously intense exploration of Lia's breasts. Her mouth traced the valley between, her teeth scraped along Lia's ribs. Only after covering every inch of them did Alex take one, then the other of Lia's rock hard nipples into her mouth. With flicks of her tongue and gentle bites, she tested Lia's boundaries of pleasure and pain. Although the pressure had been building, pushing her closer and closer to the edge, the orgasm surprised her.

Alex lifted her head and fixed Lia with a smoldering look. "No fair. You cheated."

Lia laughed and let her head fall back onto the pillows. "That's funny. I was about to say the same thing."

Lia took advantage of the break in Alex's concentration to roll onto her side.

"Hey, I'm not done."

Lia nudged Alex onto her back. "I'm not saying you have to be. I am, however, going to take my turn."

Alex scowled. "It's not about taking turns."

Lia rested her chin on her hand and studied Alex. "I know, but if I'm not careful, you're going to have me in a coma before I get the chance to have my way with you."

Alex shrugged. "And what's the problem with that?"

Lia wasn't sure how to explain the needs and fears that warred inside her. She thought about all the delightful things she'd read about being femme, as well as the bad. "The problem is that I have no desire to be…" Her voice trailed off. There really wasn't a good way to say it. "A pillow princess."

Alex looked at the woman who'd given her one of the best orgasms of her life. She opened her mouth to argue, but Lia swallowed her protests with a kiss.

"Let me."

It was as much a plea as a demand. Alex wasn't sure what was going through Lia's mind, but she sensed it was something important, and deeply personal. She nodded her consent and gave herself over to whatever Lia had in mind.

She wasn't unaccustomed to being teased, but it felt a little strange to be out of the driver's seat. Lia's mouth, however, was driving her insane. Alex couldn't have pulled together a coherent thought if she tried. It was as though Lia had a direct line of communication to her body. Lia touched her, teased her, in ways she didn't even know she wanted.

When Lia's tongue glided over Alex's swollen clit, she thought she might explode. Instead of coaxing her over the edge, however, Lia shifted her focus. She traced her tongue up one side and down the other, avoiding the one spot that would make Alex come. Lia timed her strokes perfectly with the slow thrust of Alex's hips. She was overwhelmed by the sensation. She wanted to quicken the pace, to find the release that seemed to be eluding her, but she couldn't tear herself away from the rhythm that was being expertly controlled by Lia.

Without changing her pace, Lia shifted her tongue slightly so that her strokes passed squarely over Alex's throbbing clitoris. The shift alone was nearly enough to send Alex over the edge. Rather than a flash finish, however, Alex felt herself building even higher. When she thought she might come completely undone, the orgasm began to crash over her. Alex could feel her body buck and she was powerless to stop it. Lia's arms were wrapped firmly around her thighs and she could feel Lia move with her, making the orgasm go on and on.

When her body went limp, Lia loosened her grip and rested her head against Alex's thigh. "Fuck."

Alex smiled. *Fuck, indeed.*

It was after one before they collapsed on the bed, exhausted and sated. Alex pulled Lia into her arms and kissed the top of her head. "I'm so glad you're a klutz."

CHAPTER SEVENTEEN

The alarm went off at 3:30. Lia was startled at first, unsure of where she was. Alex rolled over, hitting the snooze bar.

"Five minutes." Alex pulled her close and nuzzled her neck.

Lia was surprisingly awake given the hour, but had no complaints about the few minutes of cuddling under the blankets. With Alex's arm tight around her waist Lia relished her position as the little spoon. Dani wasn't big on snuggling to begin with, and she was so thin, it made Lia feel enormous. Alex's breathing evened out and Lia realized she'd dozed off again.

She smiled and allowed her mind to wander to the night before. If their first night together was a flash point of explosive passion, last night was a low and smoldering burn. She couldn't decide which she enjoyed more.

The second time the alarm went off, Alex groaned. Lia winced and felt compelled to say, "Sorry."

Alex lifted her head. In the near darkness, she could see Alex squinting at her, only one eye open. "Why are you apologizing?"

Lia shrugged. "I feel bad for keeping you up so late. I barged in on you and kept you up to all hours."

With surprising speed, Alex moved so that she was over Lia, straddling her and with an arm on either side of Lia's head, bracing herself inches from Lia's face. "I'm going to assume you're joking, because if you would dare to apologize for last night, I honestly don't know what I would do with you."

She kissed Lia firmly on the mouth, then nipped her jaw before hopping out of bed. Lia watched her naked form walk from the room, then saw the bathroom light flick on. Lia bit her bottom lip and considered. It was playfulness. Alex was playful. Lia was utterly unaccustomed to it. How delightful. She climbed out of bed and followed Alex to the bathroom.

After quick showers and some borrowed clothes, Lia found herself in the startlingly quiet, brightly lit bakery kitchen.

"Are you sure this isn't too snug?" Lia patted the front of the dark gray chef's jacket.

"I'm sure. Your boobs are bigger than mine, but my shoulders are broader. It all works out. You look adorable."

Lia smiled and adjusted the Red Sox baseball cap she wore, making sure her hair was securely tucked beneath. "Okay. So, what do we do first?"

"First, I make us some coffee."

"What can I do? Seriously, just give me tasks and I'm good to go."

"Sheet pans." She gestured to a rack. "You can start lining them with parchment paper." She pointed to a box. "I'll be back in two minutes."

Alex headed to the front of the shop and Lia started placing pre-cut sheets of parchment, creating a stack on one end of the main work table. Thinking of her own agitation with the perpetually curling ends of the rolled stuff, she wondered if Alex might sell her a box of the sheets. Commercial kitchens had all the good stuff.

As promised, Alex returned quickly, bearing two steaming mugs. "I'm going to do bread dough first so it can start proofing. How do you feel about getting some cookie dough that I made last week in the oven?"

Lia set down her mug. "I think I can handle that."

Alex flipped switches and turned knobs and the convection oven roared to life. "It's all in the freezer, portioned and ready to go. Chocolate chip and coffee with cocoa nibs need sixteen minutes. Oatmeal toffee, eighteen. Almond sandies and lemon-lavender shortbread are twenty. Let's go with six dozen of each."

Lia offered a salute. "Aye-aye, captain."

The job was beyond basic, but Lia didn't mind. It afforded her the opportunity to watch Alex move around the kitchen—weighing and measuring ingredients, manning the massive mixer. Watching her work was beyond hot. She had capable hands and casual focus. Had there been a walk-in cooler, she would have done her best to lure Alex into it.

As each batch of dough was completed, Alex covered the oversize bowls with clean towels and set them aside to rise. Lia moved frozen pieces of cookie dough from neatly stacked plastic bins to the sheet pans she'd lined with parchment. She put the first round into the oven and set the timer.

"Do these need to be rotated halfway through?"

"Nope. Welcome to the beauty of convection baking."

Lia sighed. "I think I have oven envy."

By a little after five, the bread dough was done and Lia was sliding the last of the cookies into the oven. The kitchen smelled amazing and Lia found herself awake and energized. She didn't think she could do it every day, but she was having fun and was pretty sure it wasn't only because she was with Alex.

"And now we croissant."

Lia rubbed her hands together excitedly. "I cannot wait to learn from the master."

Alex smiled and pulled a tray from the refrigerator. "I hope you aren't disappointed, but the dough is already made. It requires multiple steps and lots of downtime in between. We'll get to roll and shape them, though."

"Of course. I'd love to learn start to finish one day, but today, I'm here to help."

"Excellent. Let me show you the first one, then you can have a go." Alex floured the surface of the table and set the square of dough in the middle. She floured her rolling pin, smacked the dough a few times with it, then started rolling. While she worked, she explained the process of making it. "You sandwich a block of butter into the middle, roll it out, and then fold it in on itself. It's the process of doing that over and over that gives you the flaky layers."

Lia nodded. It didn't seem too complicated, but it was certainly labor intensive. She knew now why she'd never attempted them on her own. "Right. And we love those flaky layers."

"Indeed we do. So, once we've got the dough about a quarter-inch thick, we cut." Using a pizza wheel, Alex cut the dough into long strips, then each strip into triangles. "Roll it up." She took a triangle and rolled it between her fingers and the table, creating a log that was thick in the middle and skinny on both ends. "Move to the pan and shape." She placed the dough on a tray, curving it and pinching the ends together.

"Nice."

Alex wiggled her eyebrows. "Thank you. Now, you can leave them a little more crescent shaped, but since we also use them for sandwiches, I prefer more of a round. Ready to give it a try?"

"Yes, please." Alex stepped to the side and Lia took her place. She took one of the triangles and, using her fingertips, rolled it into a log. She moved it to the pan and shaped it. It wasn't terrible, but next to Alex's, it was lumpy and a little uneven. Lia frowned.

"You're so close. You just have to let your whole hand do the work."

"What do you mean?"

"Here, do one with me." Alex moved closer to Lia at the table and placed her hands over Lia's. She guided Lia's fingers over the dough, rolling it in a single fluid motion from the tips of her fingers to the base of her palm.

The croissant was perfect and Lia's pulse was racing. She could feel Alex's breasts pressing ever so lightly into her arm and Alex's lips close to her ear. Unable to resist, she shifted slightly so that she was pressed against Alex's pelvis. She was rewarded with a low moan.

"Wow." Her voice was barely above a whisper.

"I fantasized about having you here, like this."

Lia's breath caught. The wave of desire was hot and fast. It made her skin tingle and left a throbbing ache between her thighs. "I... um...really?"

"Oh, yeah."

Alex's mouth was on hers and Lia felt herself pressed between the table and Alex's body. The next thing she knew, Alex's hands were on her thighs, lifting her onto the table. She wrapped her legs around Alex's waist while Alex started yanking at the buttons of Lia's chef coat. She reached a hand in, cupping Lia's breast.

The arousal was so quick, the need so strong, Lia was caught off guard. She buried her hands in Alex's hair while Alex finished with the buttons and ran her hands over Lia's exposed torso. Her nipples tightened, aching for Alex's touch.

The sound of the back door slamming startled them both. Alex stepped back abruptly. "It's Jeff."

"Oh, God." Lia hopped down from the table and started doing up the buttons Alex had undone. She couldn't decide if she should be amused or mortified. After a minute of banging around, Jeff appeared in the kitchen.

"Are you quite all right?" Alex asked.

"Perfectly fine. I just wanted to announce my presence in case anyone was indecent." He winked at both of them, then breezed through the swinging door to start coffee and set up for opening.

Lia giggled, then blushed. Alex looked like she was going to call after Jeff, but she didn't. Given how close he'd come to finding them going at it, maybe she'd decided to let it go. She walked over to where Lia was standing and kissed her. "I'm really glad you're here."

"Even though I'm more distraction than help?"

"You are a distraction, but I'm having a hard time holding it against you."

Lia smiled. "I'll be extra helpful now, I promise."

"I'll hold you to it."

Alex cleaned up the mess they'd made and they started rolling croissants in earnest. They set the plain ones aside to rise and Alex showed Lia how to cut and roll the dough for the chocolate variety. Lia took over placing the long, thin bars of chocolate into each rectangle, rolling and placing the dough on the pan seam side down. Alex portioned out the bread dough, rolling it into loaves and putting it into the proofer for the second rise.

They worked quietly now. Although Alex didn't say so, it was clear they were behind schedule. She worked efficiently and with unwavering concentration. Even with the playfulness gone, Lia enjoyed watching her work. She had a level of focus that Lia couldn't help but admire.

The rest of the day flew by. When Darcy arrived at eight to start her prep, Lia went to the front to help Jeff, where he gave her a crash course in using the register. By the time Alex emerged at ten, Lia was calling orders to Jeff and chatting with customers like a pro. Alex watched her in amazement. Lia was a woman of many talents, and officially unlike any woman she'd ever been with. Because the crowd never really slowed, they took turns taking breaks to rest and refuel. Around three, a backup barista relieved Jeff and Darcy took over making sandwiches. Alex was impressed with Lia's stamina, as well as the fact that she'd remained energetic and upbeat the entire time.

"I don't know how you do it," Lia said as they climbed the stairs to Alex's loft.

"Well, in the busy season, I have a lot more regular help, so I'm much better at working only eight or nine hours at a stretch. And there's definitely more opportunity to sit down for a few minutes."

"Oh, good. I was starting to fear that you were a machine."

"No, I'm beat, too. Speaking of, are you too exhausted to go out with me tonight? If you are, I totally understand."

"As long as it doesn't involve dancing or making cappuccinos, I'm game. What did you have in mind?"

Alex grinned. "Well, the reason everyone is in town, besides holiday shopping, is for the concert tonight. It's the Gay Men's Chorus Holiday Spectacular. I was hoping you'd go with me to that and then the lighting of the lobster pot tree."

"Lobster pot tree?"

"Yes, it's a giant pile of lobster traps that they decorate and light up like a Christmas tree. It's very festive and very P-town."

"Okay, that's something I have to see."

"I thought you might like that. You're welcome to shower here if you want, and to borrow some more clothes." The thought of sharing a shower with Lia made the muscles between her thighs clench.

"As much as I'd like to shower with you, I fear it would lead to other things and we'd miss the festivities. Besides, if we're going to see other people, it's probably for the best that I'm wearing my own clothes."

Alex willed herself not to be disappointed. Did Lia not want people to know they were seeing each other? No, she probably just didn't want to wear Alex's clothes. Definitely not her style. It shouldn't matter either way. It's not like they were an item. "I'd very much like to drag you into the shower and to bed, but you're right. Take your car home, and when you're ready, just come back here and park. It'll be easier than looking for another spot and we can walk over together."

Lia gathered her clothes, purse, and baggie of cell phone and rice. "Sounds like a plan. I had a lot of fun today, not to mention last night. Thank you for including me."

Alex shook her head. "No, it's definitely me who should be thanking you. You were amazing, last night and today."

Lia shrugged, blushed. "I had a great teacher."

"With the croissants, maybe, but the rest was all you." Alex kissed Lia firmly on the mouth and watched her as she went down the stairs. "Be careful getting home and I'll see you in a bit."

At the bottom of the stairs, Lia turned to offer a wave. "I'll be back in about an hour."

On the drive home, Alex's words echoed in her mind. She couldn't get over being thought of as a skilled lover. She pondered it the whole way home, during her shower, and while she got dressed. She realized just how much she'd inflated the chemistry between Dani and her. It also occurred to her that, had Dani not cheated on her, she might have lived the rest of her life settling and not even knowing it.

Town was definitely hopping as she made her way back toward The Flour Pot, and Lia was grateful for the guaranteed parking spot. Alex was waiting for her and they enjoyed a leisurely stroll to Town Hall. Once there, they sat next to Jeff and Edwin, the guy Jeff had brought to Thanksgiving dinner. Both men were wearing bow ties. They made a cute couple and Lia hoped that Edwin stuck around.

The concert was festive and gay. She could get used to being surrounded by so much gayness. It felt so comfortable, more comfortable than she ever felt at home after coming out and certainly more comfortable than New York. It was something she was going to have to consider when her lease expired in the spring.

After the concert, she and Alex wandered over to watch the tree lighting. The crowd was large, but laid-back. There were plenty of visitors, but a lot of the crowd was local. It thrilled Lia to see and to say hello to faces that were becoming familiar. They ran into Jan from the real estate office and her wife, Lorraine. Stuart and Connie were there, too, along with their daughters, Maddie and Beth. Alex tucked Lia's hand in her arm as they walked. It was sweet and romantic and, Lia realized, felt completely natural.

"Hi, Alex."

Lia looked in the direction of the voice. It came from a woman she'd seen around town a couple of times, but didn't know.

"Hi, Sara. Good to see you."

Alex didn't pull her arm away, nor did she stop walking. Lia couldn't help but feeling, though, that the woman was more than a casual acquaintance. She didn't want to seem nosy, but she was curious. "Does she live in town? She seems really familiar, but I can't place her exactly."

"Who? Sara?"

"Yeah." Lia hoped she sounded casual.

"She works at the gourmet grocery store in the East End."

"That's it. If you want to talk to her, please don't let me stop you."

"No, no. It's cool. I'm here with you."

While it was exactly the right thing to say, Alex's comment convinced Lia that Sara was, or at least had been, more than just a friend. It didn't bother her, necessarily. If anything, it was reassurance that she and Alex were looking for the same thing.

"Okay. I just didn't want you to feel like you couldn't."

Alex leaned over and kissed her temple. "Thanks. No need, but thanks."

As promised, there was a huge pyramid of lobster traps stacked in the open square. Although covered with large red bows, it didn't look too much like a Christmas tree. When the lights were turned on, however, it sparkled and shined and a loud cheer went up from the crowd. As if on cue, it began to snow.

"Welcome to Christmas in New England," Alex said.

Lia thought about the Christmas traditions of her childhood, and of the ones she had during her years with Dani. They certainly weren't bad by any means, but they weren't like this. It looked like she was developing a thing for New England.

"I can't think of anywhere I'd rather be."

CHAPTER EIGHTEEN

I'll see your quarter and raise you another." Lia tossed fifty cents into the center of the table. She'd taken Stacia up on her offer of joining the poker group and had become a regular at the weekly games. Tonight, she was sitting on a full house and feeling confident.

"I fold." Stacia threw down her cards with a huff.

"Same here," Anita said.

"Too rich for my blood." Josie, a doctor friend of Jan's, shook her head. She set her cards facedown on the table.

"I don't know. I think our little Southern belle might be bluffing. I call." Jan tossed coins into the pot and then raised her eyebrow at Lia. "Three queens."

Lia slumped her shoulders dramatically. "I've only got three fours." She laid them on the table faceup. Then, after a pause, she added her remaining cards. "And these two kings."

The women around the table erupted into laughter. Josie, who was sitting next to Jan, elbowed her in the ribs. "Looks like the little Southern belle just showed you how it's done."

Lia gathered all of the change from the center of the table and began stacking it. "For what it's worth, Jan, I'm a mean bluffer, too." She looked at the first woman she met when she arrived in Provincetown, a woman who'd become both a friend and sort of a butch maternal figure. "You're just no match for this girl. Bless your heart."

The laughter intensified and Jan grumbled. "I've been hustled."

"This is Lia's third time playing with us." Anita shook her head. "I don't think you can call that hustling."

"She has a point," Stacia said.

Jan sniffed. "I can see where your loyalties lie."

Stacia shrugged and shuffled the cards for her deal. "I just call them as I see them."

While Stacia dealt, Anita turned to Lia. "A couple of us are indulging in a spa day this weekend. We're going to get massages and sit in the sauna and pretend we're somewhere tropical. Care to join us?"

Lia smiled. Not only had she been welcomed into the poker group with open arms, she'd gotten to know all of the women in it. They joined her for coffee at the bakery, invited her to dinner, introduced her to their wives or, in Stacia's case, husband. It was exactly the type of neighborhood feeling she'd so desperately missed while living in New York.

"Thank you so much for the invitation, but I have plans with Alex."

"So, you and Alex have been spending a lot of time together?"

The way Stacia framed the question, Lia couldn't help but feel like she'd been waiting for an opening. "Some," she said cautiously. "I go to the café most days to work, so…"

Anita, an accountant, looked over the rim of her reading glasses. "Some? If the way I saw you looking at each other at the Holly Folly is any indication, it looks like a lot more than some."

Lia was unaccustomed to having people, other than Sally, eager to discuss her social life. While nice in principle, in reality it made her shift uncomfortably in her chair. "We're…dating."

"Is the sex good?" Anita asked.

"Anita!" Josie gave Anita a stern look.

Lia blushed, but she couldn't help the slow smile that spread across her face. She nodded. "Yeah. It is."

"Well, good for you." Although she wouldn't have solicited it, Josie was clearly going to enjoy the gossip once it was out there.

"It's good to know her reputation isn't unfounded," Anita said. It was clear that someone, although Lia couldn't figure out who, kicked her under the table. Anita winced. "Sorry. I didn't mean it like that."

"All she means," Josie said, "is that Alex does well in the women department."

Jan chimed in. "Please don't get the wrong idea. We love Alex. I consider her one of my closest friends."

"Oh, yes," Stacia said. "Alex is a wonderful person. Pretty easy on the eyes, too, and I'm not even a lesbian."

Lia, even more unsure about being the center of attention when the topic of conversation was her sex life, scratched her temple. "But?"

"But," Jan said, drawing out the word for emphasis. "Alex has an unspoken policy of keeping things casual."

Lia cringed on the inside. She'd deduced as much from the way Jeff and some of the other people at the bakery teased her, from bumping into Sara at the tree lighting. "It's okay. It's definitely good to know. I'm happy keeping things casual anyway."

Lia heard herself say the words and they weren't very convincing. Even though she'd made the decision to have a fling, it felt weird saying as much. Looking around the table, she didn't think her friends were convinced either.

"We just don't want to see you get hurt." At Anita's words, everyone around the table nodded.

"It really is okay." Lia did her best to sound definitive. "Y'all know I just got out of a ten-year relationship. I'm in no position to start anything serious. I'm certainly not looking to fall in love."

Stacia reached over and squeezed her hand. "We know, dear. It's just that falling in love isn't always about whether or not you're looking for it."

Lia squeezed it back and squared her shoulders. "It means a lot that y'all are looking out for me. Alex and I are having a good time, enjoying each other's company. It's exactly what I want. I promise I won't get my heart broken."

"Okay, then," Stacia said. "That settles that. Ante up ladies. The game is five-card draw. Deuces and one-eyed jacks are wild."

Everyone made a point of focusing on their cards and Lia breathed a sigh of relief. She wasn't sure if her last statement was more for their benefit or her own. Either way, it was a good reminder of where she stood. She looked at her hand and found a pair of jacks, each of them with only one eye. She kept her face straight and started raising the bet slowly, not wanting to scare anyone away from throwing their dimes and quarters into the pot. If only she was as lucky in love as she was in cards.

It was a little after nine when the poker game ended. She was ahead almost twelve dollars—quite a haul for nickel-dime-quarter. She pulled up behind Alex's car and sat for a moment. She'd meant what she said. She and Alex were having a good time, and that's exactly what she needed right now. If it felt a little unnatural, it was only because that wasn't how she usually thought about relationships. She really wasn't looking for anything more.

As she was getting out of the car, Alex emerged from the back door with Murphy. "I thought I heard a car. Go on in and make yourself comfortable. We'll be up in a few minutes."

Lia went upstairs and thought for a moment, then went into Alex's bedroom and opened the closet doors. She smiled at the neat rows and perfectly stacked piles—T-shirts and chef coats and at least a dozen pairs of jeans. She selected a simple white oxford.

After she changed, Lia went to Alex's nightstand for matches to light the candles scattered around the room. She pulled open the drawer, but instead of matches, Lia found herself staring at a flesh-colored dildo and a black leather harness. Her breath hitched; she resisted the urge to touch it.

Lia closed the drawer, opened the other one, and pulled out the matches. With her mind racing, she went around the room, lighting candles. Her friends at the poker game had made it pretty clear Alex never wanted for company. This just proved the point. Alex wouldn't have such a thing handy if she didn't use it on a regular basis.

Really, though, was that so bad? Alex knew what she wanted and she went after it. For the time being, she wanted her. There was no reason not to enjoy it, to revel in being desired. Lia wanted to live up to that desire.

She wondered why Alex hadn't suggested they use it. Was Lia supposed to know, to be the one to request it? Alex was probably used to confident and experienced women, women who knew their desires and didn't hesitate to ask for what they wanted. How could she ask if she didn't even know what she was missing? She paced around the room, aroused and a little anxious, trying to decide what to do.

When Alex came in with Murphy, Lia was standing in the doorway to the bedroom, trying to look casually sexy. She was wearing nothing but the shirt she'd pulled from Alex's closet. The bottom hem grazed the tops of her thighs and she'd left it unbuttoned. She hoped she looked more confident than she felt.

"That's a good look for you."

Lia offered a slow smile, willing herself to be cool. "Thanks."

Alex crossed the short distance between them and slid a hand under the shirt and around Lia's waist. "That doesn't mean I don't want you naked."

Alex began walking her backward toward the bed. Lia complied, tugging apart the button fly of Alex's jeans. Alex stepped back and stripped off the sweater she was wearing. She pulled Lia to her, started kissing her neck and breasts. There was an urgency, an insistence that wasn't like their previous times together. Alex's hands were possessive, a little rough.

Lia had a flash of Alex tossing her on the bed, nudging her thighs apart, thrusting into her. She wanted that. Her insides ached for it. She tried to focus on that instead of the doubts it stirred up.

"Wait." When she got no response, Lia lifted her hands to Alex's shoulders and pushed against her. "Alex, wait."

Alex froze, lifted her head. "What is it? What's wrong?"

Oh, God. She wanted that cock, as much as she wanted to be the kind of woman Alex desired. Did she have the guts to do it? "Do you enjoy having sex with a…um…strap on?"

Alex pulled further back, looked at her searchingly. "Where did that come from?"

Lia flushed. "I was looking for the matches you keep in your nightstand. I wasn't trying to snoop, I swear, but I opened the wrong drawer."

Alex nodded. "It's okay. Are you into that? Is it something you want?"

Lia resisted the urge to look away. "Maybe?"

"Maybe?"

"Yes."

Alex looked at her quizzically. "Yes maybe, or yes it's something you want?"

"Yes, it's something I want."

"Okay. It kind of sounds like you aren't sure."

"I'm sure. It's just…" So much for sophistication. She was basically outing herself as having no experience. "I haven't before."

Alex looked shocked. "You haven't…ever?"

This was a terrible idea. "Never mind. Forget I said anything."

Alex swallowed and looked at her in a way Lia couldn't read. "No…God…I'd love to. Give me one second."

Alex went to the nightstand, then disappeared into the bathroom. Lia stood where Alex left her and tried not to fidget. Was it that simple? She bit her bottom lip, as much out of nervousness as arousal. When Alex emerged, she had stripped down to a pair of tight, black boxer briefs. Lia could make out a distinctive bulge and it made her mouth water.

Alex walked over to her and slipped the shirt from her shoulders. It fell in a pool on the floor. "We'll go slow. Okay?"

"Okay." She was doing this. There was no turning back now.

Alex guided her to the bed. She nudged Lia onto her back, then climbed in. Bracing herself on one elbow, she started kissing her way down Lia's torso. "I want to make sure you're really wet."

Lia let out a shaky laugh. "Oh, I don't think that's a problem."

When Alex slid her fingers over her, Lia was nearly dripping. Alex slid off her briefs and positioned herself between Lia's thighs. "You're sure?"

Lia looked at the silicone cock, held in place with a black harness. The muscles inside her began to clench in anticipation. Her breath hitched. "I'm beyond sure."

Alex moved closer and Lia felt the tip of the cock ease inside her. The feeling was exquisite, unlike anything else she'd ever felt. Her brain screamed more and deeper; she had to fight to remain relatively still. She locked eyes with Alex. "Yes."

Alex eased farther inside, then stopped, as though she was trying to give Lia a moment to adjust to the sensation. Lia groaned and arched her hips. Alex eased out just a little and then back in. After what felt like an eternity, Alex filled her the rest of the way. Lia pulled her in and held her tight.

Eventually Alex began to move, with strokes that were slow and even. Lia lifted her hips, rising to meet her each time. Her thrusts became longer and deeper.

"You okay?"

"Oh, yes."

Alex leaned down, pulling her into a kiss that felt equal parts reassuring and possessive. It was like she'd flipped a switch or, somehow, granted Alex permission to take what she wanted. Alex's movements became more forceful, more demanding. Lia hadn't realized how badly she wanted to be taken.

She opened her eyes and stole a glance at Alex. Her eyes were closed and she seemed completely carried away, lost in the moment. The rhythm grew increasingly frantic, and Lia couldn't help making little noises each time Alex filled her completely. Lia dragged her nails down Alex's back, begging to be driven harder, higher.

The pressure built quickly and the orgasm pounded through her. She felt Alex grow rigid, heard her groan. When the spasms finally ebbed, her bones felt liquid and her muscles quivered.

"I'm crushing you." Alex had collapsed on top of her.

"No, you're fine. Don't go."

Alex obliged, but propped herself slightly on one elbow. She looked down at Lia and smiled. "That was hot."

Yeah, it was hot. Lia was a little shocked by just how hot it was. Alex knew exactly what to do, and made Lia feel things she didn't even know she could feel. Now didn't seem like the time to be emotional, though, or philosophical. "Mmm hmm."

"You're really sexy."

"Ditto."

Alex got up to blow out candles and slip out of the harness. She climbed back into bed, pulled Lia close and kissed her shoulder. She was asleep almost instantly. Lia remained awake, Alex's words playing over and over in her mind. It had been beyond hot, but she had a hard time believing it had anything to do with her. Alex had the kind of skills that could only come with lots of practice. Lia didn't want to think of how much practice—with how many women—Alex had. She needed to keep perspective and remember that, no matter how good the sex was, it was still just sex.

Chapter Nineteen

Lia continued to spend most of her days at the café, most of her nights with Alex. It wasn't that there was an expectation. More often than not, though, they'd have dinner together. Dinner inevitably led to kissing, which led to lovemaking, which led to neither one of them wanting to leave the warm cocoon of each other's arms.

She would get up at five with Alex, go home to shower and change and putter, then return to the café around eight. She wasn't hiding it from anyone, and she was pretty sure Jeff knew exactly what was going on, but it was a routine that worked. If she had moments of wondering what the hell she was thinking, they were few and far between. As long as they didn't talk about feelings or futures, she figured she was all right.

On one of what had become a typical evening for them, Lia was cooking dinner in Alex's kitchen. The mushrooms at the market that day looked promising, so she had decided on a risotto. In one pan she cooked the mushrooms in batches so they'd brown. In another, she sautéed onions and leeks and garlic in a mixture of butter and olive oil, then added the rice.

"May I?" she asked, gesturing at the bottle of wine Alex had just opened.

"Of course. There's a second in the fridge if we need it."

"Perfect." Lia added wine to the rice and vegetables, stirring as it bubbled vigorously. When most of it was evaporated, she added the cooked mushrooms and two ladles of vegetable stock and continued stirring. "I'm pretty much stuck here for the next twenty minutes, so I'm going to leave entertainment up to you."

Alex sipped her wine, looked like she was considering her options. "Okay. Let's play twenty questions. I'll go first. Why did you come to Provincetown?"

Lia cocked her head. "That's not how that game works, you know."

"It's my own special version. Do you want to play or not?"

"Why do I get the feeling this is more like Truth or Dare?"

"Well, if you answer the questions, you don't have to worry about dares."

She considered. They really hadn't talked too much about their pasts. This might prove enlightening. "Okay. I'm game. What was the question?"

"Why did you come to Provincetown? I know you were getting out of a relationship, but moving here in the winter seems a little extreme."

"It wasn't really extreme. I wanted to get out of New York City as much as I wanted to get away from Dani, and I refused to move anywhere below the Mason-Dixon line. I love it here, so it felt like the perfect place to come for peace and quiet, and to figure out what I wanted to do next."

"Is your ex the one who wanted to live in New York?"

At this point, thinking about Dani wasn't nearly as painful as it had been. It was more that talking about her felt intimate. Thus far, they'd talked only casually about past relationships. For Lia, it was one of those lines in the sand that kept things with Alex from teetering into serious relationship territory. She crossed it with trepidation.

"Oh, yeah. Power suit lesbian all the way." It was an accurate description, Lia realized, although she hadn't used the phrase before. She sipped her own glass of wine. "This is very good, by the way."

"Thanks. The new guy at the wine store recommended it." Alex crossed her arms and leaned forward. "Power suits. Really?"

Lia set down her wine and resumed stirring the risotto. "Really. She's a financial analyst in the International Securities Division of Goldman Sachs."

"That sounds intimidating."

"One of the reasons she likes it. It also supports her love of designer suits and technological gadgets."

Alex frowned. She hadn't really known Lia long enough to know her type, but Alex had a hard time imagining that designer clothes and expensive toys was it. "How did you get together?"

Lia put her hands on her hips. "Am I going to get a turn?"

"I promise, but we're on a roll here. Give me a few more." For some reason, it felt really important that she know the answer.

Lia rolled her eyes in what Alex hoped was mock annoyance. "Fine. In college. We both went to Smith. Even though she was an Economics major, it was a pretty small place. We bumped into each other often enough. She was gorgeous and quite the mover and shaker on campus."

"And you're drawn to the Wall Street types?" Alex tried to keep her tone light.

"No, actually, not at all. Danielle was always ambitious, but she was more idealistic while we were in school. She wanted to change the world."

Alex nodded, relieved. She tried to conjure an image in her mind of a young Lia, wrapped up in young love.

"She had presence, you know? When she walked into a room, everyone's eyes were on her. When she spoke, everyone listened. I was a little bit star struck. She paid attention to me and I was gone. She didn't go 'Wall Street' until grad school. She worked as a finance associate, then analyst, for a couple of years, made the right connections, and got into the MBA program at NYU."

"The Stern School."

Lia raised her eyebrows. "You know it?"

Alex chuckled. "Indeed. While I was busy pursuing my Iron Chef fantasies, Meg was earning her MBA. Her area, however, is organizational behavior."

"Small world it is. When was she there?"

"Um, eight or nine years ago. Yes, because she worked for a couple of years after undergrad."

"Danielle was there at the same time. Freakishly small world."

Alex laughed at that. "They could have had a class together. How weird is that?"

"Weird. I know you were at the Culinary Institute. Where did Meg go to college?"

"She was a UMass girl. She got a full ride and used her share of the college fund to buy a car. She's always been very practical. I just realized I don't know anything about your family. Do you have siblings?"

Lia smiled. "Do I ever."

While Lia continued to add stock and stir the pot, Alex asked her far more than twenty questions about her family. It was easy to get her to talk while half of her attention was on her pot. When it was done, Lia served it up and they stayed at the bar to eat.

"I can't believe you have three brothers."

"I think it helped that I was the baby. Michael, the oldest, was ten by the time I was born. They went the protective older brother route instead of tormenting me. Not that they didn't occasionally torment me."

"That sounds really nice."

"It was. And although they didn't quite know what to do with me when I came out, I think it's probably for the best that I didn't have boyfriends in high school. They would have been brutal."

Alex chuckled. "I'm sure. Meg was never super girly, but I was most definitely the tomboy. I liked to think of myself as a brotherly figure, getting all puffed up and serious when she brought boys around."

Lia looked at the woman who'd awakened a whole new level of sexuality in her. She could so easily imagine a teenage Alex, full of bravado and swagger. She would have had such a crush on her. "Did it work?"

"Meg seemed to attract chronically nice guys, so it was a bit of a moot point. She was the homecoming queen who preferred the quiet, intellectual types over the football stars."

"And what about you? Did you attract chronically nice girls?" Lia had the distinct feeling that Alex was a heartbreaker from a young age.

"Sort of? I think because I was so obviously a lesbian, a lot of straight girls decided to do their experimenting with me. Sometimes that was thrilling, other times less so."

"Did a straight girl break your heart?" Lia was thinking of her own high school years and a tall, blonde volleyball player named Mary Louise. She'd invite Lia over to study and they'd spend hours kissing and, eventually, more. When Lia came out, though, Mary Lou shut her out completely. According to Sally, she'd married a Methodist minister and moved to Tennessee.

Alex sighed. "Her name was Jennifer. She was a cheerleader and the first girl I really fell for. After almost a year, Jenny decided she was straight, hooked up with the first baseman of the varsity team, and never spoke to me again. It's a rite of passage, I suppose."

"I believe you're right." Lia reached over and gave her leg a squeeze. She thought it might be a good time to change the subject. "Speaking of families and rites of passage, I booked a flight to visit mine for the holidays."

"What? You're leaving?" If Lia didn't know better, she would have sworn there was a trace of panic in Alex's voice.

"Just for a few days. I got away with not going home for Thanksgiving, but Christmas, it seems, is non-negotiable." In a gesture that was unusually thoughtful and assertive, Lia's parents had insisted that she come home for Christmas. They'd gone so far as to buy her a round-trip plane ticket from Boston to New Orleans. It was a sweet gesture, but she was already anxious about spending four solid days with her family.

"That sounds nice." Alex couldn't figure out why Lia's announcement put a lump in her throat. She did her best to ignore it.

"It is, it is. It's just that four whole days with them seems like kind of a lot."

"Do you not get along with your family?" After their mother's death, she and Meg had grown even closer to their dad. They still spoke several times a week and she always looked forward to spending time with him. The idea of not being close to family gave her a pang of sadness for Lia.

"Oh, we're far too Southern and civilized not to get along."

Alex raised a brow. "But?"

"We have somewhat of a 'Don't Ask, Don't Tell' policy. They love me, but my being a lesbian makes them extremely uncomfortable. Keeping a certain distance has been easier, for them and for me."

"Do you go home very often?"

"Once every year or two. I usually plan it around my best friend, Sally. She lives in New Orleans now, which is just about an hour from my hometown. I went down for her wedding, after each of her kids was born. I see my parents, my brothers and their families, but I don't spend so much time with them that we run out of things to talk about. She'll be with her in-laws for the holidays, so it's just me and the whole Brooks clan."

The pang of sadness Alex felt grew into a full wave of sympathy. She wasn't naive about how much homophobia there was, but having a supportive family and living where she did shielded her from dealing with it on a daily basis. "I'm sorry."

"It's okay. They really do mean well, and they do love me. To be honest, it was as much me as it was them. I got comfortable in New York, and my ex hated what she called the 'backwoods.' With her distaste, it became easier to avoid the whole thing." Lia paused for a moment and frowned. "It's actually kind of horrible of me."

Alex offered her a reassuring smile. "Not at all. The path of least resistance can be an effective survival mechanism."

"I guess. Thanks."

Alex rinsed their empty dishes and loaded them into the dishwasher. She notched another black mark in her mind against Lia's ex. The marks were starting to add up. She wanted to make her feel better, though, and harping on what a raging bitch the woman was likely wouldn't accomplish that. Instead, she said, "So it might be a really great chance to reconnect with them."

Lia visibly brightened. "It might just."

"When are you going?'

"I fly out on the 23rd and back on the 27th."

Alex scooped the leftover risotto into a container and put it in the fridge, then ran hot soapy water into the pot. "That's perfect. I can give you a ride to the airport."

Alex smiled as she scrubbed the starchy pan. In her thirty-three years, she'd never dropped off or picked up a girlfriend from the airport. She liked the idea of being the last person Lia saw when she left and the first when she returned.

"That's a long drive for you just to give me a ride."

"It's not. I'm heading to Boston for the week. It's my present to myself for not closing a single day in the summer." Alex didn't know why, but it suddenly felt important that she be the one to see Lia off.

"That is so thoughtful, but my flight out is at like six in the morning."

Even better. "Well, then, clearly the best plan is for us to go to Boston the day before. You can stay at Meg's with me and then it's only a twenty minute ride to Logan from there."

"I really don't—"

Alex interrupted her. "It's no trouble at all. Besides, my dad will love you. Since he retired and started spending winters in South Carolina, he likes to say he's developed a thing for Southern women."

"If you're sure."

"I'm sure."

Lia refilled their wineglasses and led the way into the living room. "I'm not going to lie, not having to drive from here to Boston in the wee hours of the morning makes me very happy. Almost as happy as the prospect of seeing Meg again and meeting your dad."

Alex gave Murphy a chew bone for being good and they both followed her. He stretched himself out on the living room rug and happily went to town. Lia curled up on the couch while Alex lit a fire. Once the flames had taken hold, Alex joined her. "It's going to be great, and it's always nice to have company for the ride."

"Agreed. So, what about you?"

"What about me?" Alex had pulled Lia's feet into her lap and was rubbing them lightly.

"Do you have an ex? A string of exes?"

Lia had been very open, so she wasn't not going to answer, but chose her words carefully. "I wouldn't say a 'string.' I had a girlfriend in college, and one serious relationship shortly after, with my first boss."

"Oh."

"Exactly. Let's just say it didn't end well. Since moving here, I've mostly kept to casual dating. It seems to be easiest, considering how much of the population is transient."

That was not the thing to say to the woman she was currently dating. They really hadn't talked at all about what their relationship meant or where, if anywhere, it was going. Still, it sounded bad, even if Lia was only around for a few months herself. She watched Lia, looking for signs of irritation or worse. What she did, however, was crawl into Alex's lap.

"Well, I'm glad there aren't a lot of transients around at this time of year. I imagine the competition can get pretty stiff."

"Lia…" Alex wasn't sure what to say. She didn't want to make empty promises or to start talking about feelings, but Lia was so different from the women she usually dated. Her feelings for Lia were, too, although she didn't want to slap a label on them.

"Shhh." Lia put a finger to her lips. "I'm teasing you. I like what we have. I like that it's fun and uncomplicated."

For some reason, that made Alex feel worse rather than better. But before she could think about why that might be, Lia's mouth was on hers. Thoughts quickly turned into needs and Alex allowed herself to be swept away by touch and taste and the heat that poured from Lia into her.

CHAPTER TWENTY

With only intermittent snow flurries, the drive to Boston was uneventful. They arrived at Meg and Rob's house late in the afternoon. Alex pulled into the driveway behind an old Buick, looked over at Lia, and smiled. "I'm really excited for you to meet my dad."

Lia tried to imagine the man who'd raised both Meg and Alex from the time they were toddlers, the retired-cop-slash-single-dad. To say she was curious was a massive understatement.

They grabbed their things and walked into the house. She instantly recognized Patrick McKinnon from the photos scattered around Alex's loft. He was sitting in an easy chair in jeans and a flannel shirt; there was a pair of reading glasses perched on his nose and he appeared to be working on a crossword puzzle. The resemblance was striking, and she imagined she was getting a sneak peek of what Alex would look like in thirty years.

He bounded out of the chair like a man in his prime. "Ali! It's about damn time you showed up."

Alex got swept up in a bear hug. When she pulled away, she punched him in the arm. "Just because you got nowhere to be, old man, you think the rest of us spend our time lounging about?"

Lia watched them tease one another. It was obvious the harassment was an essential part of their relationship. The bond, the love, between them was palpable. It made Lia's heart beat uncomfortably in her chest and she couldn't decide if it had to do with Alex or with her own anxiety around seeing her family. Before she could start ruminating, Meg breezed in from the kitchen.

"You're here." Meg hugged her, then Alex. "Your timing is perfect. I just put on the afternoon coffee."

"I'm sure you mean after-nap coffee, with Pop here."

Patrick swatted at his daughter with a rolled up newspaper. "I never did manage to beat the sass out of you, did I? Aren't you going to introduce me to your pretty friend here?"

Alex rolled her eyes, but with affection. "I don't know. Are you going to treat her the way you treat me?"

"Of course not. She's a guest."

"Right. What was I thinking? Pop, this is Lia." Alex turned to Lia. "Lia, this is my dad, Pat."

"It's a pleasure to meet you, Mr. McKinnon." Lia extended her hand.

Pat took Lia's hand, brought it to his lips for a kiss. "Please, you must call me Pat. And the pleasure, I assure you, is all mine."

Lia decided to risk Alex's ire by egging him on. "Why, thank you." She turned on a little bit of drawl. "Alex never mentioned that her father was so charming, or so handsome."

"All right, all right. That's enough out of you two."

"You're just jealous that she likes me." Pat winked at Lia while elbowing his daughter in the ribs. "I can't help it if I'm still a looker."

"Ah, but what are you looking at?" Meg poked him, then headed back into the kitchen. She returned with a tray loaded with a pot of coffee, mugs, and a plate of cookies.

If Meg was a treasure trove of stories about Alex, Patrick was the mother lode. Throughout the afternoon and evening, he spun tales of his daughters' mischief and mishaps, interspersed with their accomplishments and his proudest moments. Lia learned that Alex was the star catcher of her high school softball team and graduated third in her class. A distaste for physics resulted in her losing the salutatorian slot to Meg by a fraction of a point. And while she'd never been girly, Alex went through a brief phase in middle school during which she sported a perm and wanted to join a girl band. After getting her first job at a local donut shop, she abandoned dreams of playing the electric guitar in favor of becoming a famous chef.

It grew dark and they switched from coffee to wine. At around seven, Meg pulled a gorgeous lasagna from the oven. The conversation moved to the dinner table and they were joined by Rob, home from his job at one of the local architecture firms.

As they took their seats, Meg dished lasagna onto plates and passed them around. Rob passed around a giant bowl of salad, followed by a basket of garlic bread. Alex emerged from the kitchen with a second bottle of wine and started refilling glasses.

"Meg, where's your glass? Did you leave it in the kitchen?"

"No, I'm fine with water."

Alex looked at her sister. "That's not like you, especially once the semester is over."

Lia had an immediate suspicion about Meg's abstinence. She'd had an almost identical interaction with Sally right before Sally told her she was pregnant with her first son. Lia looked from Meg to Alex and back to Meg.

"Well," Meg said finally, "I'm not supposed to drink wine again until after the baby is born."

Lia watched Alex, then Pat, respond to the news. There were shouts, a couple of happy expletives, hugs, and a few tears. It was so touching to watch. She was happy for all of them, and a little sad that she'd not been present when her brothers and their wives made similar announcements. If her eyes were a little misty when she raised her glass to toast the impending arrival, no one seemed to notice.

They ate and drank and, by the time they called it a night a little before eleven, Lia's sides ached from laughing. She'd developed a full-blown crush on the entire McKinnon clan, even if half of them were technically Sullivans. Since Patrick was only in town for the week, he was staying at Meg's as well instead of his own house in Boston. With him in the guest room, Alex and Lia were bunking on a futon next to a computer desk and a weight bench. Meg had made it up nicely, though, and Lia wasn't about to complain about having to snuggle up close.

"The next time we're here, this room will probably be a nursery."

Even though it was just a figure of speech, Lia got a flutter in her stomach at Alex's assertion of a next time. "It's very exciting. I remember how giddy I was when I found out Sally was pregnant. You're going to be an amazing auntie."

Alex climbed in against the wall and motioned for Lia to join her. "If by amazing, you mean spoil them rotten and drive their mother nuts, then yes."

"That is exactly what I mean." She slid in next to Alex. "Just don't tell Meg I said that."

When they were burrowed under the covers, Lia found herself saying, "I don't want to go to my family anymore. Can I just stay with yours?"

Without hesitating, Alex replied, "Of course."

Lia sighed. "I know you know I'm just kidding, but that's very sweet."

"I know you're just kidding, but I mean it nonetheless."

Alex looked at Lia in the silvery light coming through the sheer curtains. She loved the way Lia's hair fell across her forehead and the pillow. She had never been big on a woman's hair, but every time she was around Lia, all she wanted to do was bury her hands in Lia's unruly tumble of curls. She took a lock of it, wrapping it around her finger. Lia smiled at her.

"I have a very serious question to ask you."

"What is it?"

Alex saw a flicker of concern in Lia's big brown eyes, but kept her face stern. "Are you at all capable of being quiet?"

Understanding dawned and Alex enjoyed watching Lia's expression go from concerned to confused to aroused before returning to a state of concern. "With you, I have absolutely no idea."

Alex grinned. "Well, I guess we're going to have to try it and see."

Lia was completely quiet. Almost. She let out one tiny moan, then managed to contain herself. When she came, she bit her fist. It was one of the sexiest things Alex had ever seen.

When the alarm went off a few hours later, it was clear Lia did not want to get out of bed. After some subtle encouragement, she grudgingly extricated herself, took a quick shower, and dressed. Alex was waiting for her in jeans, a sweatshirt, and a Red Sox cap.

"You're going to be fine."

Alex's words eased her unspoken worries. Lia smiled and nodded. "Thanks."

When they arrived at the airport, Alex pulled up to the ticketing and departure area for Delta. Before Lia could stop her, she hopped out of the car and pulled Lia's suitcase from the back.

"Very chivalrous. Thank you."

"I had an ulterior motive." She gathered Lia in her arms and indulged in a long, lingering kiss.

"No complaints here."

Alex leaned back, but didn't let her go. "I'm going to miss you." She hadn't meant to say it, hadn't planned on letting their parting get weighed down with any sort of significance. Yet, there it was.

Alex's assertion took Lia by surprise. It was the kind of thing a girlfriend would say. It was exactly what she'd been thinking, but was afraid to say out loud. "Me too."

"Good, because if it was just me, we'd have a problem."

Alex kissed her senseless again and then let her go. Lia mustered a smile. "Have a wonderful Christmas."

"You too. Let yourself have fun, but not too much fun."

"I think I can manage that." Somehow, Lia had come around to the idea of spending time with her family. She was pretty sure Alex had more than a little something to do with it.

"Text me, call me, and eat a beignet for me."

Lia saluted. "I will. See you soon."

She gave Alex another quick kiss and then hurried into the terminal so that she didn't have the chance to get sentimental or, worse, clingy. She stole a glance back and saw Alex standing where she'd left her. Alex lifted her hand in a wave that she returned. It was that image she took with her as she made her way through security and boarded the plane.

CHAPTER TWENTY-ONE

Much to Lia's relief, her flights, and the connection in Atlanta, were uneventful. It was early afternoon when she landed and she easily made her way to baggage claim, then the new rental car facility built as part of the reconstruction after Katrina. The temperature was in the low fifties and felt downright balmy compared to the near zero it was when she left Boston that morning.

After claiming her car, Lia pulled out of the garage and made her way to Airline Highway, turning off to take the Gramercy Bridge across the river. As she wound her way along the River Road, she was hit with the sweet and pungent smell of burning sugarcane. She rounded a bend and saw the line of fire in the field, the smoke billowing up and across the road. It was a common practice on the sugarcane farms—burning what was left after the stalks were harvested. It helped to feed the soil for the next season. It was one of those things, she realized, you sort of forget about when you're away for a long time. As a kid, she and Sally would complain about the smell. Now, she welcomed it and allowed herself to be glad that she was home.

When Lia pulled into the driveway, her parents came out to stand on the porch and welcome her. They did the same thing when she was in college and came home for winter break or summer vacations. It always made her feel special. This time, it made her feel special, but a bit guilty as well.

She climbed out of the car and they exchanged hugs and kisses. Her dad took her suitcase and she followed them inside. Mama had a penchant for painting and sewing curtains, so it wasn't surprising to find new colors in the living room and kitchen. Lia admired the choices and made a mental note to seek her advice when she had a place of her own to decorate.

She went to her room and found it unchanged. The pink and green quilt she'd chosen for her sixteenth birthday was still on the bed; the white eyelet lace curtains Mama made dressed the windows. She crossed the hall to the bathroom she used to hate having to share with her brothers. The counter, once crowded with toothbrushes and hair products held only a vase of silk flowers and a decorative soap dispenser. She did, however, spy a basket of toys in the bathtub. Clearly, Mawmaw and Pawpaw were equipped for sleepovers with the grandkids.

Lia spent most of the afternoon helping her mother get food ready for the family's annual Christmas Eve party while her father and brothers finished building the bonfire. Theirs would top fifteen feet and be one of hundreds that burned along the levees, lighting the way for *Père Noel*. Probably close to a hundred aunts, uncles, cousins, and family friends would stream in and out for hours—eating, drinking, and making merry. As a kid, she'd loved Christmas Eve even more than Christmas morning.

It felt good to be in the kitchen of her childhood. Mama filled her in on all of the local goings on and gossip. Lia worked to put faces with names as she learned of marriages and births and deaths and divorces. After a while, Louise paused, wooden spoon in hand. "And how are you, honey? How are you holding up?"

"I'm good. The breakup was hard, but the longer I'm out of it, the more I realize it was overdue. You know what I mean?"

"I do. And I want you to know that I'm proud of you. It took courage to walk away from that life, a life that was familiar and comfortable."

She'd focused so much on feeling like a failure, the words really hit home. "Thanks, Mama. That means a lot to me."

"Well, I mean it. Are you seeing anyone now?"

Lia blushed. "Sort of."

Louise looked over the rim of her reading glasses. "What kind of answer is that?"

"Well…" Lia suddenly felt sixteen again. If she wasn't so mortified, she might be able to laugh at herself. "I've been spending time with someone I met in Provincetown. She owns the café where I go most days to work."

It was an honest answer, Lia assured herself, even if it left out the detail of all the amazing sex. Her mother narrowed her eyes. "Works there or just owns it?"

"It's a bakery and a café and she does all of the baking herself. She's a pastry chef." That was a strange question. Lia wondered why she wanted to know.

"That's good. She sounds grounded. What's her name?"

Lia swallowed. She wished she didn't get so tense when talking with her family about her personal life. She wondered if it would be different if she was straight, talking with Mama about men. Probably. "Alex. And yes, grounded is a good way to describe her. She works hard, but still manages to have fun."

"That sounds like exactly what you need." Louise winked as she said it, taking Lia by surprise. Before she could say anything else, her dad and brothers came in, congratulating themselves on building their tallest bonfire to date. She took the opportunity to excuse herself to freshen up before supper.

The next evening, people started arriving at the house by five o'clock. There was gumbo and potato salad, cheese dips and homemade boudin, a whole table of sweets and another filled with soda and liquor and wine. Coolers were stacked on the floor and held bags of ice and cases of beer. She'd forgotten how seriously Cajuns took their parties.

She kissed great uncles and let them tell her how pretty she was. She admired the growth spurts of her younger cousins, nieces, and nephews. She was also introduced to the two newest members of the family, a niece named Ella and a second cousin named Noah. She was teased about becoming a Yankee, but it was generally good natured. She assured them all that she still said y'all and rooted for LSU football. For the most part, it seemed like a satisfactory response.

A little before seven, they flowed across the street and up the levee. Her dad held a lighter to the kerosene-soaked newspaper stuffed in strategic places that would get the fire going. A cheer went up and, in a matter of minutes, the towering structure ignited. Everyone moved back to accommodate the radiating heat. Lia leaned back and watched the line of fires coming to life as far as the eye could see. She saw a bottle rocket go up here and there, looked over at the dark, slow moving water of the Mississippi River. It was Christmas, and she was home.

About an hour later, Lia found herself in a circle with her three brothers. She realized, suddenly, that it was an arrangement that had been orchestrated. Not knowing what they were thinking, she employed her usual strategy of asking them questions about themselves.

Mike raised a finger. "We're on to you, peanut. We want to hear about you."

Peanut was the name Lia's parents had used with her brothers to refer to their new brother or sister before she was born. It was a nickname that stuck. It made Lia smile to hear it now. "What do you want to know?"

Joe looked incredulous. "Uh, everything. You left Dani, moved, apparently are dating someone, and we haven't seen you in almost a year."

"Right." They weren't a subtle bunch. "I'm good. Really. Breaking up with Dani was hard, but it was the right thing to do. Getting out of the city was the right thing to do, too. I'm working and making friends. I'm happy."

Mike interjected. "Is it true you have a new girlfriend?"

Lia hesitated. The one time Dani had come home with her, meeting her brothers had not gone well, on either side of the equation. She did not relish the thought of an inquisition, or of their judgment.

"Just dating. Nothing serious. Nothing worth mentioning." Even if it didn't feel like that the last couple of weeks, that was still her official story, and she was sticking to it.

Jaime didn't look convinced. "Why are you holding out on us?"

"I'm not holding out. I'm just…" What was she?

"Being squirrelly." Joe folded his arms across his chest.

"Not squirrelly. It's Christmas. I don't want to make things weird by talking about my personal life."

Jaime jumped back in. "You know, Lia, we have no problem with the fact that you're gay."

Lia nodded. It wasn't the first time her brothers had said as much. Yet, ever since she'd gone away to college and been in actual relationships with women, there was a lingering awkwardness that prevented her from believing it entirely. She looked from Jaime, who'd spoken, to Mike then Joe. They were all staring at her. She forced a smile. "I know."

Jaime scowled. "I don't think you do. None of us liked Dani. We all thought she was stuck up and not nearly good enough for you. That has nothing to do with you being into women."

"I...I had no idea." She struggled to process what he was saying, trying unsuccessfully to reconcile it with Dani's assertions that her family, although nice on the surface, was homophobic. It had been so easy to attribute the tension, and avoidance, to the fact that they were fundamentally uncomfortable with her, and the fact that she was a lesbian.

Joe uncrossed his arms and lifted them defensively. "We wanted to be supportive, but it was hard when the person you were with made it seem like she couldn't stand to be around us. And when you stopped coming down, it kind of felt like you were picking her over us."

If there'd been a chair anywhere nearby, Lia would have sat down. It never occurred to her that her family was not uncomfortable with her sexuality, but with her specific choice of partner. That they'd seen Dani for what she was so long ago was painfully ironic. Lia was suddenly overcome with the feeling that she'd wasted so much time, done more damage than she'd ever considered. She looked down at her plastic cup of Crown Royal and Diet Coke for a long minute. "I'm so sorry."

She looked up and locked eyes with Jaime. He was the one who had carried her home from the playground when she'd fallen from the monkey bars and sprained her ankle. He'd been proud that she got into a fancy college up north. The idea that she'd pushed him away, let him down, made her feel terribly small. She'd been such a fool.

"Oh, peanut, don't cry."

The next thing Lia knew, she was completely enveloped in a hug. All three of her brothers, and all six arms, surrounded her with so much love and so much warmth that she couldn't believe she'd gone without it for so long. "I love y'all so much."

Mike poked her in the ribs. "We love you, too, peanut. We're glad you're home."

❖

The next morning, Lia went with her parents to Mass, then returned home to make Christmas dinner. Her brothers came over mid afternoon with their families. Over ham and praline sweet potatoes, she learned everything that Santa had brought, from boring socks to the coolest bikes ever. After the meal, her oldest niece, Abby, offered to read one of her new books. Lia learned all about why pigeons should not drive buses, no matter how desperately they might want to.

Late that afternoon, she texted Alex and almost immediately got a "Merry Christmas, Southern belle" in return. She didn't hear from Dani at all, nor did she send a greeting of her own. She found herself wanting to tell Alex all about the conversation with her brothers, as well as the one she had with her parents. It was like a huge weight had been lifted, and Alex was the person she wanted to share it with.

She decided to wait until they were together again. Although she was no longer anxious to leave Louisiana or her family, she did find herself ready to be back. Whether it was her apartment or her friends or Alex, she was starting to think of Provincetown as home.

When she landed in Boston two days later, Alex was waiting just on the other side of the security screening area. She had parked and come in and it made Lia feel special. It was silly perhaps, but one of those things Dani never did.

During the three-hour drive from Boston to Provincetown, Lia related the events of her trip. Alex gave her thigh a reassuring squeeze when Lia teared up about how much misunderstanding there was and how, had she not left Dani, she might have spent the rest of her life distant and detached from her family. Alex told her about her Christmas, the continued excitement and planning for the baby, her dad's girlfriend in Charleston.

As they drove, Alex found herself stealing glances at Lia. She tried not to focus on how much she'd missed her, or thought about her during their time apart. It was easy to distract herself with thoughts of having Lia naked and under her, skin flushed and hips arching to meet her.

When they finally arrived back in town, Alex offered to take Lia home, although it was the last thing she wanted. In response, Lia ran her hand up the inside of Alex's thigh, pressing her thumb against the seam of Alex's jeans and making her more turned on than she already was. "I was hoping to stay at your place, if you don't have any other plans."

They were hardly up the stairs before they began tearing at one another's clothes. With Murphy at Jeff's until the next morning, there was nothing to do but make their way to bed.

CHAPTER TWENTY-TWO

A re you ready for our hot night on the town?" Lia wiggled her hips in a way that made the sequins on her dress shimmer in the light of Alex's kitchen. It was New Year's Eve and she was ready to party.

"As ready as I'm going to be. I can't remember the last time I was out after midnight."

"I somehow find that incredibly hard to believe."

Alex gave an exaggerated shrug. "I'm a baker."

"Mmm hmm. Well, I promise I won't keep you out too late."

"You can keep me out as late as you want, just promise to come home with me in the end." Alex sent her a smoldering look that made her insides flutter.

"Deal."

It wasn't snowing, so they braved the short walk to the Crown & Anchor. She felt silly wearing boots with her cocktail dress, but Alex was adamant. "I refuse to have you break your leg, or worse. Carry your shoes and I promise you can check your boots in the coat room."

They had dinner with Jan and her wife, Lorraine, before heading over to Paramount for the dance party. The crowd was definitely a mix—young and old, men and women, gay and straight. Everyone was dressed to the nines and the mood was festive.

The DJ created a perfect mix of fast and slow dance music, old and new. Although most of her time was spent with Alex, she had one dance with Jan and another with Josie, the doctor from her poker group. She was sweaty and her feet hurt and she couldn't remember the last time she'd had so much fun. Even dressed up, there was something that felt more casual, more laid-back, than most of the parties she'd attended with Dani. She kicked off her shoes at one point in the evening and she hadn't sucked in her stomach once.

As midnight approached, she and Alex made their way to the bar for requisite glasses of champagne. Flutes in hand, they stood in the middle of the dance floor and counted down the seconds until the new year began. When the hour turned, a cheer rose from the crowd and confetti fell from somewhere in the ceiling.

Alex wrapped an arm around her waist and pulled her close. The kiss was hot, and it lingered. When Alex eased back, Lia's vision was blurred and her legs wobbly. She wondered if there would be a time that Alex didn't have that much of an effect on her.

The next thing she knew, Lia found herself turned around and pulled into a friendly kiss with Jeff. Jeff led to Josie, then to Jan and Lorraine. The crowd was friendly and exuberant. More than once, Lia received a peck on the cheek from someone she didn't even know. Eventually, she wound her way back to where she'd left Alex. She wasn't there, so Lia began to look around the room. What she discovered was Alex standing about fifty feet away in the arms of a redhead wearing a barely-there black dress.

Lia tried to move, but she was frozen. She swallowed and willed herself to, at the very least, tear her eyes away from what she was seeing, but it was no use. The woman's arms were around Alex's neck and she had the entire length of her body pressed against Alex. Alex ran her hands along the woman's tanned and perfectly toned arms. Lia stood there for what felt like an eternity, watching the two of them kiss.

Someone brushed past and it was enough to snap her back to her senses. She turned around and weaved her way through the crowd to the restrooms in the corner. Although tempted to lock herself in a stall, she was afraid that doing so would release the tears that were burning her eyes and threatening to escape. Then her makeup would be ruined and the whole thing would go from awkward and unpleasant to humiliating. Instead, she ran cold water over her hands and wrists and willed herself to calm down.

She stood for a long time with her hands under the tap. The freezing water shocked her system and pulled some of the heat from her cheeks. It was fine. Seeing Alex kiss another woman was nothing like walking in on Dani and her assistant. For starters, both Alex and the woman wrapped around her were clothed. There was also the fact that she and Alex weren't together. They were barely dating. By Lia's own definition, it was only a fling.

The reasoning with herself worked, at least enough to keep her from bursting into tears. Feeling as though she had regained control of herself, she shut off the water. As she was drying her hands, a woman in a dapper, gunmetal gray suit walked in. She had rich brown skin and her hair was almost a buzz cut. Lia had a sudden impulse to push the woman against the wall, kiss her.

She smiled at Lia. "Great party, isn't it?"

"Absolutely." Lia was neither brave enough nor drunk enough to act on it. She tossed the paper towel in the trash.

"Don't go too crazy out there." The woman winked at her and disappeared into one of the stalls.

Relief, tinged with self-loathing, washed over her. Lia rolled her eyes heavenward. "I'm not the one I'm worried about."

Lia exited the bathroom. Looking around the room surreptitiously, she saw Jan and no sign of Alex. She made her way over to her.

"Hi, gorgeous. Are you having a good time?"

Lia mustered a weak smile. "Yes, but I'm not feeling well all of a sudden. Could you tell Alex I'm heading home?"

Jan looked at her with concern. "Oh, no. Sit for a minute and I'll go find her. I'm sure she'll want to take you."

Lia waved her off. "No, we walked over. I already called a cab." She hadn't, but it sounded good. "Tell her to stay and enjoy the party. I'm sure she won't have trouble finding other company."

The last bit was too much. Jan's eyes narrowed, her concern morphing into suspicion. "Honey, what's going on? What's wrong?"

"I really don't feel well." It's not like that was a lie. "I want to go home and I don't want to make a big production of it. Please just tell her?"

She must have pleaded just the right way. Jan shook her head slightly and sighed. "Of course. Will you let me take you home? I'm sure Lorraine is just about ready to leave anyway."

"I'm fine, really. Thank you. I owe you one."

Lia squeezed Jan's arm and hurried over to the coat check, hoping not to be seen. She collected her things and hurried out without bothering to pull on her boots. When she was a block away from the bar, she looked behind her. Alex was nowhere to be seen. She breathed a sigh of relief.

The sidewalk was slippery and her feet were already freezing, but she walked on, replaying the events of the night and trying to situate them in the context of the last month and a half. Under normal circumstances, Alex wasn't the kind of woman she'd get involved with. Of course, what the hell were normal circumstances? And since she'd spent so many years with one person, how could she even know what kind of woman she would get involved with? That was the problem. Everything she thought she knew about relationships was utterly screwed up.

She stepped off the curb and hit an icy patch. She flailed her arms, but there was nothing to grab. Her feet came out from under her and she landed in a heap on the slushy street. The shock of falling gave way to a stinging in her hands and right ass cheek where she'd hit the pavement. Swearing under her breath, she scrambled to her feet, mortified that someone might have seen her go down. Relief that she didn't seem to be hurt was replaced with dismay. Her dress was torn and her stockings were shredded. The veneer of calm was gone. Hot tears started spilling down her cheeks.

By the time Lia got home, her feet were frozen, her makeup was a mess, and she was angry. Really angry. It bubbled up, hot and fierce. Given her inclination to avoid conflict, it wasn't something she was used to. Where hurt was her typical M.O., indignation took center stage. She wanted to yell and throw things. It was powerful, and oddly energizing. She wanted to ride it, to see where it might take her.

She was pacing around the kitchen when there was a knock at the door. She stalked over and yanked it open. Of course, Alex was standing on the other side.

"Jan said you weren't feeling well. Why didn't you tell me? I would have brought you home."

There was a moment in which Lia considered sticking with the story. She could smile sheepishly and say she didn't mean to make Alex worry. She could send Alex away, crawl into bed, and try not to think about how wretched she felt. It passed quickly. She had no desire to let Alex off the hook.

"Oh, my God. What happened? Are you okay?" Alex stepped inside and closed the door.

Lia had forgotten how pathetic she must look. Anger mixed with humiliation was a dangerous combination. "Don't pretend to be concerned. It's just insulting at this point."

"What are you talking about? Of course I'm concerned. You ran off in the middle of the party, and now you look like you've been in a street fight."

Lia huffed. "That might have been a fairer fight."

"What?"

Alex's confusion, and her worry, only made Lia angrier. "I get that we aren't exclusive. We never discussed it and I'm not looking for it. But I think it's something of a common courtesy that you don't hook up with someone while you're on an actual date with someone else."

She watched the realization flash in Alex's eyes.

"Lia, I don't know what you saw, but it was nothing."

"I saw you with a woman who was stuck to you like Velcro. She had her tongue down your throat." She sure as hell hadn't imagined it.

"That's not what happened."

Lia put her hands on her hips and fixed Alex with her most withering stare. She tried to ignore how unnatural it felt. "Well, then, why don't you tell me exactly what happened?"

"Look, Kim accosted me."

"Accosted?" Her voice was thick with contempt. "You didn't look accosted. You looked like you were having a perfectly good time."

"She came out of nowhere and latched onto me. The kiss took me by surprise."

"I see. And how would you explain the fact that your arms were around her, that you were stroking her arms and back the whole time?" Alex didn't answer right away and Lia took it as a passive admission of guilt. "That's what I thought."

"No, no. Wait. I did have to pry her off of me, literally. It must have looked like I was touching her, but I wasn't, at least not in the way you think." Alex's voice was pleading.

Lia's head was throbbing and her blood was racing through her veins like she'd been running for hours. She was shaking, but couldn't seem to make it stop. "So you're trying to tell me someone you don't even know threw herself at you that fervidly."

"I never said I didn't know her. We had two dates last summer. She was too much of a party girl, even for me. I don't know what got into her tonight, aside from the fact that she was wasted."

"Oh, well, if she was wasted, then by all means…"

Alex scrubbed a hand over her face. "I was there with you. I wouldn't hook up with someone else."

If there was a shred of believability in what Alex was saying, Lia ignored it. Being the rational one had come back to bite her in the ass again and again and again. "Wouldn't you? From what I gather, you're pretty open to whatever good time presents itself."

For a moment, Alex looked as though she'd been slapped. It gave Lia pause, made her think she was being unfair. The look passed, though, and was replaced with one of defiance.

"Oh, yeah? And where did you gather that little nugget?"

"It seems to be common knowledge."

"I see. If you think so little of me, why did you sleep with me in the first place?"

Because you're ridiculously sexy. Because I wanted to try something different and adventurous. Because you make me feel amazing and more alive than I've ever felt. "Clearly, it was a lapse in judgment on my part."

"If it was such a mistake, maybe you're the one who's been looking for whatever good time presents itself."

Having the accusation turned back on her stung. Maybe Alex was right. Maybe she'd walked right into this, invited it. The idea took some of the fight out of her, but left a raw knot in her core.

"I think you should leave now."

"Lia, this whole thing has been a misunderstanding."

"I asked you to leave. Please." To make her point, she marched to the door and yanked it open.

Alex threw her hands in the air, as if admitting defeat. "And this is why I don't do relationships."

Lia didn't know if the comment was aimed at her or merely Alex's observation to herself. It didn't matter. Alex strode through the door without another word. Lia slammed it behind her and stood in the kitchen, breathing hard and not knowing what to do next.

She stayed there for a long time, staring at the door and half expecting Alex to come back. When she didn't, Lia poured a too big glass of bourbon and stalked upstairs. Although she wasn't in the mood, she ran a hot bath. She peeled off her dress and what was left of her stockings and climbed in. As always, it was the right decision. The warm water brought feeling back to her toes and loosened some of the knots that were twisting in her stomach.

After pulling on sweats and two pairs of socks, she looked at her bed and headed back downstairs. She knew better than to try to sleep. She wrapped herself in a blanket and powered up her laptop. There was no chance in hell she was going to work, so she logged in to Facebook to see if her friends were having better New Year's celebrations than she was managing to have.

There were posts by friends with kids—pretend countdowns, complete with five and six-year-olds in pajamas and party hats. There were some earnest resolutions posted shortly after midnight. A few of her friends from college and her life in New York seemed to be partying. She scrolled through photos of well-dressed people smiling, drinks in hand, couples kissing, the ball dropping in Times Square.

And then Dani's face appeared. It was a post by a mutual friend, taken at a party in a swanky martini bar in Tribeca. She was wearing a silver sequined top under her Gucci suit and her arms were around someone Lia had never seen before. The girl—really, she couldn't be a day above twenty-three—wore an electric blue dress and was practically draped across Dani's lap.

She knew it was a bad idea, but she clicked on the image. The girl, Kaitlin was her name, was tagged. Lia downed the rest of her bourbon and clicked over to her profile. Kaitlin didn't think much of privacy settings, and Lia found herself sliding down a wormhole of photos and status updates detailing exactly what Dani had been up to in the two months she'd been gone.

Chapter Twenty-three

Lia didn't remember falling asleep. When she woke, her computer had slid to the floor. She was half sitting, half slouching on the couch and had such a crick in her neck, she could hardly move her head. It was just as well, since any movement made it feel like there was an avalanche in her skull. She opened an eye, squinting at the sunlight pouring into the room. Her mouth felt like something had crawled into it and died.

As awareness of her surroundings sank in, images flashed into her head. Alex kissing that woman. Dani with her flavor of the month. Alex's back as she left, the door slamming behind her. She wondered vaguely whether the hangover was fueled more by alcohol or the emotional brouhaha of the night before. Either way, she felt like shit.

She sat on the sofa for a while, willing the throbbing in her head to subside. When it didn't, she accepted that she would have to seek out relief, no matter how painful the process. She slowly pulled herself to a standing position, grateful that the room didn't spin. In the kitchen, she took three ibuprofen with as much water as she thought her stomach could handle. She set a pot of coffee on to brew and headed upstairs.

The hot shower and clean clothes made her feel semi-human, and the toast she made to go with her coffee helped to settle her stomach. Unsure what to do with herself, she curled back up on the sofa and turned on the television. She found the pregame show for one of the bowl games starting that afternoon and willed herself not to think about Alex or Dani or anything else.

The funny thing about trying not to think about something is that it becomes the only thing the brain will do. She wondered when exactly she'd become a magnet for women without conscience or integrity. Maybe it was something about her, something that advertised she was needy and gullible.

And the fight. It was such an ugly argument. She'd been shrill, unwilling even to listen to Alex's version of the events. Even if Alex was a complete and total player, her reaction had been over the top. Alex wasn't even her girlfriend, at least not in any official sense of the word. The flash of satisfaction from the moment was long gone and she felt worse than if she'd done nothing at all.

Then there was Dani. Really, she hardly mattered. If anything, seeing her picture had only reinforced how completely wrong they were for each other. Adding insult to injury, that's what it was. Seeing Alex with Kim made her feel like a convenience, the woman kept around until something better came along. The photo of Dani only reinforced the fact that it wasn't the first time Lia'd felt that way.

Alex's words came back into her mind. *I had to pry her off me. I wouldn't hook up with someone else.* Did she believe her? Did it matter? Lia didn't want it to, but it did. It wasn't just feeling disposable. Alex mattered. She'd gotten under her skin in ways Lia hadn't expected. Being with Alex made her feel desirable, alive. As much as she'd like to chalk it up to being on the rebound, she knew deep down there was something profound about the connection they'd made. Maybe admitting as much to herself would help. She could process the feelings, put them into perspective.

When the game started, it was a little easier to shut off her mind and focus on the TV. She did that for the rest of the day, eating toast and drinking more coffee than she should. She didn't hear from Alex, didn't reach out to her. Part of her wanted to apologize, but she feared doing so would make her feel pathetic instead of like the bigger person.

She forced herself to go to bed by nine. Afraid she'd lie awake and brood, she took an antihistamine that she knew would knock her out for at least eight hours. She climbed under the covers wearily, hoping the morning would bring clarity, and with it a plan of what to do.

❖

Alex wasn't surprised that she didn't hear from Lia on New Year's Day, which was just as well because she didn't have much to say. She went over to Stuart's for one of the football games, allowed herself to get sucked into an epic game of Monopoly with Maddie and Beth. It was impossible to remain grouchy in their company and she was grateful for the distraction.

The next morning, she opened the bakery and went about her routine, expecting Lia to show up and set up camp at her usual table. When she didn't, Alex started to stew—on one hand wanting to reach out and, on the other, clinging to her ire. Sure, the whole thing with Kim looked bad. Nothing had happened, though, and she resented being penalized for something she didn't do.

She also resented having her integrity called into question. Just because she steered clear of serious relationships, it didn't mean she was a total ass. Lia hurled that accusation as if it were an accepted fact, a conclusion she hadn't come to on her own. The idea of it didn't sit well. She should cut her losses and walk away. She'd gone through winter alone before and could certainly do it again.

What she couldn't decide was why it seemed impossible to let it go. Did she suddenly value what others thought of her? Or was it something about Lia? As much as she might not want to admit it, it was Lia. She wasn't ready to let Lia, and whatever had developed between them, go. That was probably the most disconcerting thing of all.

She picked up her phone. Lia hadn't called or texted. Part of her was tempted to show up at her house, but the last thing she wanted to do was make things worse. She didn't relish the possibility of more yelling, either. She'd start more delicately.

Can we talk? She hit send and put down her phone. Watched pot and all.

Not sixty seconds later, there was a reply. *Yes. Take a walk? 4:30?*

Neutral territory—Alex couldn't decide whether or not that was a good thing. *Sure. I'll meet you in front of town hall.*

She arrived early and resisted the urge to pace. It was cold, but the sun was out and much of the snow they'd gotten on New Year's Eve had melted. When she caught sight of Lia walking down Commercial Street, a lump formed in her throat. She did her best to swallow it and the thing bordering on panic churning in her gut.

Lia looked beautiful as always, but there were dark circles under her eyes. There was a small satisfaction in knowing that the previous two days had taken at least a little bit of a toll on her, too. Still, she felt an overwhelming desire to gather Lia into her arms, to find a way to make it all better.

"Hi." She had to start somewhere.

"Hi."

"Thanks for meeting me." Offer an olive branch.

"Of course."

Alex took a deep breath. "I want to start with an apology. I was so focused on convincing you that nothing happened. You saw Kim practically on top of me and, regardless of context, that must have felt really shitty. I'm sorry about that."

Lia looked at her. She sort of expected that Alex would apologize, since she'd been the one to text first. Yet, Alex's words caught her off guard. There was a sincerity in them that she wasn't used to. "Thanks. It was really shitty."

Alex offered her a sheepish smile. "Yeah."

Okay, it was her turn. "I'm sorry, too. I didn't even give you the chance to explain and, when you tried, I refused to listen. It's not how I usually am, even when I'm mad."

"That's good to hear."

Since Alex had reached out first and accepted responsibility for what happened, Lia figured she owed her the rest of the apology. "I'm sorry that I called you a player."

"Sorry you said it out loud or sorry you have that opinion of me?"

Lia swallowed. Alex wasn't going to let her off the hook that easily. "Both. I know you tend to date casually. You've said as much and it's been reinforced by others."

Alex glowered.

Lia continued. "Don't be upset by that. It was said to me by people who like you, respect you. It was more about me being in a potential rebound place than about you."

Alex sniffed.

"More importantly, you've never given me a reason to think that."

"I just don't understand why you wouldn't even listen to me."

Lia sighed. She should probably be honest, but man, she hated being such a cliché. "My partner of ten years had an affair. I found out by walking in on them in bed together, in our apartment."

"Oh, God."

She cringed. "Please don't feel sorry for me. I can't stand being the object of pity."

Alex nodded. "Okay, I won't. I get it."

"I'm only telling you so you can understand why I was so... reactive. If you could do your best to forget I said anything in the first place, I would really appreciate it."

"Fair enough. I'm sorry I stirred all of that up for you."

Lia realized they were still standing in front of the town hall. It was sort of an awkward place to have a conversation. "Can we walk?"

"Oh, sure."

Lia turned and headed up a side street, then onto Bradford. The cold air was nice. Combined with getting the gigantic weight off her chest, it made her feel better than she had in two days. They walked for a while in silence. As they approached her street, she thought she should say something, but didn't know what.

Alex broke the silence. "I don't know where things with us are going, or even if they're going anywhere."

"Yeah." Lia braced herself for the letdown. Maybe it was for the best.

"I do know that I'm not ready for them to end."

"Yeah?" That was not what she was expecting.

"I love spending time with you, and not just the time we spend in bed."

Alex's green eyes were fixed on her, intense and searching. Lia blushed. Why did she suddenly feel shy? "I do, too."

"So, maybe we can hit the reset button. We don't have to figure everything out today. We can just go back to the way things were."

And just like that, Alex offered her a lifeline. The relief was palpable. Lia didn't realize just how much she'd been dreading the idea of breaking up, or whatever it was when you stopped seeing someone you weren't technically dating. "I think that sounds like a good plan."

"I'm going to a pee-wee hockey game tomorrow. Stuart's kids are playing. Want to come with me?"

"Sure?" It felt like an odd invitation, but she wasn't going to split hairs.

"It'll be easy and relaxed, then maybe we could grab dinner somewhere."

If Alex was looking to keep things light, it was fine by her. It would probably take her a few days to settle down and recalibrate anyway. Fights took far more out of her than she cared to admit. "That sounds perfect."

"If you come to the bakery tomorrow to work, we can leave right from there. It's in Truro."

It was impossible to know whether Alex said that to make sure she was at the bakery tomorrow. Still, it made her feel good, wanted. "I'll be there."

Chapter Twenty-four

A lex invited Lia to the game on a whim. It was a casual way for them to spend time together, and would be a nice distraction from serious conversation. It was also a way to be with Lia in a way she wasn't usually with the women she dated. For some reason, that suddenly felt important to her.

It turned out that Lia had never seen hockey, of any kind, live. It was a difficult thing for Alex to fathom. She said as much on the drive to the rink.

"I can't believe you've never been to a hockey game."

"Well, there wasn't a whole lot of ice where I grew up."

"That's true."

"Once, when I was eight, I asked for a pair of roller skates for my birthday. My mom ordered them from the Sears catalog and they sent ice skates instead."

"Seriously?"

"They were so pretty, pristinely white with glinting steel blades. I was in awe of them."

She pictured an eight-year-old Lia, full of excitement. "What happened?"

"I had a fleeting fantasy of becoming a figure skater, then Mama sent them back and got the roller skates she ordered. I was devastated for about a week. Then the roller skates arrived. They had hot pink wheels and it was a fight every night to get me to take them off."

"I'm glad it turned out so well. Wait, does that mean you've never even gone ice skating?" Alex understood that growing up in the South was different, but she'd always thought of ice skating as universal. Not like ponds froze over or anything, but the rinks were mostly inside.

Lia rolled her eyes. "Oh, I've gone ice skating, if what you mean by ice skating is falling on my ass and providing lots of entertainment for my friends."

"I see. Did you not like it or did you just never get the hang of it?"

"Oh, definitely the latter. It was fun, but I couldn't seem to keep my balance for more than a minute or two at a time. Perhaps you've noticed, I'm not the most graceful person in the world."

"Nonsense. I could totally teach you."

Lia looked incredulous. "Really? You skate?"

"Not seriously, but I played hockey when I was a kid. I don't know if you can grow up in Massachusetts and not ice skate. I bet I could manage to keep you on your feet."

"Easy for you to say." Lia laughed as she said it.

The easy, rich sound reminded Alex why she'd developed a thing for Lia in the first place. She pulled into the parking lot of the ice rink. Whether she was prepared to admit it or not, this woman had seriously gotten under her skin. What she was going to do about it was another matter altogether.

Unable to stop herself, she made a mental note to schedule an ice skating date. It was so easy to imagine Lia, in a sweater and a scarf, holding on to her for dear life. She would hold Lia's hands and skate backward; Lia would giggle in that way she had. They'd go home and share a nice hot shower to take off the chill. She thought about the hot water sluicing over them, Lia's full breasts in her hands. Alex cleared her throat, prompting Lia to look over at her.

"Are you okay?"

Alex chuckled, shaking off the fierce arousal that gripped her so quickly when she thought of Lia. "Yes, yes. Just a little tickle."

As they walked in to the building, Alex took Lia's hand. Although Stuart had met a number of the women she'd dated, this was the first time that Alex specifically brought a woman to meet her best friend and his family. It seemed very official all of a sudden. She hoped her idea of an easy date didn't backfire.

Once inside, they found Stuart and Connie in the stands. Lia asked Connie to point out Maddie and Beth in the sea of little bodies warming up on the ice. She then launched into a series of questions about their ages, interests, and how their first season as hockey girls was progressing. No tension, no awkward silences. Most importantly, no talking about feelings. It was perfect.

Lia fell into an easy rapport with both Connie and Stuart, just as she'd done on Thanksgiving, and with Alex's family in Boston. Watching her fit in so seamlessly was reassuring and disconcerting at the same time.

Lia watched the game with complete fascination. The players, boys and girls ranging in age from seven to eleven, skated around with far more focus and skill than she expected, especially given the bulky padding and helmets they wore. Maddie, taller even than most of the boys playing, was definitely the star of her team. When she scored the only goal of the game, Lia cheered, feeling like part of the family.

When the game was over, Connie turned to Lia and Alex. "I don't know if Stuart told you, but we promised the girls we'd go out for pizza after. We'd love for you to join us."

Lia glanced at Alex, who was looking to her to make the call. She turned back to Connie. "That sounds like an offer we can't refuse."

At the restaurant, Maddie and Beth talked a mile a minute, and it seemed like most of their chatter was focused on getting and keeping Alex's attention. Lia watched as Alex carefully divided her focus between the girls, asking them detailed questions about school and friends and their favorite things about playing hockey. It was evident within about ten minutes that both girls were madly in love with her. Really, Lia couldn't blame them. Alex had a way of making whomever she was with feel like the center of the universe.

What did surprise Lia was the extent to which Alex seemed genuinely interested in their stories. It wasn't that she expected Alex to dislike kids. It was just...what? It was that watching Alex with the girls was enough to make Lia's uterus skip a beat. It was unsettling, given how the last few days had played out and the fact that she'd never been baby obsessed.

There was quite a stir at the table when Alex let it out that Lia didn't know how to ice skate.

"We can teach you," Beth said with enthusiasm. "Can we all go skating on Saturday, Mom, please?"

Lia looked at Connie, who seemed to be leaving it to her to make the decision. Lia considered declining, unsure if something that so resembled family time was a good idea. But the girls were so sweet, it would be rude to say no. "Oh, you can definitely count me in."

Alex was quick to chime in. "Hey, I want to come, too."

Beth lifted her hands in the air triumphantly. Maddie followed suit and said, "It's a date!"

❖

When Saturday arrived, Lia felt significantly less brave. She had the fear of falling down, but even more alarming was the possibility she would make a complete fool of herself. Her fear was not assuaged when they arrived at the rink and she headed over to the rental area while Alex laced up her very own skates. It was amplified when she laced up the pair given to her and stood.

Despite the handful of misadventures in college, Lia had convinced herself it would be like a slipperier version of roller skating. She hadn't done that in years, but thought she knew what to expect. When her ankles wiggled uncertainly, Lia was forced to face the reality that she was balancing her entire weight on two quarter-inch thick steel blades. She listened as Maddie and Beth offered their best advice.

"Don't look down."

"Stick your arms out."

"If stopping scares you, just skate to a wall and grab on."

Lia thanked them and sent them off to warm up while she pondered exactly how she was going to go about things. When Alex appeared behind her and said "hi," it was all she could do not to tumble over on the spot. Lia blushed, then hung her head dramatically. "This is not going to go well."

"I have an idea. Do you trust me?"

Lia thought about the question, and all of its broader implications. Whatever those might be, she decided that, for the moment, it was by far her best bet. "I put myself in your hands."

Alex offered her a devilish grin. "Oh, really?"

They hadn't entirely regained their flirtatious banter, but it was getting better. "Now. I put myself in your hands now. If I make it through this without any broken bones, we can see about later."

Alex took her hand and guided her slowly to the ice. "I promise that you will not break any bones."

Lia wobbled after her, amazed by how warm Alex's hand felt despite the chill radiating from the ice. "I'm going to hold you to that."

Alex stepped onto the ice and turned to face Lia. She took her free hand, asking, "You've roller skated, right?"

Lia nodded.

"Perfect. The movement is the same, just a gentle push of the feet as you shift your weight from side to side. If you feel shaky, just squeeze my hand. I'll keep you balanced."

Lia gingerly stepped onto the ice. Slippery was an understatement. Had she not been holding onto Alex, she was sure she'd already be on her rear end. Alex was there, though, and showed no signs of letting go. "Is this where I tell you how impressed I am that you can skate backward?"

Alex chuckled. "Baby, you ain't seen nothing yet."

Lia looked up from staring at her feet and locked eyes with Alex. A wave of warmth spread through her belly. She wondered if that immediate, insatiable desire she had for Alex would lessen over time. It seemed impossible that it could last, but it showed no signs of fading.

She was so caught up in thinking about getting Alex into bed, Lia hardly realized that they had made their way around the entire perimeter of the rink. "Hey," she said. "I'm ice skating."

"Yes, you are," Alex said encouragingly. "Would you like to let go?"

"Well, no. I suppose I should try, though."

Alex slowly let go of one hand, then the other. "Just because you let go, it doesn't mean I have to go anywhere."

The warmth between Lia's thighs spread throughout the rest of her body. She reminded herself to take Alex's words at face value, without meaning beyond the moment.

Things went well for about twenty minutes. She slowly crept around the perimeter of the rink, resisting the urge to grab onto the wall. Alex showed off a little, doing turns and showing Maddie and Beth how to change directions quickly so they could fake out their opponents. Stuart and Connie held hands as they skated and looked like a pair of high schoolers in love.

Feeling bold, Lia ventured a little bit further from the wall. She resisted the urge to look at her feet, instead scanning the rink for Alex. Seeing her, Lia raised her hand in a wave. Just as she did so a little boy skated directly across her path. Terrified she might plow into him, she frantically tried to stop.

Lia turned the blades of her skates, effectively stopping her feet. Inertia, however, had other ideas for the rest of her. She lurched, flailing desperately for something to grab. There was nothing there, and she plunged forward.

The ice was painfully hard. Splayed on her stomach and a bit disoriented, Lia's first thought was one of embarrassment. That feeling was quickly replaced with pain. Her palms stung and her whole chest ached. She must have hit her head, too, because it hurt like a bitch and she couldn't see straight.

Lia rolled over and pulled herself to a sitting position, torn between wanting to see Alex and wanting to melt right into the ice. Alex didn't leave her a choice. When she opened her eyes, Alex was on her knees in front of her. The look of absolute horror on Alex's face did more to freak her out than the sharp pain above her left eye.

"Don't move. I'm calling an ambulance."

Had she severed a limb and not realized it? "No. Wait. I'm okay."

"You're bleeding."

She lifted her fingers to her head and then pulled them away. Sure enough, there was blood on them. It was a small amount, though. "I'm okay, really. Will you help me up?"

"Not until you tell me how many fingers I'm holding up."

Although tempted to argue, it was probably faster to play along. "Three."

"Wiggle your legs. Make sure nothing feels broken."

She complied. "Just my ego. Please, help me up."

They made their way off the ice and to a bench. Stuart came over to them while Connie, thankfully, kept the kids off to the side.

"Can you please tell her she needs medical attention?"

"Can you please tell her to relax?"

Stuart looked like the last thing he wanted was to be in the middle. "It was a nasty spill. You should have yourself looked at, at least. You might have a concussion."

Lia didn't want to admit it, but going to a doctor seemed less daunting than arguing. And she was still struggling to bring her vision into focus. "Okay, okay. Is there an urgent care or something nearby? I really don't want to go to the ER."

"Yes, there is. I'll take you." Alex was on the floor unlacing her skates.

Lia looked up at Stuart. "Please tell the girls I'm fine and I had a lot of fun."

"Will do. Let us know if you need anything."

"Thanks."

Alex slid Lia's shoes onto her feet and helped her stand. The process made her dizzy, although she refused to admit as much. They slowly walked to the parking lot and Alex insisted on helping her into the truck. The whole thing made her feel pathetic.

When they arrived at the Provincetown Health Center, Alex took over. She got Lia signed in, filled out the paperwork, fished the insurance card out of her purse. Lia didn't think anyone had fussed over her so much since she had her appendix out when she was twelve. Alex had a way of doing it so matter-of-factly, it was hard to focus on being embarrassed or annoyed or anything else.

The P.A. who saw to her was a beautiful, dark-skinned woman named Maria. Her accent made Lia wonder where she was from—the Dominican Republic, maybe, or Puerto Rico. She asked Lia a series of questions, then examined and cleaned the cut on her head. Lia was immensely relieved when she determined stitches wouldn't be necessary.

Maria placed a couple of butterfly bandages over the wound. "You'll have quite a lump for a few days, but it shouldn't leave much of a scar."

"Thanks. I'm pretty sure my ego got the worst of the bruising."

Maria chuckled. "Well, I don't have anything for that, but ibuprofen should take care of the other aches."

"Any special instructions? Things to look out for?" Alex asked.

Alex sounded like a worried parent, or girlfriend. Hearing it gave Lia a funny quiver in her chest.

"No, other than no contact sports for the next couple of weeks."

"I think I can manage that." Lia followed her to the receptionist desk to check out.

Alex helped her into the car again, then climbed into the driver's seat and started the engine. "I can't believe I gave you a concussion."

She seemed genuinely distressed by the prospect, which Lia found very sweet. "Honey, you didn't. I managed to do that all on my own."

"But I promised you wouldn't get hurt."

"Actually, you promised I wouldn't break a bone."

"Oh. Well, then I feel much better now. Thank you."

"Good. You are hereby absolved of all guilt."

Something shifted in Alex's demeanor and she got a glint in her eye. "You couldn't just fall on your ass like a normal person?"

Lia laughed and it turned the dull throb in her head into a shooting pain. She winced, then glared at Alex. "You're a jerk."

With that, the tension of the previous two hours, and the previous week, seemed to melt away.

"Come home with me?" Alex asked.

Lia could think of nothing she'd rather do. "Yes, please."

CHAPTER TWENTY-FIVE

After the whole concussion incident, things returned to normal, or at least what Lia liked to think of as normal. If anything, she and Alex spent even more time together. The sex was still amazing and the ease of conversation had returned. It was a good thing, too, because Sally was coming for a visit and she'd see through any pretenses quicker than Lia could make them up.

She drove along Route 6, thinking about the day she told Sally she was moving to Cape Cod for the winter. Sally had wanted her to come home, but understood that Lia needed to be on her own and her reluctance to become the subject of hometown gossip. Being the big city lesbian whose life imploded left a bad taste in her mouth, on several levels. In the end, Sally was so thrilled that she was leaving Dani, she was supportive of any plan that got Lia as far out of New York City as possible. As soon as Lia picked Provincetown, Sally started planning her trip.

Alex offered to drive, but Lia insisted she could handle it. There were only a few flurries and Lia made good time to Logan. At the airport, Lia parked in the short-term garage. She typed the level and row number of the parking spot into the notepad on her phone. Roaming around for an hour in search of her car was a mistake she only planned to make once in her life. She made her way into the terminal and checked the monitors. Sally's flight, a connection from Atlanta, was on time and due to land in twenty minutes.

To pass the time while she waited, Lia perused the gift shop on her side of the security checkpoint. T-shirts and shot glasses and magnets, all emblazoned with Boston's historic sites and sports teams, were artfully arranged on every available surface. She walked past them to the wall of books and magazines. When she and Dani had traveled, Dani would pick up *Forbes* and *The Economist*. Even on vacation, she never seemed able to, or interested in, turning off that part of herself. Lia, on the other hand, bought *Southern Living* and *Bon Appetit* and indulged fantasies of being a food writer. Since she hadn't in a while, she picked up the latest copies of both.

With her purchases tucked in her purse, Lia headed over to the security area through which all arriving passengers in the terminal were funneled. The monitor on the adjacent wall indicated that Sally's plane had landed. Lia waited, enjoying the hugs and kisses and reunions between other passengers and their loved ones.

Eventually, she spied a petite woman with shoulder-length black hair weaving her way through the crowd. When they made eye contact, Sally threw up an arm and waved enthusiastically. Lia returned the gesture, finding it impossible to suppress a wide grin. Once Sally was through the swinging security gate, she hurried over and flung her arms around Lia.

Lia stood for a moment in the crushing embrace. For all that Sally was five-foot-one and weighed a hundred pounds soaking wet, the woman could give a hug. When Sally stepped back, Lia took in the full sight of her. Effortlessly glamorous—that's what she thought every time she saw her best friend. "You look amazing, as always."

Sally waved away the compliment and looked Lia up and down. Lia felt like she was getting the once over from her mother, but in a good way.

"You look pretty amazing yourself. New England, or perhaps some New England baker, seems to agree with you."

"Probably a little bit of both. Do you have a checked bag?"

"Despite my better judgment, I took the minimalist route." She gestured to the small, wheeled suitcase at her feet. "This is it."

Lia nodded. "I'm impressed."

"I thought you would be. I try."

"Well, let's get out of here. I'll do my best to get you back to my place in one piece."

Sally gave her a quizzical look, but instead of answering, Lia walked through the doors leading out of the terminal. Even expecting it, she nearly had the wind knocked out of her by the gust of frigid air and swirling snowflakes.

Sally stopped dead in her tracks. "Oh, my God."

Lia spread her arms out Vanna White style. "Welcome to Massachusetts."

They got into Lia's car quickly and got on the road. As they drove south, the snow began to fall more heavily. By the time they crossed the bridge onto the Cape, Lia could hardly see the road in front of her. She drove at a crawl, gripping the wheel.

"Are you okay?" Sally asked for the fourth time.

Lia tried to stretch out the kink developing in her neck. "It's just that, for as long as I've lived up here, I haven't had to drive much in the winter."

"You're doing far better than I would. I'd have given up ages ago. Should we stop somewhere? Will it let up after a while?"

Lia snorted. "You'd think. Sadly, I learned pretty quickly that it can snow like this for hours, if not days. I'm afraid if we stop, we'll never get started again."

They drove along, making slow and steady progress. Just as they were about to enter Truro, a car came up behind them. It pulled into the left lane, sped past, then cut back in front of them. Sally was giving the driver a piece of her mind when the brake lights flashed and the car started to fishtail. Lia panicked and hit the brake hard. She immediately felt the back end of her car lose traction. She attempted to steer in the direction of the skid, as she'd been taught to do but never actually tried, but it was too late. The car turned perpendicular to the road and slid onto the shoulder. Fortunately, they didn't hit anything. They weren't even off of the road entirely. Lia looked over at Sally, whose eyes were as wide as saucers.

"You okay?"

Sally nodded, but didn't speak. Lia took a few deep breaths and tried to slow her racing pulse. It was okay. They were both okay. Even the car was okay. They sat for a few moments in silence.

"What a fucking asshole!" Sally, it seemed, had found her voice.

Lia smiled, then she snickered. Sally was always one to tell it like it was. She also swore like a sailor. Within seconds, Lia was laughing hysterically. When she finally stopped, she had to wipe tears from her eyes. "I love you."

"I love you, too. I do not love that fucking lunatic that just about killed us. Seriously, what the fuck?"

"Seriously." Lia tapped into her drawl, mimicking Sally. "I hope you don't swear like that in front of the kids."

"Of course not. That's why I do it so much when they aren't around. I have to get it out of my system."

Lia rolled her eyes. "You're ridiculous."

"You're ridiculous."

"Okay, let's try to get our ridiculous selves out of here." When Lia tried to pull back onto the road, however, the car didn't budge. She tried again, pressing harder on the gas pedal. "It's no use. I'm just making it worse."

Sally made a face. "Should we call a tow truck?"

As if on cue, Lia's phone started to ring. It was Alex. She showed Sally who was calling, then swiped a finger across the screen to answer. "Hey."

"Hi. I wanted to make sure you got home okay. The snow is getting worse."

Lia debated how much to share. She'd been so adamant she could handle driving in the snow. "Well, we're not quite there. We had a little incident."

"What do you mean? Where are you? What happened?"

Alex's voice sounded more worried than judgmental. "We're fine. Some jerk passed us, then swerved in front of me and started fishtailing. I braked to avoid hitting him, but slid off the road in the process."

"Where? Are you still in the car? Are you sure you're not injured?"

"I promise. We're barely off the road, but I can't get any traction. We're stuck on the far side of Truro."

"Don't move. Don't get out of the car. I'll be there in fifteen minutes."

"You don't have to come out. I think we just need a tow truck."

"I'll take care of it. Do. Not. Move."

Lia looked at the screen of her phone. *Call Ended.* She looked over at Sally, who was regarding her with a raised eyebrow. "What?"

Sally shrugged. "Sounds like someone has a hero."

"I don't…It's not like that."

"Yeah, we'll see about that. I can't believe we're stranded in a blizzard. It's so exciting."

"It's not a blizzard. And we aren't stranded." Lia tried unsuccessfully to keep an edge out of her voice.

"If you say so, Miss Cranky Pants."

It was the perfect retort. Lia couldn't deny being cranky without sounding more cranky. She had to laugh—only Sally would combine a third grade insult with the panache of a criminal prosecutor.

True to her word, Alex arrived less than fifteen minutes after ending the phone call. She pulled up next to Lia's car and climbed out. Lia motioned to Sally and they both stepped out into the blowing snow.

"Alex, Sally. Sally, Alex." After the introductions, Lia turned to Alex. "You really didn't have to—"

Alex cut her off. "I wanted to. Is there stuff in the back?"

"One suitcase. Can we just leave the car here?"

Alex picked up the bag and carried it to her truck. "A friend of mine owns a garage. Leave the keys under the front seat. She'll be here in less than an hour and will tow it home for you."

Sally hopped into the back seat of the truck before Lia could argue. Lia climbed into the passenger seat next to Alex. "I'm sorry to put you through so much trouble."

"Don't apologize. I'm happy to help. I wish you'd called me."

Lia frowned. "Well, we didn't not call you. We were trying to figure out what to do when you called."

Sally chimed in from the back seat. "My friend has issues with being seen as helpless. I, on the other hand, have always relied on the kindness of strangers."

Lia rolled her eyes. "Cool it, Blanche."

Alex chuckled and Lia turned to her. "Thank you. Really. I appreciate your coming to our rescue."

Alex looked at her so intensely that Lia's heart started to race again. "I'm happy to. Call me. I mean it."

Lia nodded her agreement as Alex put the truck in gear and pulled onto the road.

They pulled up in front of Lia's and Sally leaned into the space between them. She turned to Alex. "Have you eaten? You should join us."

Alex chuckled. "A very tempting offer, but I'm going to give you two some time to catch up. You're coming to dinner at my place tomorrow, right?"

"That's the plan. We might come to the bakery in the morning."

Sally put a hand on Alex's shoulder. "She means absolutely, most definitely. She says your croissants are better than the ones at la Madeleine."

"I'll be sure to keep one with your name on it."

"Perhaps you should make it two."

"Deal."

Lia and Sally made their way down the snowy sidewalk. Alex didn't pull away until the door was open and they were inside. They peeled off their coats and boots.

"I'm sorry that was such an ordeal."

"Nonsense. It was an adventure, and I got to meet Alex."

"Well, I'm glad you see it that way instead of a near death experience. Are you hungry?"

"Ravenous. How about you make me a grilled cheese and try to convince me again that this is just a fling?"

They sat on the couch in sweatpants, eating sandwiches and drinking red wine. At first, Lia was able to keep the conversation focused on Sally. They talked about Logan and Charlie, who were devastated that they were missing out on a chance to see real snow, and about Sally's husband, Will, who was planning a golf weekend with his buddies in exchange for parenting solo for the better part of a week.

"He's not really solo. Between my mom and aunt, I don't think he's going to have to cook once. If anything, he'll have to banish the mother hens so he and the boys can get the man time he promised them."

"What does man time consist of?"

"I think it involves video games and junk food mostly, perhaps some inappropriate scratching."

Lia snorted. "I'm glad I'm a lesbian."

"Speaking of lesbians, let's talk about you."

"Did you really just say that?"

Sally shrugged and took a bite of her sandwich. Lia shook her head.

"Things are good. Physically, at least. And we have a great time. At this point, I'll take it."

Sally didn't seem convinced. "I'm not sure people brave a blizzard to come to the rescue of someone they only think of as a roll in the hay."

"Again, not a blizzard. She does nice things. A lot of nice things. It doesn't mean anything."

"Are you falling for her?"

"I told you, we're keeping it casual."

"You didn't answer my question."

Lia continued, "It's kind of beside the point. After the whole New Year's fiasco, we pretty much agreed to keep it light, no strings attached. She doesn't do relationships and, for now, I don't either."

Sally gave her a look. Lia imagined it was the one she used with an uncooperative witness. "Okay. Let's try this again. Put aside the idea that Alex might be a player. Put aside the idea that you have no business falling in love with anyone."

Lia huffed. "Okay."

Sally let a long moment pass and then asked again, "Are you falling for her?"

"Yes." Lia closed her eyes. There it was, whether she liked it or not. "I don't know what that means, and I'm pretty sure it's a terrible idea, but yes."

Sally smiled. "That's my girl. At least we know what we're dealing with. We can sort out later whether or not it's a terrible idea."

Lia slumped back on the sofa. "I don't see how it could be anything but a terrible idea."

"It means, my darling, that your heart is intact. It means you're ready to leave the train wreck that is Dani behind."

"I guess you have a point."

"I usually do. That's what they pay me for."

"Thanks, counselor."

Sally slung an arm around her shoulder and squeezed. "Your bill is in the mail."

When they'd finished the bottle of wine and were struggling to stay awake, they made their way upstairs. They crawled into the big bed together, just like when they were ten. With Sally asleep next to her, Lia stared into the darkness. Whether she was prepared for it or not, she was well on her way to falling in love.

CHAPTER TWENTY-SIX

Lia and Sally arrived at The Flour Pot just after nine. Most of the morning crowd was already gone. When they walked in, Jeff was perched at a stool behind the register, staring intently at a clipboard with a pencil stuck behind his ear. He looked up and flashed them a broad smile.

"Southern belles, two of them. Alex promised you'd be in. Lia, introduce me to this beautiful creature."

"Jeff, this is my best friend, Sally. Sally, this is Jeff. He's the manager here."

Sally extended her hand. "Pleasure to meet you."

Jeff took her hand. "Oh, honey, the pleasure is all mine. I've been hearing stories about you for weeks."

Sally rolled her eyes. "Oh, Lord. That sounds dangerous."

"Only good things, I swear. Except for that time you borrowed your daddy's car without asking so you could go to some frat party at LSU and got yourself ticketed and towed."

"Well, if that's the worst you heard, I'm thinking we can still be friends." Sally winked at him.

"Girl, if you have worse stories, we might just be the best of friends. Now tell me why you have such a delightful accent and Lia hardly has one at all."

"It's because she never left," Lia said. "College at Loyola, law school at Tulane. Girl is a tried and true gem of the Mississippi Delta."

Jeff's eyes suddenly got big. "Did you have a debutante ball?"

Sally shook her head. "I did not. That was more of a rich, city folk thing. Lia and I were country girls."

Jeff looked genuinely disappointed. "So sad."

"She was the queen of a Mardi Gras ball, though." Lia knew Sally hated when she brought that up, which was why she did so every chance she got.

"Really?"

"I was, although I think it was because the Louisiana Bar Association thought having a woman of color as their queen would be a nice notch in their diversity belt."

Lia shook her head. "Although that might, sadly, be true, you are without a doubt the most beautiful attorney in a hundred mile radius of New Orleans."

"I haven't even been to New Orleans and I'd put money on that," Jeff said.

Alex emerged from the kitchen. "Good morning, ladies."

Lia's gaze instantly went to her, as it always seemed to do. She heard Sally say, "Well, look at you all chef-y and handsome."

Alex grinned at the compliment. "We've been anxiously awaiting your arrival. What can we get for you today?"

"I'll have a latte," Lia said.

"Do y'all do mochas?" Sally asked.

"Yes, indeed, I'll get right on those for you." Jeff moved over to the espresso machine to start their drinks.

Before Lia could ask for two chocolate croissants, Alex leaned under the counter and pulled out a beautiful glass cake stand with a domed lid. On it there appeared to be at least half a dozen chocolate croissants. "I believe I promised to put your names on a few of these. I do hope initials will do."

She removed the lid with a flourish and Lia realized that each of the pastries was marked with an S or an L in chocolate. It was silly and thoughtful and decadent and Lia knew that Sally would love it. It was just the kind of thing that would lead Lia to fall in love with a person, if she were inclined to fall in love.

Sally looked at the plate and smiled. "Ohhh. Those look good."

Lia nodded her agreement. "They're beautiful, and completely over the top."

"We aim to please. Now go make yourselves comfortable and we'll be over with your coffees."

Lia led the way to her usual table. Jeff brought over two large coffee cups and Alex placed the plate of croissants and two saucers on the table. Alex bowed. "Of course, we are happy to bring you anything else you might desire."

"Oh, I think this will do us just fine," Sally said.

"Well, enjoy. Darcy is out today, so I've got to go finish prepping for lunch."

"Okay. Good luck, and thank you." Lia meant it in more ways than one.

They managed to polish off five croissants between the two of them and Lia was afraid she might burst. They carried the plates and cups back to the counter.

"Leaving so soon?" Jeff asked.

"Well, there is no way we could possibly eat lunch. And I promised Sally we'd walk down to the beach no matter how cold it was."

Jeff whistled into the kitchen. "Today might be your best bet. The sun is out and the wind isn't too bad."

"My thoughts exactly." Alex emerged and Lia filled her in on their plans. "We'll be at your place at six. Are you sure we can't bring anything? Wine?"

"Just your lovely selves." Alex walked around the counter and gave Lia a kiss. "Enjoy your afternoon and be careful at the beach."

Lia and Sally strolled through town, stopping in the handful of shops that were open. Sally picked out some souvenirs for the boys at the Marine Specialty, along with a couple of vintage military pins for Will. They put in an appearance at the real estate office to say hi to Jan and Stacia. Sally bought two of Damien's photographs for her office, then lamented her decision to bring a small suitcase. After Lia assured her they could be shipped, Sally made them backtrack to one of the boutiques they'd stopped in so she could buy two sweaters and a pair of pants. Lia had almost forgotten how much Sally liked to shop.

At around two, Lia determined that it was as warm and sunny as it was going to get. They walked down to the beach in town, admiring the boats and the calmness of the water. They walked back to Lia's and drove along the road at Herring Cove. Lia pointed out her favorite spots, realizing she was more excited to show off Provincetown than she'd ever been to show off the sights of New York.

❖

Lia and Sally rang the bell at Alex's a few minutes before six o'clock. Despite Alex's directions, they each carried a bottle of wine. Neither of them were raised to show up for a meal at someone's house empty handed.

"Even if she is your girlfriend," Sally said.

"She's not my girlfriend."

Alex opened the door to find Lia glaring at Sally. Sally flashed Alex a brilliant smile and whatever it was seemed to pass. She led the way upstairs, then took the bottles of wine each of them offered. "You really didn't have to."

Sally shrugged. "And that's why we did."

Alex opened wine and put out a plate of cheese and olives for them to eat while she finished dinner. Much like Lia, Sally was smitten with Murphy. They sat on the floor and lavished him with belly rubs and ear scratches.

"He's going to be incorrigible for the next week," Alex said.

"He doesn't have an incorrigible bone in his body," Lia said. "What's for dinner?"

"Shepherd's pie and roasted Brussels sprouts with walnuts and cranberries. It's just about ready."

Sally stood. "That sounds amazing. After this morning, I was sure I wouldn't want to eat for days, but you've proven me wrong."

"I do my best."

They sat at the table and passed dishes. Alex studied Sally. She was anxious to learn about the woman who'd been Lia's best friend for so long. She also hoped to learn a thing or two about Lia along the way.

Instead, Sally expertly plied her with questions. She didn't ask anything intrusive, but it was clear Sally was feeling her out, probably deciding with each response whether or not Alex was worthy. She didn't know whether or not she passed, but she was pretty sure the flourless chocolate torte she served for dessert helped. Despite feeling like she was on the witness stand, Alex couldn't help but like her.

"So what does the rest of your night hold?"

"Well, I promised Sally a night on the town, so I'm thinking we'll go to the Crown?"

"You know the Governor Bradford has karaoke."

Sally's eyes lit up. "No way!"

"Way." Alex nodded, feeling like she'd stepped into an old Wayne's World sketch.

"Can we go there?" Sally asked Lia. She turned to Alex. "Will you come with us?"

Alex glanced at Lia, who looked a little queasy. "It's okay. I don't want to crash your girl time."

"No, no, no," Lia said quickly. "You should definitely come. That way Sally can pester you to sing with her instead of me."

Lia's comment made Alex realize that her squeamishness was more about karaoke than the prospect of her tagging along. She found that to be quite comical. It also made her curious to see Lia in such a setting. "It's only a few blocks from here. We can walk over if you don't think you'll freeze your buns off."

Sally was already standing up. "Let's go."

At the bar, Sally insisted on buying the first round. "And don't try to argue. I argue for a living."

"I'll have a bourbon," Alex said. "Neat."

"Same here." When Sally was out of earshot, Lia turned to her. "You didn't let me buy the first round."

"That was different. I'm not trying to get Sally to sleep with me." She was rewarded with a blush. She loved how easy it was to put color in Lia's cheeks.

Sally returned with three glasses. There were a few other patrons in the bar, but no one was singing, at least not yet. Sally picked up a binder with all of the music selections. "Let's see what we have here."

Alex looked over at Lia, who smiled. "She sang the lead in every musical we had in high school, even as a freshman. Had her parents not insisted on something practical, I think she might have majored in musical theater."

Sally shrugged. "I probably could have convinced them to let me, but I had no interest in waiting tables and hoping for my big break. There are just so many roles for a short black girl who can't dance. It would have taken all the fun out of it."

Within minutes, Sally had a list of songs she wanted to do. She brought her selections up to Heidi Treasures, the drag queen who was serving as emcee. Sally accepted the microphone and Alex watched as the tiny woman belted out back-to-back Patsy Cline and Beyoncé numbers.

"Wow."

Lia shook her head. "I know. I can't carry a tune in a bucket. It's wretchedly unfair."

Sally returned to the table and Alex offered her compliments.

"Thanks," she said. "So, who's next?"

"I'm trying to help Lia relax a little so she'll do a duet with me."

"I think that's a fabulous idea. And since my friend here is such a lightweight, it shouldn't take much." Sally elbowed Lia in the ribs good-naturedly.

The tables began to fill and other people started taking turns with the microphone. The crowd was mostly older and the selections ranged from Elton John and Culture Club to Melissa Etheridge and Madonna. Most people were good if not great; a few were clearly singing with the abandon that comes with a few cocktails.

Even after the bourbon, Lia was hesitant. "I'll go get the next round."

While she was gone, Alex leaned over to Sally. "I have an idea."

After hearing the plan, Sally nodded enthusiastically. She walked back over to the side of the stage and slipped in her request before Lia could see what she was doing.

Lia returned to the table with three highball glasses and looked at them suspiciously. "What? What did you do?"

A couple of middle aged men singing a duet of "Don't Go Breaking My Heart" finished and Heidi took the stage. "I'm not sure which one of them was supposed to be Kiki," she said, earning claps and laughter from the audience. "I've got a special request now, for a shy girl who loves show tunes. That's silly, we're all shy girls who love show tunes."

She stepped from the stage and the opening strains of "Seasons of Love" came pouring out of the speakers. Alex and Sally stood, each taking one of Lia's hands. They pulled her to the stage. Sandwiched between them, Lia seemed to find her courage. Watching her made

Alex think of the first time she'd gone to Lia's house, how sexy and ridiculously charming she'd been belting out "Don't Cry for Me, Argentina" in the middle of her kitchen.

Sally made a sweeping motion with her arm and the entire crowd joined in. When the song ended, there was clapping and cheering and even a few whistles. They returned to their seats and Heidi stepped back into the spotlight. She raised her glass in their direction. "See, honey? We're just a bar full of shy girls dying for a show tune."

Lia turned to Sally. "That was very clever."

"Don't look at me. It was her idea." Sally hooked a thumb in Alex's direction.

Alex shrugged. "I had a feeling that musicals were the way to your inner diva."

Lia chuckled. "Touché."

Sally narrowed her eyes. "What am I missing?"

"You didn't tell her about the first time I came to your house?"

"No. No, she did not." Sally planted her fists on her hips.

Lia sighed and rolled her eyes. "I was cleaning."

Before Lia could continue, Sally jumped in. "It was *Evita*, wasn't it?"

"I really felt like I was outside the Casa Rosada," Alex said earnestly.

"I'm quite the diva when I don't have an audience." Lia looked at her. "Or when I don't think I do."

"I thought she was gorgeous the moment I laid eyes on her, but that was the moment it turned into a full-blown thing."

Sally smiled. "Alex McKinnon, I think I like you."

CHAPTER TWENTY-SEVEN

I hope you found Provincetown all you expected." Lia drove along Route 6. Morning sunlight filtered through the pines and dappled the road. The pavement was clear and dry, allowing her to relax.

"Oh, I'd say it exceeded my expectations. Now I really want to come back in the summer."

"Well, you just say the word and I'm in for a girls' vacation. We could get a place for a week or just a few days depending on how long you can get away. It's been a few years since I was here during the high season and I miss it."

"So, you don't think you'll be living here come summertime?"

Lia sighed, wondering if Sally had been waiting for a chance to bring up her future plans. "I don't see how that's possible. My lease expires at the end of April. I could probably find something reasonable for another few weeks, but once mid-June hits, there's nothing I could afford. It's the blessing and curse of a tourist town."

"And things with Alex?"

Of course that was what Sally really wanted to know. "I don't know. I don't want to think about it ending, but I think it might be sort of inevitable. Even if I admit that I have feelings for her, I don't really trust myself in that department. And even if she has feelings for me in return, I'm pretty sure Alex isn't the settle-down-with-one-woman type."

And even if the Kim incident was a misunderstanding, the underlying facts were there. Alex didn't do relationships. And as relieved as she'd been to, as Alex had said, hit the reset button, Lia felt like she was living a bit of a fantasy. Given how blindsided she'd been by Dani's infidelity, it felt critical she not forget that.

"I know the whole Dani thing messed with you, honey, but it was her, not you. She was the lying, cheating bitch."

Lia knew that was true, but still. She struggled to clearly articulate the ways she felt genuinely responsible for the way her relationship evolved and, eventually, fell apart. "I know that she was in the wrong. There's no excusing her behavior. It's just…I was complacent, you know? I didn't really like the Upper West Side lifestyle, but I didn't press the issue. I was bothered that we virtually stopped having sex, but I didn't do anything about it. I just sat on my hands and pretended everything was fine, hoped it would somehow get better. I hate myself for that."

"Lia, you were trying to hold a relationship together all by yourself. Trying, being optimistic, doesn't make you a bad person, or weak. You can't always know that someone doesn't deserve your heart."

Lia sighed. Sally always said just the right thing. "You're right. It's weird. Sometimes I don't know if I'm more afraid of having my heart broken or of being so terribly wrong about someone. Does that make sense?"

"Absolutely. And I can see why that makes you skittish about Alex. You've been forewarned that she gets around and you feel like it might turn into some cosmic I-told-you-so."

Lia chuckled ruefully. "Fool me once…"

Sally shook her head. "I hear you. Look, I know the whole point is for you to trust your gut and do what is right for you, and that's exactly what I want you to do. I only want to say, for the record, I like Alex. I'm pretty damn good at reading people, if I do say so myself, and I think she's in love with you, or close to it. Promise me that you'll trust yourself enough to be open."

The way Sally framed it, it didn't seem unreasonable, or dangerous. "Okay. I promise."

"Good."

She glanced over at Sally. "You never liked Dani, did you?"

"Nope. Not a lick."

"I'm sorry I didn't listen."

Sally patted her leg. "It was your life. And, to be fair, I technically didn't dislike her in the beginning. She was a bit flashy for my taste even then, but she was smart and passionate and over the moon for you."

Lia allowed herself a moment of nostalgia for the early years of her relationship with Dani. "It's easy to forget all that sometimes."

"Lia, you're not dumb, or naive. You wouldn't have fallen for her in the first place if it wasn't amazing."

"Yeah. It was after we moved to New York that things started to change."

"Things change, and so do people. Sometimes that sucks and sometimes it's wonderful. Remember that. Maybe Alex has just been waiting for the right woman."

Lia wasn't quite ready to hope for that, but it was nice to hear.

At the airport, they exchanged a long, tight hug. "Thank you so much for coming. You are so good for me."

"The feeling is mutual, my friend. Let's spend a few days in Provincetown this summer, no matter what."

"Deal. Travel safe and give my love to Will and the boys."

"I will. You drive carefully getting back. I'll call you this weekend."

"Sounds good. Bye, Sal."

"Bye, Lia." Sally squeezed her again and then made her way inside the terminal.

On the drive home, Lia's mood was reflective. Sally was astute. She'd picked up on Lia's feelings pretty quickly, and for some reason seemed to think Alex's feelings were the same. It might not mean anything, but, then again, it might.

She was about halfway home when her phone rang. When she saw Dani pop up on the screen, she was tempted not to answer. Avoidance was part of her problem, though, and she was trying to turn over a new leaf. She pulled to the side of the road and swiped a finger across the screen.

"Hello." Lia wanted to lead with "What do you want?" but her upbringing had her keeping her manners.

"Hi, Lia. It's Danielle."

"Yes, I know."

"How are you?"

"I'm doing very well. What can I do for you?"

She hadn't heard a peep from Dani in nearly three months, and from the look of some of the Facebook photos she'd seen, Dani wasn't wanting for company. She couldn't fathom what Dani could possibly have to say that she would want to hear.

"I wanted to see if you were okay. Things were so messy when you left. I've been thinking about you, worrying about you."

Lia took a deep breath. Dani sounded sincere, but she couldn't help but feel suspicious. She kept her answer vague. "I really am doing well. I've been working a lot, but I'm having fun, too. I've made friends."

"I'm really glad. I think getting out of town for a while made a lot of sense. Work's been really nutty. I wouldn't mind a little vacation myself."

The choice of words made Lia's jaw clench. "I didn't go on vacation, you know."

"I know, I know. I'm sorry. I didn't mean to make it sound like that."

It was unlike Dani to whip out an apology so quickly. She didn't know what to make of it. Everything about the conversation seemed off. "It's fine. I just…"

"My father is in the hospital."

Dani shifted gears so abruptly, Lia almost missed it. "What? Your father? What happened?"

"He had a heart attack. He underwent emergency triple bypass this morning." There was the slightest hint of a quiver in her voice.

"Oh, Dani. I'm so sorry to hear that. Is he going to be okay?" She had met Dani's father a number of times. He'd left investment banking for private wealth management and lived in Greenwich, Connecticut with his third wife. Dani was so much like him, Lia found it unsettling.

"They think so. Fortunately, he was at work when it happened and people were around. His secretary gave him an aspirin and the EMTs were on scene in less than ten minutes."

"That's good. And he made it through surgery without extra complications?"

"Yes. All things considered, he was lucky. I was in the middle of a presentation when the call came in. My assistant interrupted. She was as white as a sheet and I was convinced someone had died. I don't know if I've ever been more scared."

Lia believed it. Even after the fact, Dani's voice seemed small and far away. It was so rare for her to admit any kind of weakness, especially fear. It reminded Lia of pre-Wall Street Dani. Lia felt the part of her heart she'd frozen off melt slightly. "How are you holding up?"

She heard Dani take a deep breath. "I'm okay, or at least I will be when he's completely out of the woods. I thought you'd want to know, and you're still the person I think of when something really good or really bad happens. Do you know what I mean?"

Lia felt herself soften a little further. She did know. It was hard to be with someone for ten years and not know. Even with the hurt, even with the feeling that she was moving on, Lia held a small amount of fondness for her former partner. "I do, and I'm glad you called me. I'll keep him in my thoughts."

"That would be really great. It's good to hear your voice."

"You, too." Lia wasn't sure that was true, but it didn't seem like the time to split hairs.

"I'll let you know when he's released from the hospital?"

"Sure."

"Okay. I should go. I'll talk to you."

"Bye."

"Bye, Lia."

Lia sat for a long minute after the call ended. She couldn't decide what to make of it. Rather, she couldn't decide whether or not to make anything of it. It was likely that Dani, in a moment of feeling worried and helpless, reached out to something familiar. Lia felt like she'd been able to provide a small amount of comfort and reassurance.

Despite everything they'd been through, Lia didn't begrudge her that at a time like this.

Either way, it was over and done. Lia doubted that she'd hear from Dani again and that was fine with her. She put her car in drive and got back on the road. Whatever worries or misgivings she had about the future were easily brushed aside. She was more than happy to have something that made her feel good and was, for the most part, uncomplicated.

Uncomplicated and sexy. She had a vision of Alex, with her flashing green eyes, braced over her, fingers sliding into her. Alex had a look of such fierce intensity, coaxing Lia to open wider, give her more. The clarity of the fantasy was potent, and left her shifting uncomfortably in her seat.

Suddenly aroused and anxious to be home, she had to keep checking her speed and easing off the gas pedal. When she pulled into the parking spot next to Alex's truck, it was just after four. Alex should be done with cleanup and upstairs. Lia fumbled with both the seat belt and her purse in her haste. Once inside, Alex greeted her with a hug and a long, smoldering kiss.

Lia leaned back and smiled. "I love her to death, but I swear I thought she'd never leave."

"That's horrible. You're a horrible person. I mean, I completely agree, but you're horrible." Alex wound her arms around Lia's waist and pulled her close.

"It really was nice to have her visit. The funny thing is, I'm pretty sure she'd have strongly approved of a booty call."

"Why the hell didn't you say so?"

Alex teased and nibbled her way up Lia's neck, then made her way over to Lia's mouth. Although the conversation was light, the kiss was both hot and hungry. It had only been five days since she'd been alone with Alex, but in that moment, it felt like an eternity. Lia was consumed by the urgency of her need. She began tearing at Alex's clothes, desperate to touch.

Hooking her fingers under the hem on Alex's sweatshirt, Lia pulled it up and over her head. The tank top she wore under it revealed her broad shoulders and strong arms; it stretched tight over her breasts. Lia admired for a moment, then pulled it off as well. Underneath,

Alex's skin was warm and smooth. Lia scratched her nails lightly across Alex's back as she leaned in to take one of Alex's nipples into her mouth. The scent of Alex's skin, the taste of her, sent pulses of lust through her.

Lia pulled herself away long enough to look into Alex's eyes. "Take me to bed."

"I thought you'd never ask."

CHAPTER TWENTY-EIGHT

At first, Lia was hesitant to make plans for Valentine's Day. Doing so seemed to imply a relationship status that she was still very much trying to avoid. Alex asked though, so it wasn't like she was going to refuse. In the end, she suggested they stay in, and offered to make dinner. She decided it would be a nice break from the showy celebrations—more about status than romance—she was used to with Dani.

She spent a fair amount of the afternoon on preparations, then indulged in a long bath. Since she was spending so many nights at Alex's place, she'd had significantly less time for them. Really, it was a small price to pay.

After the bath, she slathered lotion on her damp skin. She did her hair and makeup leisurely, relishing the pampering. There was a unique thrill in getting all dressed up for someone else's pleasure as much as her own. She put on the new lingerie she'd ordered, enjoying the satin and lace against her skin. She was a firm believer in the power of sexy underwear, even if no one else knew she was wearing it. Thinking about Alex's eyes and hands and mouth on her, however, really did heighten the effect. She was aroused already.

She slipped on a dress she'd bought a couple of years ago, but had never been brave enough to wear. The neckline plunged to reveal an amount of cleavage that had always seemed like too much. She smiled to herself. No time like the present.

Lia headed downstairs, fussing where no fussing was needed. The crab cakes would go under the broiler for a few minutes. The spicy remoulade sauce was made, as was the dressing for the salad assembled and waiting to be tossed. The bread pudding for dessert was fresh out of the oven and the bourbon sauce for it just needed to be warmed before serving.

Feeling very impressed with herself, Lia went around the kitchen and living room lighting candles. When her phone pinged, she figured it was Alex saying she and Murphy were en route. When she picked it up, however, it was Dani's name that appeared on the screen.

Miss you. Would like to talk/see you. Call me.

Lia scowled at her phone. She hadn't heard from Dani since the phone call almost three weeks prior. Lia's first instinct was to worry that something was seriously wrong. She started typing a concerned reply when she caught herself. It was Valentine's Day. She read the text again. It didn't allude to any type of emergency. *Miss you.* When she heard the knock on the door, Lia hastily silenced her phone and threw it into her purse. She'd deal with it tomorrow.

She opened the door to find Alex and Murphy waiting on the other side. Alex was wearing a pale gray sweater over a white shirt and striped tie, with dark gray pants. She looked effortlessly sexy, as always. She was holding a bouquet of bright red tulips. Murphy held a matching red and white polka-dot gift bag in his teeth.

A wave of warmth, part desire and part something else, washed over her. She decided thinking about Dani at all classified her as bat-shit crazy. She bent down to Murphy. "For me?"

As if on cue, he released the bag into her hands. Alex said, "He's hoping you'll be his Valentine, too."

Lia peeked in the bag and saw a box of sea salt caramel truffles. She gave Murphy a kiss on the top of his nose. "You're my favorite boy. Y'all come inside out of the cold."

Once they were in, Lia took the tulips and beamed at Alex. "How did you know they're my favorite?"

She shrugged. "I have my ways."

"Well, they're gorgeous, and they make me hopeful about spring. Take off your coat and stay a while. I was about to open wine."

Lia took the flowers into the kitchen and put them in a vase. She ran a fingertip along the curve of one of the petals. She loved that Alex handed them to her instead of sending them through some overpriced delivery service. It made her feel special. She mooned over them for just a moment, then took a bottle of dry rosé out of the fridge. Lia handed Alex the bottle and opener, then went back to finishing dinner.

When the wine was poured, Alex picked up the glasses and handed one to Lia. She lifted hers in a toast. "To Valentine's Day."

Lia clinked her glass against Alex's. "To Valentine's Day."

Alex put a hand on the small of her back and pulled her close. The kiss was light at first, sweet. It still managed to send ripples of desire from her center to the tips of her fingers and toes. She leaned into it, loving the way Alex's tongue teased hers.

As the kiss deepened, Alex wrapped both arms around her. The heat and firmness of Alex's body made Lia ache for bare skin. She grabbed Alex's ass, pulling her even closer.

"God, you make me want you." Alex whispered the words against her ear.

"Yes. I mean, me too." Lia found it difficult to string a sentence together. She started tugging at the back of Alex's shirt, anxious to get her fingers under the fabric. Alex's skin was warm and promising. Rather than satisfying her, it made Lia want more.

Without warning, Alex pulled away.

There was a look of concern and confusion on Alex's face that made Lia worry. "What is it? What's wrong?"

Alex sniffed the air, made a face. "Is something burning?"

As if on cue, the smoke detector began emitting a high, shrill beep. Lia turned to see traces of smoke coming from the oven.

"Shit." She raced over, opened the oven door, and was greeted by a much larger cloud of smoke. "Shit. Shit. Shit."

She yanked out the pan. Her perfect crab cakes were perfectly black. One of them was on fire. After blowing out the small flame, she set the pan on the top of the stove and turned off the oven. She turned her attention to the smoke alarm and found Alex standing beneath it, waving a dish towel.

It showed no signs of stopping, so she went to the door and started opening and closing it in rapid succession. Bursts of frigid air swept into the room. Murphy got up from his makeshift bed and looked at her like she'd lost her mind. When the noise didn't stop, she dragged a chair over and climbed onto it. She twisted the contraption off the wall, then pried open the back. Only when she popped out the nine-volt battery did the noise stop. Alex stopped flailing and looked at her.

Mortified. She was completely mortified.

"So, dinner's ready?"

With that one question, Alex made the entire fiasco ridiculous. Lia bit her tongue, weighed her options, then broke into laughter. After helping her down, Alex slung the dishtowel over her shoulder, walked over to the stove, and regarded the pan. "What is it?"

"Don't you mean 'what was it?'"

"I would never."

Lia shook her head. "Crab cakes. They only need—needed—a couple of minutes under the broiler."

"So, really, it's my fault. I distracted you."

"No, I should have set a timer. I'm horrible at setting timers. I think, it's only a few minutes, I'll keep my eye on it."

"Who doesn't set a timer?"

"Idiots. Idiots don't set timers and I am an idiot."

Alex looked at her earnestly. "You're not an idiot."

"Says the professional chef."

"Babe, I've been there. Trust me."

Lia did her best not to look dejected. "There's salad, still, and dessert."

Alex looked her up and down slowly. "Will the salad keep?"

"Yeah, it's in the fridge."

"And dessert?"

"Yes. I managed to make it without burning the house down."

Alex shrugged. "I'll be honest, I'm not all that hungry."

Lia sighed. "You're just saying that to make me feel better."

The next thing she knew, Alex's arms were around her, hands cupping her ass. "You have a way of whetting an entirely different appetite."

Lia smiled slowly. Never before had she felt so desired, never had she felt such a sense of power in her own sexuality. She suddenly couldn't care less about her charred crab cakes. "In that case..."

She walked around the room blowing out each of the candles she'd lit. Murphy eyed her, as though he knew what she had in mind and was resigned to the antics of his humans. Once they were extinguished, she took Alex's hand and led her up the stairs.

Alex followed without a word, happy to go wherever Lia beckoned. Lia had clearly readied the room before she arrived. The covers were turned down and tea lights were set on the dresser and nightstand. After lighting the candles, Lia went to the stereo and slow, sensuous jazz filled the room. Alex reached for her, anxious to peel away her dress and find the warm skin beneath.

"See, this is far better than dinner."

Lia took her wrists and pulled her hands away. "Patience."

Alex swallowed and wondered what exactly Lia had in mind. She didn't have to wait long to find out. Lia pulled Alex's sweater over her head, tossing it on a chair in the corner. She undid the tie, sliding it slowly from her neck. Her shirt followed, then pants and socks and everything else she had on. When Alex was completely naked, Lia nudged her so that she sat on the edge of the bed.

"Sit back, get comfortable."

Alex did as she was told.

"Let's see if I can get something right this evening."

Lia walked to the center of the room. As if on cue, the music went silent for a moment. When it started again, Lia locked eyes with Alex, and she offered a quick wink. Then, she began to move.

Alex watched Lia's hips dip and twist in time with the music. She licked her lips as Lia's hands moved over her body, up her sides and across her breasts exactly where Alex wanted so desperately to put her own hands. Lia turned around and glanced at Alex over her shoulder as she unzipped her dress, sliding it first from one shoulder and then the other.

Alex shifted slightly on the bed and realized how insanely turned on she'd already become. Lia turned again, this time to face Alex. She slid her arms from the dress, then raised them over her head. The motion, combined with a little hip shimmy, caused the dress to slither down Lia's body and fall in a silky pile at her feet. Lia was left wearing a deeply plunging bra and a pair of low-rise panties in navy blue and cream.

It had been only two or three weeks ago that she and Lia had been talking about lingerie. Alex jokingly complained that it was always red and black, black and red. "What's wrong with blue?" she'd protested.

That Lia remembered that conversation was one thing. That she'd gone out of her way to find what Alex decided was hands down the sexiest set of lingerie she'd ever seen was another. To have Lia, the woman she was, for all intents and purposes, nuts about, turn it into a sensual strip tease was almost more than her system could handle. She made to get up and Lia lifted a finger, stopping Alex in her tracks.

Lia milked the last few seconds of the song, making her way to the bed with deliberate slowness. The music switched back to an insistent bass and a pleading trumpet. Lia knelt on the bed and crawled toward Alex. She made her way up Alex's body until she was on Alex's lap, straddling her thighs.

Alex lifted her hands and brought them to hover an inch above Lia's breasts. She could see Lia's breath hitch in anticipation. Rather than touching, however, Alex held them there. She waited until Lia looked her in the eyes.

"May I?"

By way of answer, Lia leaned forward, pressing her breasts into Alex's waiting hands. It was her first real attempt at a seduction and she felt triumphant. In a flash, however, the tables were turned. Alex shifted so quickly that Lia didn't even process what was happening until she was pinned beneath her.

"That was exquisite, but also excruciating. I'm going to show you just how crazy you make me."

Lia opened her mouth to protest, but Alex didn't give her the chance. She swallowed Lia's words, coaxed Lia's tongue with her own, pulling her into a kiss that was both a demand and a challenge. Grasping Lia's wrists, she pinned Lia's arms over her head. Lia didn't struggle, but she did writhe, trying to test Alex's will to remain in control. Her efforts proved fruitless.

Over the course of the next hour, Alex mounted a calculated assault on Lia's senses. She teased and tortured, with tongue and teeth. She sucked Lia's erect nipples, gently bit the insides of her thighs. With hands and mouth, she drove Lia to the edge, again and again. Alex had a way of filling her and stroking her simultaneously that drove her mad. Each time Lia orgasmed, Alex merely shifted positions, never allowing her to come down. Each time Lia tried to catch her breath, to switch places, Alex laughed softly in her ear.

"Not yet. One more."

After the fourth orgasm, Lia lifted her hands feebly with the plea, "No more, please. You win. I mean, I won, but you win."

Alex chuckled and rolled to her side. As much as her own desire burned, she felt sated. Having Lia so completely and thoroughly give herself to her was more satisfying than Alex thought possible. In that moment, she would have been completely content to pull Lia into her arms and drift off to sleep.

Lia, however, seemed to have other things on her mind. She propped herself up on her elbow and looked at Alex. "That was not fair."

Alex grinned. "Given your performance earlier, I'm not really sure how else it could have gone."

"Really? You have no idea?"

Lia kissed her, then proceeded to kiss her way down Alex's torso. The contentment Alex felt evaporated, leaving in its place a pulsing urgency. When Lia pressed her tongue against her clit, Alex exploded. It was instantaneous and left flashes of light dancing behind her closed eyelids. She felt Lia slide up her body, her breath against her neck. Alex wrapped her arms around her, wanting to pull her close for the rest of the night. She could feel Lia's mouth curve into a smile.

"Not yet," she said. "One more."

CHAPTER TWENTY-NINE

Alex looked around and spied a T-shirt and pair of sweatpants tossed over a chair in the corner of the room. They smelled faintly of Lia's perfume, which made her smile. She pulled them on and headed downstairs.

In the kitchen, she opened cabinets at random until she found a bag of coffee beans and filters. She prepped the pot, then switched it on. While the coffee brewed, she went to the fridge to see what there was. She expected to find the leftovers from dinner, possibly a bottle of wine and some half-and-half. She was pleasantly surprised to find an array of fruits and vegetables, herbs, cheese, eggs, and more. She pulled out the eggs and a block of Gouda, a shallot, and a few spears of asparagus. She cracked and whisked half a dozen eggs, then started on the vegetables. She poured herself a cup of coffee and resumed chopping.

The frittata was in the oven and Alex was slicing bread—multi-grain from the bakery, she noted with pleasure—when Lia came padding down the stairs. Her hair was a mess and she'd put on Alex's shirt from the night before.

"Good morning, my little sex kitten. Coffee?"

Lia nodded. She was blushing. It seemed impossible that the woman who'd fulfilled her sexual fantasies a few hours before could be blushing now, but there it was. Alex felt a swelling in her chest that she tried to ignore.

She poured Lia a cup of coffee, added cream. "Breakfast will be ready in a few minutes."

Lia sipped. "You didn't have to make breakfast. It's your morning off."

Alex topped off her own cup and smiled. "I love to make breakfast, especially for two instead of two hundred. Besides, I was awake."

"Well, you're very sweet. You're also adorable in my clothes."

"You like?"

Lia watched as Alex struck a pose, then sashayed around the kitchen. The Tulane T-shirt was just a little bit snug and the sweatpants a bit loose. She found the combination oddly sexy. Part of her wanted to forget breakfast and drag Alex back to bed. For better or worse, her thoughts were interrupted by the kitchen timer. Alex maintained her exaggerated walk over to the oven. She made a display of bending over to remove the pan.

"I'd come over there and grab your ass if I wasn't afraid you'd burn yourself."

"I promise there will be plenty of time for ass grabbing later."

Alex put the bread on the oven rack to toast while she peeled a couple of clementine oranges and served the frittata. When the toast was done and buttered, she carried the plates over to the table and set them down with a flourish.

"Show off."

"It's all about the timer, baby."

"That's mean."

"I'm sorry. I shouldn't make fun, especially since you were much more delicious than any meal."

Lia felt her belly tighten. After last night, it seemed impossible that she could still be consumed with want. Yet, in an instant, Alex had that power over her. She swallowed and tried not to think about what that might mean. "The feeling is mutual."

Alex put her elbows on the table and leaned forward. "Well, then, if you aren't sick of me yet, I'd love to spend the day with you."

She really shouldn't be surprised by such a thing, but hearing Alex say it sent a little flutter of excitement through her. "Yeah?"

"Oh, absolutely. The question is, what do we do?"

Lia smiled. "I put myself entirely in your hands."

Alex eyed her suggestively. "God, I love when you say that."

"I'll have to remember to say it more often."

"Promises, promises. The way I see it, we can do one of two things."

"Do tell."

"One is that we can stay in, pretend to watch movies, and make love all day."

More flutters. What had gotten into her? "Oh, that sounds awfully tempting."

"The other is that we can have an adventure."

Lia set down her fork. "I hate to seem unadventurous."

"True. It's a very tough decision."

"Well…" Lia loved how playful Alex could be. It was a trait that Dani didn't seem to possess, even when having fun. "Could we have a mini adventure and then come home and make love all afternoon?"

"Genius. Pure genius." Alex stood and carried their empty plates to the sink. She loaded the few dishes she'd made into the dishwasher, wiped the counters and dried her hands. "Okay, I know what we're going to do. I'm going to go home and get ready. I'll be back in under an hour. You should dress as warm as you can, including boots and at least two pairs of socks."

Lia narrowed her eyes. "What are we doing?"

"You said you put yourself in my hands. Don't you trust me?"

"The last time I did that, I got a concussion."

Alex cringed, but recovered quickly. "It will be fun, I promise, and safe. And we'll have all afternoon to warm ourselves."

"Well, when you put it that way."

"That's the spirit. Mind if I return these later?" Alex gestured to the clothes she'd pilfered.

"Not at all."

"Great. I'll see you in a little bit. Come on, Murph." Murphy hopped up from the blanket Lia had for him near the heat vent, tail wagging. Alex slipped on her coat and shoes and gave Lia a quick kiss before heading out the door.

Lia headed upstairs to shower. She allowed her mind to wander to the night before. She'd been so upset when she ruined dinner, but Alex had a way of making it seem like a comical distraction. She'd still managed to pull off her little performance, and if the way Alex made love to her was any indication, it wasn't half bad. Alex had a way of making her feel brave, adventurous; she hadn't felt either of those things in a long time.

As instructed, she dressed in layers, putting on a pair of leggings under her jeans, a long-sleeve T-shirt and sweater, two pairs of thick socks. She pulled out the puffy ski jacket Dani insisted on buying her for a weekend trip to Vermont, along with a hat and mittens. Just when she thought she might have to step outside to prevent herself from overheating, there was a knock on the door.

Alex looked ridiculously sexy in jeans and hiking boots, a black cap, and dark green North Face jacket. Even with the burst of cool air from the outside, Lia found herself flushed. "Well, hello."

"Hello, yourself. Ready?"

"Are you still not telling me where we're going?"

"It's a surprise. It isn't far, so you'll know soon enough."

Lia pulled the door closed behind her. As they walked to Alex's truck, she noticed a furry face in the back seat. Murphy was wearing a coat of his own. It was dark blue with a wooly collar and reminded Lia of a horse blanket. "Is Murphy joining us?"

"He is. We're doing one of his favorite activities, so it seemed mean to leave him at home."

As far as Lia knew, Murphy's favorite activities were sleeping, eating, and chasing sticks. "I see."

"Have a little faith."

Alex drove them up Shank Painter Road to Route 6, but only stayed on it for about half a mile. She turned left onto Race Point Road which, as far as Lia knew, led only to the tiny airport and the beach. They passed the airport entrance and the small, unmanned booth at the driveway to the beach parking lot. There wasn't another car there.

Lia had ventured to the beach on the harbor side of town a few times since her arrival. It was beautiful and serene, the water a disarmingly dark shade of blue. She'd given it up, though, once the snow started to accumulate. "Isn't it a bit snowy for a walk on the beach?"

"Patience, grasshopper." Alex put the car in park and walked around to the back. Lia couldn't see what she was doing, so she opened her door and climbed out to join her. Alex was holding a pair of metal frames with rubber-looking mesh and straps.

"Are those snowshoes?"

"Yes, ma'am, they are."

Lia experienced a wave of excitement laced with trepidation. "I've never gone snowshoeing before."

"It's as easy as walking."

"That's what they said about cross-country skiing." She thought back to her awkward and exhausting attempts to slog along the trail in Vermont.

"Ah, but it's actually true about snowshoeing. Just step into these and I'll tighten them for you."

Lia did as she was told and Alex bent down, turning a knob that tightened the contraption around her boot. She stood in place, staring at her feet, while Alex walked back to the back of the vehicle. She looked up as Alex pulled out a second pair. "You own two pairs of snowshoes?"

"Well, technically, they are on long-term loan. Meg and Rob bought them, used them once, then realized they don't like being out in the wilderness. I promised to give them back if they ever want to try again."

"Ah." Lia thought about Alex's sister and her husband. It didn't surprise her in the least that the urbanites were not keen on outdoor winter recreation. The image of them stomping through the snow made her smile.

Alex closed the hatch then opened the back door so Murphy could hop down. While he pranced around, she strapped the second pair to her own feet. "If you hate it, we can stop anytime. You just have to tell me."

Lia smiled because it was clear that Alex meant it. She felt her nervousness melt away. She was adventurous, after all. "Let's do it."

Alex was right. With only a slight adjustment in her gait, Lia was able to walk up the path that led over the dune and down to the beach. Snow coated the slats of the wooden fence and gathered in drifts where dead sea grass blew in the breeze. When they crested the small hill, Lia saw the beach and ocean spread as far as the eye could see. There wasn't another person in sight. "Wow."

"It's amazing, isn't it?" Once they were down the path, Alex came up alongside and took her hand.

"It's beautiful."

Alex grinned. "So are you."

"I've got nothing on this."

Alex wasn't so sure. Lia's cheeks were pink and her eyes bright. It reminded her of the first morning Lia walked into her shop, the first moment Alex found herself drawn to her. "There's no trail, so we can walk as far as you're comfortable and then turn back. Sound good?"

Murphy bounded along next to them, running ahead, then circling back. Even without any sticks to chase, it was clear he was having a good time. The snow was a good six inches deep where they walked, covering the shells and seaweed that usually littered the beach. The waves crashed along the shoreline. The water seemed to be heavier, to move slower, than in the summer. There was a jagged line of ice that marked high tide.

As they walked, Lia realized what felt so different. In addition to no tourists, there were no gulls or terns circling and screeching overhead. The only sound was that of the ocean.

"I could become addicted to living by the sea," Lia said.

"I know I have. Even without the luxury of living right on the water, knowing it's close by, and having access to it anytime, is something I don't think I could ever give up."

Lia tried not to think about the spring, when her lease would be up and she'd have to leave both the ocean and Alex. Like she'd told herself so many times in the last few months, it was the moment that mattered. She'd deal with the future when the future came.

After about half an hour, they decided to head back, more from the cold than fatigue. In the car, Alex cranked the heat, although it wasn't likely to accomplish much on the short drive to town. "Come home with me? I'll light a fire and make you soup."

Lia smiled. "I don't think I could resist that even if I wanted to."

Back at Alex's, they began the process of peeling off their layers of clothing. "Do you want to shower before we eat?"

Lia nodded. "Yes, please. Will you join me?"

"I thought you'd never ask."

Alex stepped into the tub and cranked the hot water. Lia followed and Alex shifted so Lia could stand under the spray. Watching the water sluice over Lia's skin made Alex's fingers itch to touch her. To give them something to do, she picked up the shampoo and squirted a generous amount into her palm. "Turn around."

Lia did as she was told and Alex worked the shampoo into her hair, massaging her scalp and causing Lia to groan with pleasure. Alex swallowed the lump in her throat and guided Lia under the spray to rinse. She repeated the process with conditioner, then moved on to body wash. She turned Lia back to face her. When Lia blinked her eyes open and fixed her with a sultry stare, Alex gave in to the desire that had been building inside her. She ran her hands up Lia's sides and over the swell of her breasts. Lia's nipples hardened at the touch and a small moan escaped her lips.

Alex closed the short distance between them and found Lia's lips. Lia's skin was slippery with soap and it slid erotically over Alex's. When their nipples brushed, Lia bit down lightly on Alex's shoulder and tested the limits of Alex's self-control. Alex allowed her fingers to trail lower, over Lia's abdomen and into the triangle of dark hair at the top of her thighs.

Lia shifted slightly, giving Alex both access and an invitation. Alex dipped her fingers lower and found Lia already slick with arousal. "Oh, God."

Lia let out a shaky laugh. "It's you. You do this to me."

Alex was pretty confident in her abilities as a lover, but there was something about Lia's reaction to her that was different. It was so powerful, so instant; Alex found it intoxicating. "I love that."

Alex teased her with long, slow strokes. Lia braced a hand against the shower wall. The hot water continued to course over her and Alex bent to take one of her nipples into her mouth. Alex sucked and tugged in sync with the thrust of her hand, creating a rhythm that she knew would push Lia closer to the edge.

Lia was pressing against her with increasing urgency. When she shifted again, Alex took advantage of the improved access, easing two fingers inside her. The slow strokes became forceful thrusts and Lia bucked against her. Alex used her thumb to press against Lia's throbbing clit and immediately felt her entire body tense.

Lia quaked for a long time and she feared they both might tumble over. Eventually, her body stilled and Alex gently pulled her hand away. Lia looked at her, but her eyes seemed unfocused.

"How do you do that?" Lia was clearly out of breath, which made Alex smile.

"It's you," she said, turning Lia's words back on her. "You do this to me."

"Oh, I have a few things I'd like to do to you."

She was about to make a smart-mouth retort when Lia grabbed her shoulders and turned her around. Lia took her hands and placed each of them on the wall above her head. Alex could feel Lia's breath on her ear as she said, "Don't move."

Lia dragged her nails down Alex's back and over her ass. She continued to knead the taut muscles with her left hand while her right reached around front. Alex inched her feet further apart, opening herself for Lia's touch. She was hard and throbbing when Lia's fingers found her. Unused to the position, Alex pressed back, craving the feel of Lia's body against her.

What she felt, however, was Lia's left hand, sliding between her legs from behind. The next thing she knew, Lia was inside her. Surprise quickly gave way to white-hot desire. The feel of Lia's fingers sliding in and out, slightly curved to stroke her in just the right spot, made her groan. Lia continued to move along either side of her clit with her other hand, sliding up and down in time with each thrust. The pressure built quickly. As much as Alex wanted to prolong the feeling, she was powerless to hold back.

Lia could feel Alex constricting, convulsing around her. She pressed the pads of her fingers against the small, ridged spot, using all of her strength to hold them there as Alex bucked against her, screamed her name. Feeling the way Alex shuddered against her was almost more powerful than her own orgasm. When Alex went lax, Lia eased her hands away, keeping an arm around her waist for support.

She planted a kiss between Alex's shoulder blades. "Let's get out of here before one of us drowns."

"Mmm hmm."

Lia smiled and reached around to turn off the water. She stepped out of the shower, handing Alex a towel from the hook on the back of the door. As they dried off, Lia said, "I don't think I've ever done that before."

Alex stopped drying her hair and looked at her. "Had sex in the shower or been such a top?"

Lia bit her bottom lip. "Both?"

"Well, feel free to give into either of those urges anytime."

Lia flushed. She was going to have to push out of her comfort zone more often, especially if the result was anything like this. In the bedroom, Alex offered her a pair of flannel pants and a sweatshirt. Lia accepted gratefully and pulled them on. "Okay, now I'm starving."

"Ditto. I can cook something more substantial than soup, but it will take longer."

"No, soup is good. What I'd really love is a grilled cheese with it."

"I'm sorry…Are you seven?"

"I'm sorry. Are you knocking grilled cheese sandwiches?"

"Not at all. I would just never think to eat one."

"I don't know if I should be offended or feel sorry for you. You start a fire. I'll make sandwiches and we'll see who still thinks they're kiddie food."

They headed to the kitchen and Lia went to root around in the refrigerator. She wasn't disappointed. She pulled out ingredients, along with a container of soup from the café. Twenty minutes later, they sat on the couch with Alex's roasted red pepper soup and Lia's brie and pear on grilled sourdough.

"I didn't realize you were counting this as grilled cheese," Alex said between bites.

"It's grilled and it's cheese, isn't it?"

"Who can argue with that logic?"

They finished their meal, then found a rom-com marathon on television. At one point, she fell asleep; when she woke, Alex was dozing. It was, in her mind, the perfect afternoon. When the fire began to fade, Alex added logs. Lia opened a bottle of wine. They had a simple pasta dinner, invited Murphy to join them on the couch.

Flopped on his back between them, with his legs in the air, he snored like an old man and took up far more than his third.

That night, curled up under the blankets with Alex's arm slung around her waist, Lia imagined what it would be like to fall asleep like this every night. The thought made her heart beat just a little bit faster. Maybe it wasn't such a crazy idea after all.

CHAPTER THIRTY

L ia sat on the sofa, folding laundry and singing along to the *Rent* soundtrack. When her phone ringtone cut into the middle of "The Tango: Maureen," she did a solo tango across the room to where her phone sat on the counter. She looked at the screen and her heart sank. Dani was calling. Lia feared it was bad news about her father.

"Hello?"

"Hi, Lia." Dani's voice was upbeat and it caught her off guard.

"Hi."

"It's me."

"I know. What's up?"

"Not much. I didn't hear back from you so I wasn't sure if you got my text the other day. I thought I'd give you a call instead."

Lia suddenly remembered the text she got from Dani on Valentine's Day, along with the fact that she'd put it out of her mind and never responded. "Is everything okay?"

"Things are great. You?"

"Your dad?"

"His doctor hasn't cleared him to go back to work yet, but he's chomping at the bit. He says he's feeling better than ever."

"Oh. That's great. I'm so glad to hear it."

"Of course, he's downplaying the whole thing, which I suppose means he's back to normal. How are you? What are you up to today?"

"Umm, laundry."

Dani laughed. She had one of those low, sexy laughs that reminded Lia of a femme fatale in an old movie. "Can I confess something? Since you've been gone, I've resorted to sending the laundry out. All of it. I'm so helpless."

Lia couldn't help but laugh a little. She'd done most of the laundry, but she figured it was because her job allowed her to be home more of the day. "I think it's more that you can't be bothered than you aren't capable."

"Perhaps." Dani's tone seemed almost flirtatious. "I liked the way you did it, though, like you were taking care of me. It just isn't the same."

It was 11:30 a.m. on a Tuesday. There was no reason Dani wouldn't be at work. Lia tried to picture her at her desk in her corner office. It didn't make sense. Dani didn't call her in the middle of the day when they were together. She certainly didn't call for idle chatter or, Lia realized uncomfortably, flirtation.

"Dani, why are you calling me?"

"I didn't realize I had to invent an excuse every time I wanted to talk to you."

Lia couldn't tell if Dani was hurt or being defensive. She didn't want to be antagonistic, but she felt weird about where the conversation was going. "It's not about having an excuse. It's about me trying to figure out why, after all these months, you've decided to be in touch. What do you want?"

"I was trying to give you space."

"Space?" Lia thought about the pictures she saw on Facebook. New Year's Eve had been just the tip of the iceberg. Once Lia started clicking around, it was clear that Dani had been spending her time with a variety of women: at parties, on ski slopes, even on a beach somewhere. "I really don't think that's how I would classify the end of our relationship."

"Lia, I made some mistakes. I know that. I respected that you needed to leave so that you could work through it. I still care about you."

Lia's mind was turning. Was Dani feeling guilty all of a sudden? Was she after something? It simply didn't make sense. "I...I appreciate the thought, but I'm fine."

"I'm glad. Look, I didn't mean to interrupt your day. I have a meeting I have to get to anyway. Take care of yourself, okay?"

"You too."

"Thanks, baby. Bye."

Baby? Lia looked at her phone for a long while after the call ended. If she didn't know better, Lia would swear that Dani was trying to get her back. It was impossible, though. Even if Dani had decided Lia was worth fighting for, she wouldn't have waited four months to do something about it. Maybe her latest flavor of the month hadn't ended well. Maybe her father's heart attack had made her sentimental.

Regardless of the reason, Lia didn't like it. Her days of being whatever Dani needed whenever Dani needed it were over. Lia tried to put it out of her mind, but found herself feeling unsettled. Finishing her chores didn't help, nor did attempting to work. Not wanting to go to the café and try to make conversation, she grabbed her coat and headed out for a walk.

Lia walked and walked, losing track of time. Only when it began to grow dark did she realize how late it had gotten. Since she was supposed to have supper with Alex, she decided to walk there instead of heading back to her place. When she arrived, Alex was about to get in the shower.

"Help yourself to a glass of wine," she said. "I'll be just a minute and then I'll finish dinner."

Lia poured herself a big glass and curled up in the middle of the couch, patting the empty spot on her left so Murphy would join her. She sipped her wine and rubbed his ears. By the time Alex emerged from the bedroom, she was feeling significantly more relaxed. "Hey, you."

"Hey, yourself." Alex walked over to the couch and kissed her. "Stay exactly where you are. I'm going to check on dinner and I'll be right back to join you."

"Okay." Lia remained where she was, content to let the dog and the wine continue their work.

Alex returned with her own glass of wine and flopped down in the empty spot on the sofa. She watched as Lia stretched her limbs and let out a sound that was a cross between a moan and a purr. After a few deliberate blinks, she locked eyes with Alex, and smiled.

"The wine has gone right to my head."

Alex returned the smile, appreciating the curve of Lia's back and the press of her breasts against the thin sweater she wore. "I know you're a lightweight, but you're still on your first glass. Unless, of course, you started before you got here."

"Well." Lia tapped her finger up Alex's thigh as she spoke. "I did not have lunch. On an empty stomach, you could show me a glass of wine and I'd be tipsy."

"Why didn't you eat? Please don't tell me you're one of those women who forgets to eat."

Lia guffawed. "I've forgotten a lot of things—why I walked into a room, what I wanted to do with my life, my own birthday. I don't think, however, that I've once in my life forgotten to eat. Don't you know me at all?"

Lia turned to Alex, leaning in and bringing her face very close. Alex was sorely tempted to kiss her, to revel in Lia's looseness and lack of inhibition. For some reason, she didn't. "So why no lunch?"

"My ex called and it put me in a weird mood. I went for a walk to shake it off and I lost track of time. Since I knew you were making me dinner, I decided I'd save myself for that."

"I see. Well, dinner will be a little while yet. Let me rustle up something to tide us over." Alex extricated herself from the sofa and went to the kitchen. She sliced some cheese and put it on a plate with a few slices of baguette and some olives. She considered whether she should press Lia about the conversation or simply let it go. After Lia's revelation about how the relationship ended, there were things she wanted to know. Given how disinclined Lia was to talk about her ex, she thought that this might be her best opportunity.

Alex set the plate down on the coffee table and handed Lia a piece of bread and cheese. "So what about it put you in a weird mood?"

She hoped the question seemed light enough that Lia would perceive it as an invitation, and not a demand, to talk. It did the trick.

"I told you Danielle and I were together for about ten years."

"You did."

"And I told you that I ended it when she had an affair with her administrative assistant."

Alex's jaw tightened. She had an intense desire to punch the woman. Since she couldn't act on it, she tried to set it aside. "Yes, you did."

Lia seemed to be choosing her words carefully. "Well, after I found out, she apologized, she expressed regret. The regret, though, seemed more about disrupting the status quo. It was like the thing she valued most was how well our life together worked, certainly more than my heart or how much she'd hurt me."

Alex thought about what Lia was saying, about this Dani's obsession with status. "And that made it worse?"

"At first, yes. The more I thought about it, though, the more I realized that was how our whole relationship worked. It was for show. That made it easier to leave."

"That makes sense. So what happened today?"

"She called me for seemingly no reason and said that she still cares about me."

Alex's insides clenched. She tried to keep her voice from sounding as angry and suspicious as she felt. "Cares as in wants you back?"

Lia shook her head emphatically. "No, it wasn't like that. It was, I don't know, nostalgic, maybe? Sentimental. Which is strange because Dani isn't ever sentimental. I can't decide what to make of it. It was a short conversation and there probably isn't anything to make of it, but it was all rather strange."

Lia's statement was punctuated by a beeping from the kitchen. Alex picked up Lia's hand and kissed it. "Don't move."

The beeping stopped and Lia heard the oven door open, the scraping of a heavy pot on the rack, and the door close again. Alex appeared back in the living room. She sat on the couch and looked at Lia. "Why are you so sure she isn't trying to get you back?"

Lia rolled her eyes. "One, it isn't her style. Two, I know for a fact that she's been with at least half a dozen different women since we broke up. Three, she's shown absolutely no interest in getting back together."

Alex was far from convinced. In her estimation, this was just about the time remorse and regret would set in. She couldn't imagine anyone in their right mind would let Lia go and not regret it. "If you say so."

Lia squared her shoulders. "I have no interest in being with her, so it's a moot point."

That made Alex feel somewhat better. She stood and pulled Lia to her feet. "Good for you. Don't let it, or her, get under your skin. Let me pour you another glass of wine and we'll eat."

"I'm sorry I was in a funk."

"You're entitled and I asked." In the kitchen, Alex ladled beef bourguignon into bowls and carried them to the table. She grabbed the rest of the baguette, cut it into large chunks, and put it into a basket. She grabbed the open bottle of Cabernet and motioned for Lia to join her at the table.

"Thanks for listening."

"Of course. You okay?"

"Yes. I spent a lot of time thinking I should be heartbroken. I mean, one is supposed to feel heartbroken in situations like this, right?"

Alex nodded, trying to follow Lia's train of thought.

"The thing is, I didn't. I was angry with Danielle and with myself, and I was sad. The sadness, though, was that I'd been completely ready to spend the rest of my life like that—not unhappy, but not really happy either. I was devastated that I didn't know the difference, that I'd settled without even knowing it."

Alex wasn't sure she understood where Lia was coming from. On one hand, she was livid that Lia would judge herself for the fact that her ex turned out to be a liar and a cheat. She wanted to offer some comfort, a reassurance that Lia wasn't to blame. On the other hand, she couldn't help but thinking about her own choices in life and love, and what they said about her.

Lia scooped up a bite of the stew and sampled it. "Oh. Oh, this is amazing."

That Lia was able to switch gears so easily made Alex smile. She was more than happy to turn the conversation from cheating exes and bad choices. "I'm glad you like it."

"Like is a bit of an understatement. What you can do with food is dangerous."

"It's good to know I have a secret weapon."

Lia looked at her long and slow. "As good as this is, it is most definitely not your secret weapon."

Alex enjoyed the way Lia stared at her, what her words implied. It was easy to let her shift the conversation, easier to focus on the spark between them. It was fine, really; she didn't relish talking about the woman with whom Lia had spent so many years.

One thing was certain, she hadn't been this taken by a woman in a very long time. It made her nervous. She felt like she was on the cusp of falling in love with Lia and she wasn't at all sure that Lia was in the same place. Tonight's conversation had, if anything, increased that uncertainty. The whole situation left her uneasy. Something about Lia's past didn't feel resolved and she had a gnawing sense that it was a feeling Lia shared, even if she didn't want to talk about it.

CHAPTER THIRTY-ONE

Spring was in the air and the sun was shining. Although it was entirely possible that they'd see more snow before it was all said and done, the whole town seemed optimistic and energized. When Lia left to get ready for her book group, she was nearly giddy, declaring that she wasn't even going to wear a coat.

Alex decided she and Murphy would have a nice, long walk when she closed up. She might not wear a coat, either. It was probably too early to open windows, but she was tempted. She had a vision of making love to Lia, sunlight pouring through the windows and a breeze blowing in through the curtains. She was lost in thought when the door opened. When she looked up, a gorgeous blonde was standing in front of the register.

"Hey, stranger. Long time, no see."

It was true. Alex hadn't seen Sabrina since August. She'd come to Provincetown to tend bar for the summer, during which she and Alex had spent more than a few nights getting hot and heavy in Alex's bedroom or skinny-dipping in the ocean. When they parted ways at the end of the season, it was with affection and no expectations. In truth, Alex hadn't expected to see her again.

"Sabrina." Grinning, Alex jogged around the bakery case to the opposite side of the register and gave her a hug. "You look fabulous. What are you doing here?"

"I came out to talk with a couple of the bar owners, try to line up a gig for the summer again."

Alex frowned. "I thought you were going back to grad school?"

"I was, I mean, I am. I've got one more year to finish my master's with teacher certification. I'm figuring this will be the last year I can spend my summer behind a bar and on the beach and I don't want to miss it."

Alex smiled. When they met, Sabrina had been accepted to a graduate program, but was nervous about returning to school after being out of college for almost ten years. It made her happy to know that Sabrina had figured out what she wanted to do with her life and was making it happen. "That's awesome. Really, really awesome."

"Thanks. It's been a crazy year, but a good one. I couldn't resist stopping by to say hello, and to see if you might be free for dinner tonight. I don't have to head back until morning."

It was clear from the tone in her voice that Sabrina was interested in more than dinner. At any other time in her life, Alex wouldn't have hesitated. This time, she did.

"I'd love to."

"But?"

The hesitation in her voice must have been obvious. "But only if you're okay with just dinner."

Sabrina looked at her. "You're not dabbling in celibacy, are you?"

Alex looked away. "No, of course not."

Understanding flashed in Sabrina's eyes and she grinned. "You're with somebody."

"Well..." Alex wondered why it was so hard to be open about it. She wasn't embarrassed to be in a relationship. It was more like talking about it might jinx it in some way.

Sabrina's grin turned into a frown. "You don't sound sure."

Alex remembered just how perceptive Sabrina was. It was one of her best, if at times more infuriating, qualities. "It's just, I don't know. I haven't really done the serious relationship thing, not in a long time, at least."

"We're going to have dinner and you're going to tell me all about it."

Alex nodded her agreement. "Sounds good, but only if I get to hear all about the adventures of grad school."

"Deal. Squealing Pig, around seven?"

"See you then." Alex waved as Sabrina left, then went back to cleaning the espresso machine.

Over dinner, Sabrina talked about her coursework and the student teaching she was slated to begin in the fall. She loved the classes, if not all of her classmates. "I can't tell you how many twenty-two-year-olds I sit next to who have no interest in teaching. They're just biding their time until they marry a dentist or an accountant. It's so depressing."

"Just think how much the experienced teachers and principals will be vying for you over those misguided girls."

"I guess you have a point. They're just such a waste of space, not to mention resources. I swear, one of them rolled her eyes at me when I used the phrase 'make a difference.'"

"You could think of it as training for when you'll have to deal with them as parents?"

"Okay, you're officially not helping." Sabrina punched Alex in the arm.

Alex shrugged. "I do what I can."

Sabrina shook her head. "Enough about me. Tell me all about you and this new girl."

Alex told her about how Lia appeared in her shop in early November, how she began coming nearly every day to work. "We chatted. I asked her out for drinks."

"Like you do."

"Sort of. I really hesitated at first. I don't know if it was because she was getting out of a relationship or what, but she seemed different, unsure of herself."

"Wounded, you mean."

"Maybe, or at least out of practice. I didn't want to make things messy, for her or for me."

"So what happened?"

Alex thought about their first real date—the dinner, Lia's dress, the garters, the insanely good sex. "She opened the door, and I guess I couldn't resist."

Sabrina let out a low whistle. "I've been there, my friend. I've been there. So are you officially an item?"

Alex cringed inwardly. "Yes and no. We discussed keeping things casual, no strings attached. She was in like a ten-year relationship, and she's only here through the winter."

"I sense another but."

"But I'm not seeing anyone else, and I have no desire to. I'm pretty sure she isn't either."

"Are you in love with her?"

Stuart had been asking that very same question for the last month and a half. She'd yet to give him a concrete answer. There was no use denying, though; it wouldn't change the fact of the matter. "Yes. I am."

If Sabrina was taken aback by the confession, she didn't show it. "Well then, I'm happy for you."

"Thanks. I don't know exactly where it's all going, but we'll see."

When Alex and Sabrina walked out of the restaurant, it was 9:30. Sabrina, who'd sworn off drinking during the semester to help both her studies and her pocketbook, was just the slightest bit tipsy.

"I can't believe two beers are all I can handle."

Alex was surprised, too. The summer before, Sabrina could have easily kept up with her in the drinking department. "It's quite adorable, actually. I'd feel better, however, if you let me get you back to your hotel. Are you at the Boatslip?"

Sabrina nodded. "They're pretty empty still. Dylan gave me a room in exchange for covering the front desk for him in the morning."

Alex smiled. Dylan, the manager, was a good friend. He was also a master at bartering. "That sounds like a good arrangement. I'll walk you."

Sabrina took Alex's arm. "So chivalrous. Lia is a very lucky woman."

They strolled down Commercial Street. Aside from another couple walking ahead of them, it was deserted. Alex thought about the floods of people that would descend in a couple months' time. For the first time in as long as she could remember, she realized she wasn't looking forward to the high season.

"I don't know if I've ever seen the town so quiet. I love the bustle, and the income that comes with it, but this is really nice."

Alex sighed. "Yeah. I know exactly what you mean."

They meandered down the street in companionable silence. Alex allowed her mind to wander to thoughts of the future. A future with Lia. It frightened her just how easy it was to imagine.

She and Sabrina were just past Spiritus Pizza when Lia emerged from a side street right in front of them, as though she'd been conjured from Alex's thoughts. She must have tensed, because Sabrina let go of her arm and stood up straight.

"Lia." Alex had done nothing that should make her feel guilty, but that didn't seem to stop her stomach from shifting uncomfortably.

"Hi."

Lia's expression gave nothing away. Her voice was even. Unsure what to make of it, Alex said nothing. Lia said nothing. Seconds passed.

"Lia, it's so nice to meet you. I'm Sabrina, an old friend of Alex's. She's been telling me all about you."

Lia put out her hand. "It's nice to meet you, too."

Alex, who'd been holding her breath, let it out in a whoosh. "Sabrina drove out to see about lining up a job for summer and stopped by the shop. We were just catching up over dinner."

Lia nodded. "That sounds very nice. I won't keep you. Enjoy your evening."

She turned and started walking in the direction of her house. Alex watched, wanting to call after her, but unsure of what to say.

When she was out of earshot, Sabrina said, "Was it just me, or was that awkward?"

Alex sighed. "It wasn't you."

Her thoughts turned to New Year's Eve and the whole fiasco with Kim. In the nearly four months she and Lia had been dating, that was the only real fight they'd had. She had a sinking feeling that another fight was looming on the horizon.

"You should go talk to her. I'm fine."

"No, no. We're almost there. I'll go over after."

Sabrina raised an eyebrow. "Is she weird around people she doesn't know? Or really jealous?"

Alex shook her head. "Neither. I think she's experiencing déjà vu. This woman I used to date pounced on me at a New Year's party. Lia saw her kissing me and it was a big mess."

"Only you, McKinnon. Only you."

"It's never been a problem before."

"Times change, right?"

"You're not kidding."

"And she's worth it?"

"Yeah." When it came down to it, it was as simple as that.

"Well, then, good luck."

They arrived at the Boatslip and hugged their good-byes. Alex headed straight to Lia's, resisting the urge to run. She worried that Lia's cool response had been a cover for anger, or worse, hurt. Of course, there was also the possibility that Lia's reaction was genuine. Lia might not care one way or the other if Alex was seeing another woman. Both possibilities made her uneasy. She wanted to see Lia, to talk to her. She wanted—no, needed—to tell Lia how she really felt.

The downstairs lights were on when Alex knocked on the door. She saw Lia's silhouette moving toward her and breathed a sigh of relief. When Lia opened the door with a smile, a little bit of the tension in her stomach eased. "Hi."

"Hi. I didn't expect to see you again tonight. Is everything okay?"

"Yes, yes." Alex tried to keep her tone calm. "I just wanted to see you, to talk to you. May I come in?"

"Of course." Lia stepped back, allowing her to step inside.

"Thanks. Lia…" She trailed off, unsure of how to begin.

"Yes?" Lia looked at her with an expectant smile.

"Lia, about tonight. I…I don't want you to have the wrong idea about Sabrina."

"It's completely okay. We agreed that we wouldn't be exclusive. You have nothing to explain."

"No, it's not that. Sabrina and I are just friends. I mean, we dated for a little while last summer, but that's done." She hadn't wanted Lia to be upset with her, but, somehow, this was worse. It felt like Lia couldn't care less whether she was hooking up with Sabrina or not.

"Alex, really. You're free to spend time with anyone you want. We agreed to no pressure, no expectations. I mean, I think it's pretty obvious I'm in no position to be getting serious with anyone. Besides, I'm only here for another few weeks and then who knows. It's actually so much better that we're not overly invested."

Alex's heart sank. Everything Lia said made sense. Alex had been so focused on sorting out her feelings that she hadn't given a whole lot of thought to Lia's. She'd assumed Lia was on the same page. They'd practically been living together since Valentine's Day. Now, telling Lia how she felt seemed selfish, if not outright demanding. The last thing she wanted was to put that kind of pressure on her. She also didn't want to give her heart to someone who didn't want it. She'd been there before and the outcome was a disaster.

"Okay, then. It's, uh, good to know how you feel." As Alex spoke, the words rang hollow in her ears. "We are totally on the same page."

"Good. I hope you didn't think I was going to freak out or get weird or anything. New Year's was an anomaly. That's not how I usually am."

Alex shook her head at the irony of it. In retrospect, having Lia freak out would have been preferable. It would have meant, if nothing else, that her feelings were somewhere on the same plane. "I didn't think anything. I just want you to be honest with me, to tell me how you feel."

"I feel fine. Well, fine, but a little tired. Do you mind if I don't come home with you tonight? I know you need to take care of Murphy, but I think I might just want to crash here."

Again, Alex felt at a loss. She couldn't figure out whether Lia was hurt and refusing to talk about it or if she was unfazed by the whole thing and really didn't have a huge stake in their relationship. It was exactly the kind of complication that led her to swear off serious relationships in the first place. As much as she wanted to press Lia until the truth of her feelings came out, it wasn't how she operated. Alex did not push the women she dated. And since baring her soul didn't come naturally, either, she didn't.

"Sure. I just wanted to make sure you're okay."

"Absolutely."

"Okay."

"Yep."

Alex felt like she was only making matters worse. "Well, I'll go. I'm going to Red Sox Opening Day with Stuart tomorrow, so I won't see you at the bakery."

Lia nodded. "Have a great time."

"I will. So, um, good night, I guess." Alex stepped toward Lia to give her a kiss. It wasn't awkward, but it was definitely devoid of any real passion or longing. She was tempted to ask more questions. Worried things would only get weirder, she decided to leave.

When she was gone, Lia locked the door and leaned against it. That wasn't so bad, was it? She thought she'd managed to stay cool, that she'd been convincing. The one thing she couldn't bear was the idea that Alex felt sorry for her, or that she needed to be gently reminded of the rules of their relationship. Convincing herself, unfortunately, was another matter altogether.

CHAPTER THIRTY-TWO

"I can't believe you chickened out."

Stuart handed Alex a beer and took his seat next to her. They were sitting a few rows back, squarely between first base and Pesky's Pole. The tickets had been an early birthday gift from Connie, who was thrilled to send them off on a boy's day while she began prepping her garden for spring planting.

"I didn't chicken out." Alex scowled. "She made it clear that she didn't want a relationship. I don't want to pressure her into something if she isn't ready. It's the noble thing to do. I thought you of all people would appreciate that."

"Yeah, but it's not like you even gave her the choice. She's operating without all of the relevant information."

Since when did Stuart talk like a therapist? She didn't like it. "I'm not going to throw myself where I'm not wanted or, worse, convince her to stay here and be with me if it's only going to make her unhappy in the end."

The conversation was interrupted by the national anthem and ceremonial first pitch. As the Sox took the field for the top of the first inning, both Alex and Stuart cheered, offering particular shouts of encouragement for their favorite player, rough-and-tumble second baseman Dustin Pedroia. "Let's go Peedy!" they bellowed in unison.

With the first inning under way, Stuart turned to Alex. "You don't think there's a pretty big chance she only said that because she stumbled across you with another woman?"

"I wasn't with another woman. You make it sound so seedy."

Stuart lifted his hands. "I'm just saying. I think maybe it's possible she thought something was up and she was trying to play cool."

Alex rolled her eyes. "And maybe you just want me to find a nice girl and settle down."

A foul ball sailed over their heads and into the far rows of the grandstand. Once it was clear neither of them was going to be pelted in the head, Stuart resumed his case. "Even if that's true, I think you need to put yourself out there. Take a risk. Grab the bull by the horns."

"You mean grow a pair?"

Stuart shrugged, raised his hands again. "Hey, I didn't say that."

"But you wanted to."

"If the shoe fits."

Alex affectionately jabbed him in the ribs with her elbow. "You're a regular old Confucius, aren't you?"

"Does that mean you're going to do it?"

"We'll see."

"I'll drink to that." He raised his beer and bumped his plastic cup against hers.

The Sox beat Tampa four to three with a double in the bottom of the ninth inning by Mike Napoli. After three hours of game and nearly three hours in the car to get home, Alex was tempted to call it a night and crawl into bed alone. After dropping Stuart off at his house, however, his words continued to nag at the back of her mind.

It was one thing to keep her life, and her relationships, simple. It was another to be afraid of going after what she wanted. Once she hit Provincetown, she steered her car toward Lia's house instead of her own. When she pulled up, the entire downstairs was dark. A small square of light came from Lia's bedroom upstairs.

She almost drove away. Instead, she pulled out her phone and dialed Lia's number. Given that it was almost midnight, she didn't want Lia to think her house was being broken into. Alex gripped the steering wheel with her free hand and waited.

"Hello?"

Lia's voice sounded strange and far away. Alex immediately questioned her decision. "Did I wake you?"

"No, not at all. I was just reading. Are you okay?"

Alex relaxed. "Yes, everything is fine. I'm actually outside, but I didn't want to knock on the door and scare you half to death."

Lia chuckled. "You know me so well. I'll be down in one minute."

"Great." Alex ended the call and took a deep breath. She was just going to do it. Put it out there. No pressure. Then she would at least know that there wasn't a big question hanging in the air anymore. If it didn't go anywhere, it wasn't meant to, and she wouldn't have to wonder. And Stuart would get off her back. It would be good. It would be fine. She climbed out of the car and walked the short distance to Lia's door.

Holy crap. What am I doing?

The door opened and there was no going back. The sight of Lia standing in the doorway made Alex's heart thud uncomfortably in her chest. This woman, with her fuzzy pink robe and bare feet, had managed to steal her heart completely. It was time she admitted it, for better or worse. She followed Lia inside and closed the door behind her.

"I'm sorry to come by so late, but I really didn't want to wait."

Lia had a feeling of déjà vu. This was almost exactly what Alex said when she'd shown up the night before. Perhaps she was here to finish what she'd started...whatever that was. "It's fine. Are you sure you're okay?"

"Yes. I mean, I will be. I...we need to talk."

"Sure." Lia braced herself. If she hadn't fallen apart when Dani broke her heart, she sure as hell wasn't going to now. "What's on your mind?"

"When we talked last night, I wasn't entirely truthful with you."

Lia stuck her hands in the pockets of her robe to keep herself from fidgeting, determined to keep her composure. If she needed to fall apart a little bit, she'd do it after Alex left. "Okay."

Alex took a deep breath. "When I said that we were on the same page, that wasn't really how I felt. How I feel. I feel so much more than that."

"I don't understand what you mean." Lia could tell that Alex was fumbling. She didn't want to make her squirm, but she really didn't know what she was trying to say.

"When Sabrina showed up, she made it perfectly clear we could pick up where we left off last summer."

Lia set her jaw. She'd freaked out that one time and it was going to continue to haunt her. "I thought I made it clear that I didn't expect, or demand, that we be exclusive."

"I know. The thing is, when she showed up, it made me realize just how much I didn't want that. I don't want to pick up with Sabrina or with anyone else. I like being with you. I like being with you all the time."

Lia narrowed her eyes, trying to make her brain reconcile Alex's words with what she was expecting.

"What I'm trying to say is that I love you. I'm in love with you. I want to be with only you. I don't want you to feel pressured and I understand that you might not be in the same place. I'm not asking you to be or do anything you don't want to, but I need you to know how I feel." Alex shrugged and tucked her hands into her pockets.

The dull ache in Lia's chest became a skittering pulse that made it difficult to breathe. She'd spent the better part of the last two months convincing herself that her feelings for Alex were a rebound reaction—intense and unreciprocated feelings that would fade when she left town. "I don't know what to say."

"You don't have to say anything. You don't have to feel or decide anything tonight. Wait, I take that back. You do have to decide one thing. Do you want me to stay or go?"

Lia closed her eyes. She methodically went through her mind, shutting off the fears and doubts, silencing the questions. She'd figure them out when she needed to. For now, she was wanted and, if she allowed herself to believe it, loved. She opened her eyes, taking in the woman who was standing in front of her, offering her heart. For now, it was enough. She closed the short distance between them. She wrapped her arms around Alex's waist and looked into her piercing green eyes. "Stay."

Alex's mouth was on hers and her hands were in Lia's hair. Lia took in her scent, the way Alex's body molded against hers. It felt so familiar, so natural, it was hard to imagine that she'd only known Alex for a few months. She slipped her fingers under the hem of Alex's shirt and traced over the skin of her lower back. The uneasiness she'd felt for the last twenty-four hours melted away.

Alex pulled herself away long enough to kick off her shoes, then allowed Lia to take her hand and lead her up the stairs. Once in the bedroom, Alex untied Lia's robe and pushed it from her shoulders, leaving her in a thin cotton chemise. Lia raised her arms and Alex lifted it over her head.

"You are so beautiful." Alex's voice was barely over a whisper.

Although Alex had said as much dozens of times in the past few months, it still gave Lia a quiver to hear it. Instead of blushing, she allowed the words to sink in, to make her feel beautiful. Not trusting her own voice, Lia busied herself with removing Alex's shirt and bra, jeans and boxer briefs. In turn Alex slipped Lia's panties over her hips and they fell to the floor.

It was as though everything was happening in slow motion. Lia ran her fingers over Alex's chest and stomach. Alex made a trail of open-mouthed kisses down Lia's neck and across her shoulder. When Alex guided them onto the bed, Lia sighed. There were long, languid caresses over smooth skin. Their kisses were a fluid melding of lips and tongue, with none of the urgency that usually drove them.

When Alex slipped inside her, Lia felt complete. It was like a void being filled, a chasm repaired. "Please, I need to feel you, too."

Alex shifted so that Lia's hand could slide between them. Lia's fingers slid into her wetness, finding her swollen and hard center. They continued to move slowly, in unison. Lia thought their bodies might simply melt into one another, becoming one.

Alex's orgasm crested first. It was a shuddering that seemed to radiate through her. Feeling the heat pour out of her sent Lia tumbling toward her own release. As the waves of pleasure carried her, she opened her eyes and found Alex staring at her with quiet intensity. The connection in that moment felt deeper, more profound, than she believed possible.

After, they lay together with limbs entwined. With her head on Alex's chest, Lia could hear her heartbeat. It was strong and steady, offering a quiet assurance that felt more powerful than any words.

"I love you, too," Lia said softly.

Alex's hands, which had been stroking her hair, grew still. "Lia?"

Lia lifted her head so that she could look directly at Alex. "I said, I love you, too."

CHAPTER THIRTY-THREE

W ell?"
    It was a week later and Alex was sitting with Stuart at the Squealing Pig. He'd cut right to the chase, but Alex would be damned if she didn't make him work for it. "Well, what?"

Stuart drummed his fingers on the polished bar. "Well, did you tell her? What did she say? What happened?"

Stuart was a good friend. He was also as nosy as a little old lady. Alex shrugged, keeping her tone nonchalant. "Well, we aren't engaged or anything, but I'm...optimistic."

"Optimistic? What does that mean?"

Alex played coy for another minute or two before she caved and gave him the highlights of her conversation with Lia, how Lia eventually revealed that she shared the same feelings. "And I owe it all to you."

He bumped his shoulder against hers. "I'm happy for you."

"Thanks, pal."

Wanting to change the subject, Alex asked about Connie, who was contemplating returning to grad school so that she could move from teaching into administration. They talked about their hopes for the upcoming baseball season, the NHL playoffs. Alex's mind, however, remained on Lia. When there was a lull in the conversation, she took a deep breath.

"I'm going to ask her to move in with me."

Stuart raised a brow. "Wow. That's big."

"Her lease is up in a few weeks. We haven't really talked about what will happen at that point, but I know she doesn't have another place lined up."

"Are you afraid she'll leave if you don't?"

Alex was annoyed by the question, if for no other reason than it was the same one she'd been asking herself for days. She'd yet to come up with a satisfying answer. "No. I'm in love with her. I want to be with her and this makes sense. If anything, it's moving up something we'd get to sooner or later."

Alex wasn't sure whether she was trying to convince Stuart, or herself. Hearing it out loud helped to ease the worry that she was being too impulsive, getting herself into a situation she might later regret. Admitting she was in love, to herself and then to Lia, had been the dangerous part, and it had gone remarkably well.

Holding on to that feeling of certainty, she stopped by the hardware store on her way home. She had a duplicate set of keys made, including one for the back door entrance to her loft and the main door to the bakery. She popped into the souvenir shop next door and picked out the least cheesy Provincetown key chain she could find.

When she got home, she had a good hour before Lia was due to arrive. She rooted around in her closet, finding a small square box. She put the keys inside, adding a little bow. She hoped it wasn't overkill. She returned to the kitchen to start preparing dinner. When Lia knocked on the door at seven, Alex was nervous, but it was more excitement than apprehension. At least, that's what she told herself.

Lia was in a great mood. She'd finished two projects ahead of schedule, the weather was amazing, and her girlfriend was cooking her dinner. Her life was so much more than she expected when she arrived in Provincetown five months prior. When she arrived at Alex's and was greeted with a kiss that made her weak in the knees, it felt like icing on the cake.

She set down her things, bent down to say hello to Murphy, then looked up at Alex. "Tell me, darling, how was your day?"

Alex chuckled. "That's funny, considering I've only spent about three hours of it away from you."

"You have a point. How was your drink with Stuart?"

"It was good. He sends his regards, as always."

"He's such a good guy. I love that y'all are friends. I hope you told him hi for me."

Alex smiled, but seemed fidgety. "I did. Dinner will be quick. Sit with me for a minute?"

"Happily." Lia got the distinct feeling something was up.

When they were both seated on the couch, Alex took one of Lia's hands. "Before we eat, there's something I wanted to talk to you about."

It was good to know she was right about these things, that she was tuned in to Alex, but the choice of words made her nervous. Try as she might to not let it, her mind always seemed to jump to the worst case scenario. "Okay."

Alex got up and walked over to the corner where her desk was. She returned to the sofa and handed her a small box. Based on the size, Lia thought it might be a bracelet. The thought of a gift was nice, but it didn't go with the serious vibe Alex was sending off.

"Did you get me a present?" She hoped her voice sounded lighthearted.

"Sort of, just open it."

She opened the box and found a key chain of Pilgrim's Monument. Attached to it was a pair of keys. She looked at it, then at Alex.

"One is for the loft, the other is the main door to the shop. I want you to have them. I'd like you to consider moving in with me."

Lia was speechless. In the back of her mind, she'd been worrying for months about what was going to happen at the end of April. She'd had momentary fantasies about living with Alex, but she hadn't given any serious thought to what it would mean to move in with her. "I… Wow."

"I know we haven't really talked about the future, but your lease will be up soon. Finding digs in Provincetown for the summer is a challenge, to say the least."

On one hand, Alex's offer was exactly what she wanted. On the other, it felt like Alex might be doing it for all the wrong reasons. That terrified her. She wasn't sure which sentiment would, or should, prevail. She didn't want to say that out loud, but she knew she had to say something. "I love your place, and I love being with you."

"Which is exactly why you should be here all the time."

Lia smiled. As much as she wanted to say yes and to launch herself into Alex's arms, she hesitated. It was not the kind of decision she should make lightly. And if Alex was only doing it to be nice, or because Lia didn't have any other options, that had disaster written all over it. "It's very tempting."

"But?" Alex looked queasy.

"There's no but. It sounds really amazing. I don't want you to think I'm not grateful."

She saw Alex stiffen. Something she said had been the wrong thing. "I don't want you to feel grateful. I'm not doing it as a favor."

"I'm sorry. I didn't…I didn't mean it that way."

Alex didn't seem convinced, but she took a deep breath. "It's okay. I just want you to understand where I'm coming from. This isn't me trying to help out a friend. It's me wanting to be with you."

Lia wanted to believe her, trust her. The promise of it, and the risk, was almost more frightening than the prospect of moving in together. "I know."

"I hope you really do, and you're not just saying it."

"I do. I just need a little time to think. I try not to make big decisions on the spot, you know? Impulsivity has not been my friend."

"I understand. It's a big step."

"Are you sure?"

"Yes. I sprang it on you pretty suddenly. I've been thinking about it for days, so you should have a little time, too."

"You have?" The assertion was reassuring.

Alex smiled. "I have. And it truly is a big decision. You need to be sure it's what you really want. Why don't you let it sink in and we can talk about it tomorrow?"

"That sounds like a great plan." Lia took a deep breath and felt her heart rate begin to slow. "Thank you."

"Tomorrow is supposed to be gorgeous, the warmest day we've had all spring. Let's plan to go for a walk on the beach after I close the shop. If you're ready, we can talk logistics and then you can decide."

"Deal."

"In the meantime, I'm starving. You?"

"Famished."

Lia relaxed enough to enjoy the linguini and clams that Alex cooked, as well as the lemon tart pilfered from the case downstairs. Her mind, however, never stopped turning over Alex's proposal. For a moment, her heart would swell and it would feel like the easiest decision of her life. Then the nagging voice in the back of her mind would start casting doubts and it felt like the hardest.

They finished dinner and went to bed early. Lia stayed awake for a long time after they made love. She looked around the room, barely lit with the light of the moon and streetlights. Home. If she was being honest with herself, she felt more at home at Alex's than she had for much of the time she spent living with Dani.

When she finally slept, Lia dreamed that she was back in the Manhattan apartment, trying to prepare a meal. She was upset and frustrated because she didn't know where anything was, couldn't find the pots or ingredients or utensils she needed. It was like being in the home of a stranger. She woke with a start, feeling agitated and uncertain. She blinked in the darkness, letting the familiarity of Alex's room slow her racing pulse.

CHAPTER THIRTY-FOUR

There was something magical about the first open-door day of the season. With the sun shining and the temperature creeping above seventy, Alex propped open the door to the bakery and let the salt breeze blow in. Although it wasn't quite warm, the promise of summer was in the air. It was her favorite time of year. Lia was enamored with the warm spell, too, showing up wearing a sundress and sandals. As nice as the weather was, it wasn't quite warm enough for open doors or sundresses. A little before three, she decided she should go home to change into something warmer for their walk on the beach.

Alex was walking to the door to flip the sign to "Closed" when a woman walked in. She was tall and thin and stunning, one of those women who simply looked expensive. She wore a blue and white checked shirt, white pants, designer sunglasses. Even her hair looked expensive—cut and styled perfectly to look sporty and androgynous without screaming butch. Really, though, it was the shoes. Thanks to Jeff's semi-unhealthy obsession with footwear, Alex knew a Gucci driving loafer when she saw one. They were white with blue trim and had the signature gold buckle. Had Jeff been there, he would have drooled.

"Could I get a latte?"

When the woman spoke, Alex tore her gaze away from the shoes and looked again at her face. Angular jaw, deep gray eyes, diamond stud earrings. Alex got the sense that she was the kind of woman who was used to getting her way. "You caught me just in time. What size?"

"The largest you have, to go. Extra shot, nonfat."

"Coming right up."

Alex set the espresso machine to brew and started steaming a small pitcher of milk. "Are you in for the weekend?"

"Sort of. I'm here to see someone."

Alex added the hot milk to the cup. "Well, I hope you spend some time outside. You don't see weather better than this in early April. That'll be five-fifty."

The woman pulled a ten out of her wallet and handed it to Alex. "This is a cute place," she said, gesturing vaguely.

"Thank you. I'm the owner."

The woman took the cup, offering Alex a nod and a disinterested smile. "Thanks." She turned and walked out the door without waiting for her change.

Alex rolled her eyes. If there was one downside to living and working in Provincetown, it was the onslaught of detached rich people who came to play. She knew that it was the influx of those people that allowed her and the rest of the town to earn their livelihoods, but still. It was like winter—a little shocking until your blood thickened up a bit.

Alex came out from behind the counter again, this time flipping the sign and locking the front door. She whistled through her cleaning routine, thinking of sunshine and walking along the water's edge with Lia and Murphy. If they got there before sunset, it might still be warm enough to walk barefoot in the sand.

Alex thought about a summer full of walks on the beach, of blustery falls and winters huddled inside, and so much more. Since asking Lia to move in with her, she had been able to picture it so easily, and want it desperately. She hoped Lia was coming around to feeling the same.

When Lia heard the knock on the door, she was surprised. She wasn't expecting Alex for another half hour at least. She started down the stairs. "Come in," she called.

She jogged the rest of the way down with a smile on her face. She'd been thinking about Alex's proposal nonstop and was feeling more and more certain of her answer. The sight of Danielle standing in her kitchen made her come up short.

Dani smiled at her. "Hi."

Lia looked at the woman she'd spent nearly ten years with, the woman she thought for so long was her future. Dani was, as always, impeccably dressed. Although it was likely she'd just spent the better part of the day traveling, her clothes didn't seem the least bit rumpled. Lia tried to will herself to be calm. "What are you doing here?"

Dani laced her fingers together and held them at her waist. Lia imagined it was how she stood when presenting an investment strategy. "You stopped taking my calls."

"I've been busy." Lia hated herself for lying, and for sounding defensive.

Dani either didn't detect the tone or chose to ignore it. "Your lease here will be up soon and I wanted to discuss how we can move forward."

Lia wondered if Dani realized she sounded like she was looking to broker a deal. "I haven't decided what I'm going to do at the end of the month. I'll let you know when I do so you'll have my address."

"Lia, I want to work things out. I want you to come home."

What? She was dumbfounded. Either she'd been completely oblivious or Dani had completely lost it since the last time they'd spoken. Lia thought back to the weird conversation they had about laundry, the two other phone calls in the middle of the day. There had been a vaguely flirtatious tone, but Dani hadn't even hinted at a reconciliation. The whole thing had started to make her uncomfortable, so she'd let the last couple go directly to voice mail.

"Dani, when I left, it was a permanent decision. There's nothing to work out."

"I'm here to apologize, to make you see that we should be together. I know the whole Tracy situation was embarrassing for you."

Now she'd heard it all. "Embarrassing? Are you serious? You betray my trust, you break my heart, and you're worried about it being fucking embarrassing?"

Dani took a deep breath. "That's not what I meant."

"Really? Because I think it's exactly what you meant. I think our whole relationship has been more about how it looks than how it feels."

❖

Alex walked up the street to Lia's, noticing the sleek silver Lexus parked in front of the house. She wondered if one of the two empty apartments had been rented for a quick getaway weekend. The temperature was in the mid-seventies and it was forecast to be sunny all weekend. Such conditions often inspired a last minute wave of winter-weary New Englanders into town.

She headed up the driveway, clutching the bouquet she bought on a whim from the florist she passed on the way. She knocked lightly, but didn't wait for a response. They'd done away with knocking for the most part, aside from a way of announcing their arrival. When she stepped inside, she saw Lia as well as the woman from the café.

"I'm sorry. I didn't know you had company."

She could feel the woman's eyes on her; it was a cool assessment. She wondered if the woman even realized she was the same person who'd made her coffee an hour before. Not likely. There was an awkward silence while she waited for Lia to speak.

After what felt like an eternity, Lia said, "Alex, this is Danielle."

"Oh." She was stunned, but kept her tone cool. "Hello."

"I wasn't expecting her. She arrived from New York this afternoon."

"Pleased to meet you." The woman's posture was ramrod straight. Her tone made it clear to Alex there was no pleasure in it whatsoever.

"You too." Alex's reply was equally chilly. She still wasn't over the shock that this glamazon was Lia's ex, or that she was standing in the middle of Lia's apartment.

"I came to talk with Lia about our future."

"Alex, could I talk to you outside for a moment?"

You mean as opposed to asking her to wait outside? It was what Alex wanted to say, but it was petty and possessive and she refused to give Lia's ex the satisfaction of seeing her ruffled. "Sure."

Without another word, Alex walked out the door she'd just entered. Murphy followed without so much as a hand signal. He was no dummy.

Lia stepped outside and closed the door behind her. "I'm so sorry."

Alex gaped at her. A sick feeling that was part anger and part something she didn't recognize bubbled up inside her chest. "Why is your ex in your apartment? How does she even know where you are?"

Lia put a hand on her arm and she promptly brushed it away. There was a pleading look in her eyes. "I asked her to forward my mail. She showed up to talk about what's going to happen when my lease ends."

Alex realized the other feeling jockeying for position was panic. "You mean she's here to get you back." Unwilling to think about what that might mean, she shoved it aside and focused on the woman standing in front of her, the woman she loved.

"I'm telling her it's over, that it's been over. I just...I might not have...it's possible I wasn't clear enough about that when I left."

Alex tried to ignore the throbbing in her head, as well as the wave of nausea that had taken over her stomach. She needed to get away before she said something she'd regret. She thrust the flowers into Lia's hand. "I shouldn't be here. You do what you need to do."

Without another word, she turned and walked briskly down the driveway.

Lia called her name, but to no avail. She watched Alex and Murphy disappear out of sight. She felt like she could vomit. There was little she hated more than having people upset with her. Having to deal with Dani was one thing. Having Alex mad at her too was overloading her conflict-avoidance systems. As tempted as she was to chase after them, she couldn't just leave Dani standing in her living room.

"Fuck," she said under her breath, then headed back inside.

She set the flowers down on the counter and turned to face Dani, who was standing exactly where Lia had left her. "Why are you really here? What do you want?"

"I miss you. I miss us. I wanted to talk you into coming home with me, but mostly I wanted to see you, to talk."

She couldn't decide if Dani was being sincere or strategizing her next move. It amazed her how many times she took Dani's words at face value when, in reality, Dani was really just trying to maneuver—or manipulate—the situation to get what she wanted. Dani took her silence as an invitation to continue.

"Look, I didn't mean to barge in on you like this. I really did just want to see you. Will you have dinner with me tonight, for old times' sake? No strings attached."

Lia still wasn't sure whether or not she believed her. It occurred to her, though, that once Dani left, she might not ever see her again. No longer heartbroken, she found that fact to be bittersweet. So, she agreed. "Sure, let's have dinner. But let me be clear, this is not about getting back together."

"Perfect. I'll pick you up at six." Before she could decline the offer of a ride, Dani picked up her keys and her Ferragamo sunglasses and walked out the door.

Lia looked at her watch. It was just before five. She wanted nothing more than to run to Alex's place. She was really wound up, though, and the last thing she wanted was to get into a fight or, worse, get overly emotional. And she needed to deal with Dani once and for all. She tried calling, but Alex didn't answer. She drafted a text, agonized over the wording, then finally hit send.

I'm so sorry about earlier. I had no idea she would show up. I'm going to have dinner with her tonight, to get the closure I didn't when I left. I hope you can understand.

CHAPTER THIRTY-FIVE

Lia expected Dani to take her to one of Provincetown's posh restaurants. When they drove by everything in the center of town, Lia didn't know what to think. When Dani pulled into the driveway of a residential building in the East End, Lia was beyond confused.

"What are we doing here?"

Dani's smile seemed cunning. "Dinner. I promise. Trust me."

Lia snorted.

Dani sighed. "Okay, fine. Bad choice of words. We are here for dinner, though. Come on."

Lia followed her up a short path. It was a newer building, three stories. If Lia had to guess, she figured it housed six or eight high-end condos. Dani followed the path to the side of the building and started up a set of stairs. Lia almost refused to follow her, but didn't want to seem petulant. At the top, Dani slid a key into the lock and then pushed open the door. She gestured for Lia to enter.

Lia did and found herself in the middle of a gorgeous open space. Sliding glass doors opened to a private balcony and a stunning view of the harbor. The living room furniture was casually elegant and the kitchen looked brand new. On the kitchen table was a spread of crackers and cheese, olives, hummus, fruit, and more. It was enough food to feed eight people.

"I hope you don't mind a picnic style dinner. I didn't want things to get cold." She walked to the refrigerator and pulled out a bottle of wine. "Shall we?"

Lia still didn't understand where they were, or why. "Are you staying here?"

"I am. I thought it would be better if we could speak in private. I picked up things from that little market. You could walk there from here if you wanted."

"It's a beautiful place."

"Yes, it is. Wine?"

"Yes, please."

Lia sat at one of the chairs while Dani poured. It was exactly the kind of thing Lia had craved when she and Dani were together—something thoughtful and casual for just the two of them. So many nights, Dani worked late. She would come home, saying she'd eaten a protein bar and only wanted to go to bed. Other times, Lia found herself as Dani's plus one at a business event, sipping cosmos and making nice with her colleagues' wives. Lia wondered if Dani appreciated the irony of the situation.

Dani sat in the other chair. She sipped her wine and plucked an olive from one of the bowls. "This is really nice."

When Lia only mumbled her agreement, Dani took the reins of the conversation. She told Lia about some of their mutual friends—one couple was expecting a baby and another was moving to Charlotte. She talked about a couple of her projects at work, yet another promotion.

Suddenly, she shifted the conversation. "I can't stand the idea that you hate me."

"I don't hate you," Lia said after a long moment. "I'm not even angry, really. I mean, I was, but I don't do angry very well. It takes a lot out of me."

Dani's expression was sad. She seemed almost, maybe, vulnerable. "I hated you for not ever getting angry with me. It was as though you didn't care enough to fight."

Lia shook her head. "I didn't want to have to fight for your love. I wanted it outright. I wanted you to want to give it to me."

"We were so good together."

The regret in Dani's voice seemed sincere. Lia thought for a moment that she might even cry. Lia considered Dani's assertion. It wasn't entirely untrue. They'd made a nice home, had a lot of mutual friends. They managed the day-to-day business of being a couple well. "We were, in a lot of ways."

"We could be that way again. I know I treated you badly. I would need to make up for that. I would do whatever you asked to earn your forgiveness."

For weeks after she'd discovered the affair, Lia had longed to hear those words. She'd lie awake at night and think about whether she'd accept them graciously, whether she'd make Dani grovel. To realize that she no longer needed it—didn't even want it—was overwhelming. "I do forgive you, Danielle."

"So you'll come home with me, and we can put this whole nonsense behind us."

Lia sighed. "No, I'm not going anywhere with you."

Dani's eyes went dark. "You're going to make me beg."

Lia cringed. Of course that's what Dani would think. It was kind of annoying, but mostly sad. "No, that's not what I mean. What I mean is that I can forgive you, but I can't be with you. We can't be together again. I mean, I don't want to be with you. I'm not in love with you anymore."

Dani laced her fingers together. Her knuckles turned white and Lia could see the veins start to protrude on the back of her hand. She took a deep breath and braced herself.

"That's a very dramatic thing to say. Okay, let's say you go off on your own, permanently. How will you even support yourself?"

"I do have income. I own a business, if you recall."

"And you're accustomed to combining that income with another that is six times as large."

Lia narrowed her eyes and looked Dani up and down. As always, she was effortlessly chic. She'd changed from the checked shirt and white pants into buff-colored linen slacks and a black silk tank. Even her casual wear was designer label and perfectly tailored. Lia had often thought Dani would make an excellent model. She had the angular features and aloof way of looking at the world. There was a time when Lia found this woman glamorous, found being with her glamorous. Now, it all seemed like a flashy veneer on something utterly hollow.

"I don't need a two-thousand-square-foot Manhattan apartment."

Danielle sighed. Her face softened. "I know you've not relished living in the city. That has been rather selfish of me. What if we started looking for a place on Long Island, or maybe in Connecticut?"

"It's not about that."

Dani ignored her. "You know, I've actually been thinking how nice it would be to have a summer place. Although I was leaning toward something in the Hamptons, there's no reason it can't be here."

Lia expected Dani to bring up money. There was no doubt that being on her own would require a level of frugality that Lia hadn't had to think about in years. It surprised her, however, that Dani would start throwing around something as major as a piece of real estate to appease her.

"You want to buy a place in Provincetown?"

"Think about it. You clearly enjoy it here. We could spend a few weeks of the summer together. You could even come up and work sometimes while I'm back in the city. It would be the best of all worlds."

Lia's brain was struggling to keep up with processing both Dani's words and their unspoken subtext. It made her wonder how many of Dani's colleagues did just that—buy the dream home wherever the wife would be happy and live together on weekends and holidays.

"I'm prepared to buy this place for you."

It took her a moment to register what Dani said. Even when she understood the meaning, it didn't compute. "What?"

"I didn't rent this place for the weekend. I'm staying here as a potential buyer."

"I don't understand."

Dani pushed her plate aside and set her elbows on the table. "You've obviously enjoyed your time here. I get that. So before I came, I did a little research and I found this place. The renovations were complete only last year, and the furniture is included. It's a great investment."

Lia still couldn't fathom what Dani was proposing. "You're offering to buy me a condo if I take you back?"

"I'm offering to buy this condo for us and for your personal use and pleasure, as a good faith gesture toward making our relationship work."

It sounded to Lia like Dani was describing a corporate merger. Perhaps that was the crux of the matter all along. To Dani, their relationship was a business deal. It was all about negotiating terms that were agreeable to both parties, and coming out on top. Rather than making her angry, the realization made Lia profoundly sad. After a long moment, Lia shook her head. "No, that isn't the kind of arrangement I want."

"You're in love with this baker? Is that it?"

Lia knew it was important to choose her words very carefully. "She has nothing to do with this."

"Of course she does. You're infatuated with her and have talked yourself into believing that whatever is going on between the two of you is better than what you and I have."

"Whatever feelings I have for Alex, whatever feelings she has for me, they have nothing to do with the fact that I am no longer in love with you." She instantly wished she hadn't used Alex's name. It personalized it, brought her into the equation in a way she wanted to avoid.

"I asked about her, you know. Around town. She's got quite the reputation."

"You asked around town? What are you, my father?"

"I didn't have to dig very much. She hooks up with women—one or two or five—all summer long."

Dani had a habit of ignoring whatever was being said to her once she had a train of thought going. It was one of the things about her that drove Lia the most crazy. "What business do you have coming here and digging around in my life?"

"I care about you, Lia. I don't want to see you hurt. I'm sure you have her attention right now, but what's going to happen come May? What's going to happen when a parade of dozens of beautiful, available women pass through her doors?"

Lia swallowed and tried to keep her hands from visibly shaking. She unsuccessfully tried to block the image of Kim from her mind, of Sabrina, of God knows who else. She'd been prepared for Dani to pressure her. She'd been prepared for her to throw around the length of their relationship, the money disparity that in some ways gave Dani the upper hand. She'd even been prepared for, if not groveling, some heartfelt apologies. This, however, this artful injection of doubt, tapped into the fears that were already dancing in the back of her mind.

"I do not want to talk to you about this." Lia wanted to convey strength and certainty, but her voice sounded feeble.

"Lia," Dani reasoned, "you've been here in the summertime. You've seen the women in the bars, on the beach. Girls in bikini tops and tiny shorts who are up for whatever good-time lesbian comes their way."

Lia was trembling now. She wanted desperately to be alone, preferably in a dark and quiet place. She needed to calm down and try to regain some semblance of control over what was happening.

"Sweetheart, you don't even like how you look in a bathing suit." Dani said it softly and without malice. It was a talent she had, that unique brand of pity that passed itself off as sympathy. It was more undermining than any garden variety insult. Lia had always been especially vulnerable to it.

Lia looked at her. As she could have predicted, Dani wore her concerned face—head tilted and lips pursed ever so slightly. It was a look that had always made Lia crave an embrace and some words of reassurance. This time, however, rather than care and love and protection, Lia only saw manipulation. She was convinced that this was no less a tactic than the hard and imposing stance Dani used to get her way in the boardroom. It was all about leverage and getting what she wanted.

Lia stood. "I need to leave."

Dani gave a mildly impatient sigh. "Lia."

"No. No more. I'm done. I'm leaving and, honestly, I don't want to see you again."

"Lia, you don't mean that."

Lia fixed her ex with a hard stare. "Danielle, you have no idea how much I mean it. When I left, I thought the problem was that you didn't love me anymore. I realize now that the problem was much bigger than that."

"What are you talking about?"

Lia could almost see the wheels in Dani's head turning, assessing the turn of events and calculating the right next move. She wondered how she'd missed it for so long. "I'm talking about me. The real problem isn't that you don't love me anymore. It's that, when I'm with you, I don't even love myself."

Dani was stumped. Lia could see it in her eyes. Under other circumstances, she might have taken satisfaction in it. Now, however, she felt nothing. After the hurt and confusion and anger, feeling nothing was quite amazing. She no longer trembled; she felt invincible.

"I really do need to leave now. I don't care if you drive back to New York tonight, or stay until tomorrow, or buy this condo and stay here forever. We are done, and we're done talking about it as well." She stood up. "You don't need to drive me. I can walk from here."

Dani stood as well. "You'll regret this. That trashy butch is going to break your heart and you're going to be all alone and you're going to wish you could come running back to me."

Lia lifted her chin. "Whatever happens, I can assure you that your arms are the last place I'll come running."

Lia walked to the door, opened it, and left. She didn't look back and she didn't pause on the stairs or the path. Once on the street, she turned up a side street to avoid seeing anyone she might know. Her brain was going a mile a minute and she couldn't seem to quiet it enough to formulate a coherent thought.

In the time it took her to get home, Lia's mind settled, if only just a little. It seemed ironic that their final fight, the fight they didn't have when Lia left, was about Lia's entanglements and not Dani's. It hardly mattered at this point, so she tried not to let it bother her. Instead, she focused on feeling that it was ultimately her choices, her decisions, that ended things once and for all. It was a feeling of control that had been missing in the months after she first learned of Dani's affair.

She also felt free. She reveled in it for about thirty seconds before her thoughts turned to Alex. As much as she didn't want them to, Dani's words played over and over in her mind. Lia had, for the most part, quashed her fears about Alex's casual relationships, but now they came roaring back to life. Doubt was powerful like that. It didn't need to come from a reliable source to do its work.

There was also the matter of her essentially shutting Alex out of what was happening. When Lia had tried to explain how she needed to deal with it on her own, Alex agreed, but she didn't seem happy about it. Lia worried that Alex was angry with her. She feared that this was just the sort of thing that would send Alex looking for something easy and uncomplicated. Refusing to let herself hesitate, she walked out of her apartment and straight to Alex's.

When Lia arrived, no one was home. Remembering the plans they had to walk on the beach, she contemplated going in search. Given how her day was going, however, it was likely she'd miss them and end up wandering around aimlessly.

Lia decided to stay put and wait for them to return home. The keys Alex gave her sat in her purse, but she decided that now was not the time to use them. She sat on the back step and thought about what she was going to say when Alex arrived. She banged her head lightly against the door. What a mess.

When Alex saw Lia sitting on her stoop, the first thing she experienced was relief. Murphy seemed to share the feeling and his tail began to wag excitedly. Lia's eyes were closed and her head was tilted back against the door. Alex took advantage of being unseen and took a moment to study the woman she was in love with.

She hadn't gotten around to changing and was wearing the same navy blue and white polka dot dress from earlier. Her hair was loose, the curls tossed by the wind. Alex felt a lump form in her throat. The idea of losing Lia was almost more than she could stand. The thought that Lia would get back together with the woman who'd treated her so badly made her sick to her stomach.

As if she'd sensed her approach, Lia opened her eyes and glanced over to where Alex was standing. "Hi."

"Hi." Alex closed the remaining distance between them.

"May I come in?"

"Of course." Lia stood and Alex reached around her to unlock the door. It stung that Lia hadn't simply let herself in, but she could see that the circumstances were less than ideal. She walked into the living room and sat on the couch, resisting the desire to pace.

Lia followed, sitting at the opposite end. "So, more than anything, I want to apologize."

Alex narrowed her eyes. "Apologize for what?"

"For the fact that you walked in on that, for the fact that she showed up at all, for the fact that I bailed on our plans so I could talk to her."

It was a start. "Okay. Why don't you tell me what happened?"

Lia took a deep breath. "She showed up completely unannounced, which was probably a tactic on her part. She talked about trying to move forward."

"So she was trying to get you back?" In this instance, Alex felt no satisfaction in being right.

"Yes, but it was more complicated than that. She wanted to talk about how things ended. That's why I agreed to sit down with her, to talk. When I left, there wasn't really any closure. It felt important to try to get it, even if it was after the fact."

Alex understood. She didn't like it, but she understood. "Did you get what you wanted?"

There was a long pause. "Yes."

"You don't sound sure."

"She played the money card, which I kind of expected."

"Based on what you've told me about her, that's not surprising." Was Lia susceptible to that? Was she tempted?

"She offered to buy me a condo."

"She did what?"

"Instead of a restaurant, she took me to this condo in the East End for dinner. I figured it was where she was staying. And then she told me it was for sale and she would buy it—for us, but mostly for me."

Alex was speechless. Condos in the East End rarely went for less than half a million dollars. Even though she owned the bakery, the mortgage was a special arrangement. She couldn't wrap her head around having that kind of money at her disposal.

"Can you believe it?"

"I can't." She tried to sound indignant, but there was definitely a layer of intimidation underneath. She could never offer Lia anything like that.

Lia shook her head. "Not that I was remotely tempted to get back together, but that really sealed the deal. Mergers and acquisitions—that's her specialty."

Alex hoped desperately that she meant it, not just being done with Dani, but being uninterested in that kind of person. As much as she hated to admit it, there could be a certain draw in that kind of money and power. "So now what?"

Lia thought for a moment. "Well, she's gone. At least I think she is. I walked out."

It was a huge relief to hear Lia say that. Alex nodded. "Good for you."

"I'm here, with you." Lia offered an uncertain smile.

Alex was still unsettled, but wanted to offer some reassurance. "That's very good."

"Thanks." Lia let out a shaky laugh. "I'm exhausted."

"How about we have something to eat and have a low-key night? We can start fresh in the morning." At this point, she felt like she could use that as much as Lia.

"That would be perfect."

Alex grilled a steak for them to share, made a salad. They ate with the television on, not talking. Lia took Murphy out while Alex did the dishes. The easiness, the routine of it should have been comforting. Instead, it just felt flat.

Lia was leaving something out. Alex didn't know what it was, or why, but it made her uneasy. When they went to bed, she lay awake. She thought Lia might be awake, too, but she didn't whisper her name. She didn't know what she would say anyway. Eventually, the sky outside the window began to lighten. The alarm sounded and she was still awake, no closer to answers than she'd been the night before.

CHAPTER THIRTY-SIX

L ia didn't know what to do. It was nearly a week after Dani had come and gone and she couldn't seem to quiet her mind. It kept replaying the conversation in the condo overlooking the water. Dani essentially offered her the option to be kept, and lavishly kept at that. Days later, she couldn't wrap her head around it.

Clearly, something in their decade-long relationship had given Dani the idea that she would consider such a proposition. The more Lia thought about it, the less she liked the possible reasons. As much as she valued her work and took it seriously, it was never a major factor in their household budget. Dani covered the mortgage and many of the bills, the fancy restaurants and the vacations. Lia never objected because they weren't things that she chose, or even necessarily wanted.

But still. She didn't object to them and often enjoyed them. She paid for her own car, the groceries because she did the shopping and cooking, and her own clothes, except for the designer label things Dani gave her as gifts. It seemed so paltry now. It was like she'd been kept all along. The idea was repugnant.

All that combined with Alex asking her to move in with her. She knew it wasn't fair, but she couldn't manage to separate the two. A little voice in the back of her mind taunted her that she'd merely go from being dependent on one woman to being dependent on another. In the moments she was able to quiet that voice, to see that Alex and Dani were nothing alike, she was overcome with other doubts. The most insidious was that Alex pitied her, offering her a place to stay because she had nowhere else to go. It was followed closely by the fear that Alex would tire of her, as Dani had. If that happened, she'd be worse off than she was now.

She tried meditating, she talked to Sally, she made lists. It was useless. She couldn't shake the churning in her stomach and the feeling that she was on the verge of making a terrible mistake. It didn't help matters that she was running out of time. She had to vacate her apartment in five days.

On a Tuesday morning, she arrived home from spending another tense and restless night at Alex's and began packing. In four hours, she filled the same boxes and suitcases she'd unpacked nearly six months before. She arranged them in her car before cleaning out the refrigerator and pantry, making sure everything was left as she'd found it. She took down the two photographs from the wall, her first purchases in Provincetown that she'd come to think of as a symbol of her independence.

When she was done, Lia checked her watch. It was quarter to three. She'd be able to catch Alex just as the café was closing. There was no point in putting off the inevitable.

On the short walk, she thought about the fact that it would be the last time she did so. Even if things somehow managed to work out, she would never again call the little apartment on Vine home. She'd come to escape and had found so much more than she bargained for. Feeling her resolve start to weaken, Lia dug her fingernails into the palms of her hands. When she arrived at the café, she would do her best to explain and hopefully Alex would understand.

Alex flipped the sign to "Closed." Five days ago, she'd been doing the exact same thing when a tall, beautiful woman walked in the door and changed everything. Five days since Lia had been herself.

As far as she was concerned, Lia's ex showing up and offering to buy her a condo was almost laughable. Yet, Lia remained edgy and quiet. She didn't talk about Dani, nor did she bring up Alex's proposal that they move in together. She offered half-smiles and repeatedly had to be pulled back into conversations.

With each passing day, Alex became increasingly worried that Lia had more unresolved feelings for her ex than she admitted, maybe even to herself. Alex wanted to press the issue, but feared she might inadvertently pick a fight. One minute she was angry with Lia for throwing a wrench into what had been the best and easiest relationship she'd ever had. The next, she wanted to kick herself for letting down her defenses, for caring so much in the first place.

Lia hadn't even come in that day, which made her surly and a little paranoid. She contemplated showing up on Lia's doorstep and refusing to leave until Lia put her out of her misery one way or the other. Of course, that could open the floodgate on a whole different kind of misery. She tried not to think of that as an option.

When Lia showed up, looking pale and tired, Alex knew something was wrong. Barely pausing to take a breath, Lia launched into a speech about needing to get away, take some time, sort out her feelings. When she was done, Alex gaped at her. "You're leaving? Leaving leaving? I don't understand."

"I need to think, and I can't seem to do it here. I need to go somewhere neutral for a little while and figure everything out."

"But you've cleaned out your apartment. You're taking everything with you."

"I have to move out in a few days anyway. It's purely logistical."

Even if what she said made sense, the only message getting through to Alex's brain was that Lia was leaving. A little voice in her head added that it was for good. "You're running away."

"It's not running. I'm clearing my head."

It was a feeble excuse, and Lia had to know how unconvincing she sounded. Maybe she didn't care. The anger and frustration of the last few days were replaced by terror. Alex contemplated begging, as well as stealing Lia's keys. It was a level of desperation she had never felt. Before she could stop herself, the ugliness of it came tumbling out.

"I'm not asking you to marry me. I'm not even asking you to buy a house with me. You're about to become homeless. I love you and I want you to stick around. Is that really so shocking? Or so difficult?" Alex regretted the words the moment she said them. Lia looked like she'd been slapped. "I'm sorry. I didn't mean to say it like that."

"I just can't. I'm not ready. I need to think. I need to sort everything out."

Hearing the same phrase did nothing to make it sound any better. Panic licked at her and it took all of her self-control to keep her voice calm. "Are you going back to New York?"

Lia squared her shoulders. "No."

She wasn't convinced. "Where then? Where are you going to go?"

"Louisiana."

To Alex, it felt a world away. As wretched as it was, as much as she wanted to do something about it, she knew in her gut that it was beyond her control. "I wish you'd reconsider."

"I know. I wish it was different, too. I have to do this."

"Do you have to leave right now?"

"If I don't, I'm afraid I might not ever."

"Would that really be so bad?" As hard as she tried, Alex couldn't keep the hitch out of her voice.

Lia offered a sad smile. "I'll be in touch, I promise."

She hurried out without looking back. Alex went through her cleaning routine in a fog. Over and over, she wondered if she'd somehow imagined the whole thing, that it was some sort of bad dream and Lia would be waiting for her at her usual table, or upstairs on the sofa. Reality was always there, however, like a crushing weight on her lungs. Lia wasn't waiting for her; she was gone.

She made her way upstairs and found Murphy with his tail wagging, blissfully ignorant of the fact that his second favorite human wasn't coming over later, or tomorrow, or the day after that. She changed her clothes and picked up his leash. They headed straight for the beach and she spent the next hour trying to run off the hurt and anger churning through her.

Rather than clearing her mind, she only managed to spin scenarios that became more and more lurid. When she finally sat down on the warm sand, Alex was convinced that Lia had decided to return to Dani, that she was trying to escape without having a big fight. The logical part of her knew that was unlikely, but it didn't keep her brain from generating images of Lia in Dani's arms, or worse.

CHAPTER THIRTY-SEVEN

When Lia crossed from Connecticut into New York, she veered north slightly toward White Plains and the Tappan Zee Bridge. She'd easily make up the additional miles by avoiding the worst of New York City traffic. She also wanted to avoid Manhattan altogether. She wasn't tempted to stop there, but she felt the need to keep as much distance as possible.

She spent one night in Pennsylvania, another in Tennessee. Her body was exhausted enough to sleep, but it was fitful and filled with strange dreams. She fought the urge to text Alex. There was nothing useful to say and a casual greeting seemed cruel to them both.

She arrived at Sally's house exhausted. Every muscle in her body ached from the hours spent sitting in the same position. Her stomach was both empty and unsettled. She'd been subsisting primarily on crackers and Diet Coke for the better part of three days. Although she'd not wanted anything else, it was starting to catch up with her.

With only the most basic of questions, Sally welcomed her with open arms. She had Logan bunk with Charlie and set Lia up in his room. Lia spent the weekend playing with the boys and catching up with Will, whom she hadn't seen in over a year. Lia couldn't forget why she was there, but she slept better and had moments of feeling almost like herself. Always looming, though, were thoughts of Alex and the question of what she was going to do.

On the morning of her third day at Sally's, Sally put her sons on the bus and called in to work. She didn't tell Lia it was an intervention, but Lia knew. Subtlety wasn't really Sally's thing. Once the house was clear, she made breakfast and a big pot of coffee. "Let's sit out on the patio."

Although only April, the temperature was already pushing eighty and the humidity made everything feel damp. Lia realized just how much she'd lost her tolerance for Southern weather. She sipped her coffee and looked over at her friend, who looked as cool as a tall glass of iced sweet tea. Sally was one of those women who didn't sweat; she glistened.

After they ate, Sally set aside their plates and leaned forward on the glass-top table. "What are you doing?"

If it was anyone but Sally, she might have played dumb and given a literal answer. Since it was Sally, she slumped back in her chair and told the truth. "I'm getting away. I'm giving myself some space so I can figure everything out. Where I can figure myself out."

"It seems to me like you've figured yourself out just fine."

Lia huffed. She'd filled Sally in on the Dani debacle and the tense, restless days that followed. "Have I? It feels like I've just allowed myself to get swept up in something that feels good. I don't know if I can trust it and I sure as hell can't control it."

"And?"

"And I feel like, with Dani, I was sort of kept." It still disgusted her to think about it. "I really don't want to rid myself of that only to be beholden to Alex."

Sally sighed. "You realize those two things and those two people have absolutely nothing to do with one another."

Lia cringed. The women were most definitely different. The situations still bore some eerie similarities. "Yes?"

"And that they were asking you for completely different things."

"Were they? Both involve me relying on another woman for the roof over my head."

Sally shook her head. "I get that you have a penchant for being down on yourself. I hate it, but I get it. Do you really think so little of Alex?"

She hadn't thought about it that way. In her angst, it was so easy to focus on everything wrong with herself, all the reasons she shouldn't—couldn't—trust herself. Alex had laid her heart on the table, along with the keys to her home. All she'd asked Lia to do was take them. How was it Sally always knew the right button to push? "Well, fuck."

"Mmm hmm. Exactly. Are you in love with her?"

She didn't hesitate in her answer, didn't need to. "Yes."

"Do you believe she is in love with you?"

"I do." She did. Whatever she was afraid of, whatever horrible scenarios her brain invented, she believed that Alex loved her. And that love felt more genuine than what she'd ever had with Dani or anyone else.

"Well, I think you have your answer."

Could it really be as easy as that? Lia rolled her eyes. She did over think everything. It was one of her most consistent and annoying habits. "So now what do I do?"

Sally folded her arms. "She isn't going to chase you. You're not a possession to her, something to be retrieved. She laid her cards on the table, went all in. You have to decide what to do with it."

"Since when do you use poker metaphors?"

Sally glared at her, clearly unamused. "Since when do you not go after what you want?"

The question hung between them. Sally held her gaze. Lia thought about being eight and wanting to play baseball with her brothers. She settled for the "Lassie League" softball team, but she insisted on practicing with her brothers. Staying out with them long after the street lights came on, she learned how to run harder and throw further than any of the other girls. She thought about deciding to go away for college. She submitted applications and entered scholarship competitions and became the first member of her family, as well as the only girl in her class at Sacred Heart, to attend school outside of the southeast. She used to pride herself on being fearless.

When had that gone away? She realized with distaste that it was one more casualty of her time with Dani. Leave it to Sally to bring her to her senses. She looked at her friend, a woman who'd loved her and stood by her better than any sister she could have ever wanted. She felt her eyes fill up with tears. She blinked them away and lifted her chin, just as Sally had encouraged her to do when girls at school called her "dyke" and "lezzy."

"Since too long."

Sally punched her on the arm affectionately. "That's my girl. So, what are you going to do about it?"

She thought about the three miserable days it took her to drive to Louisiana. Although driving back would take the same amount of time, at least she wouldn't have the discomfort of riding the whole way with her tail between her legs. She smiled. "I guess I'll get back in my car."

"Ha. Aren't you glad you didn't unpack?"

She thought about the boxes and suitcases filling her car. Aside from a single duffel bag of clothes and toiletries, she'd left everything where she'd put it when she left Provincetown. What had been an act of avoidance turned out to be a saving grace. "I most certainly am."

With the decision made, Lia was tempted to get on the road right then and there. She relented, however, and spent the rest of the afternoon with Sally, then drove to Vacherie and had supper with her parents. She spent the night in her childhood bedroom, allowing herself to feel comforted, rather than smothered, by it.

Her alarm was set for six, but Lia woke at five. She'd slept well, felt rested and ready. She drove out of her parents' driveway and began the long journey northeast just as the sun began peeking over the horizon.

CHAPTER THIRTY-EIGHT

When Lia took the exit ramp for the Sagamore Bridge, traffic was at a near standstill. She'd stopped in Connecticut for a few hours of sleep so she wouldn't be a danger to herself or others. The unfortunate side effect was that she approached Cape Cod at noon on a beautiful spring Saturday. The last ninety miles of her journey would likely take hours.

Lia took a deep breath and tried not to panic. She would see Alex; she would make her case and offer her heart. The rest would be up to Alex. Considering she'd been gone for over a week, a few hours would unlikely make a difference one way or the other.

It took her an hour to get over the bridge, but once on the Cape, traffic eased noticeably. If all went well and Provincetown became her home, she would have to become strategic in planning any ventures onto the mainland. Lia allowed herself to imagine what it would be like to settle in the town she'd grown to love. She'd enjoy the high season, and respect the prosperity it brought that sustained life throughout the rest of the year. Likely, though, she'd always be partial to the winter months when the locals hunkered down and enjoyed each other and the quiet.

Realizing she was getting ahead of herself, Lia brought her attention back to her surroundings. Although she'd been mindful of the road and the vehicles around her, she'd stopped paying attention to signs and mile markers. She was pleasantly surprised to find herself almost to Wellfleet.

Excitement gave way to anxiety as she registered the possibility that the next few hours might determine not only her future with Alex, but also her connection to Provincetown. As much as she loved it, the thought of living there without Alex in her life was something she couldn't even contemplate. Even if she could find a way to afford it, which she probably couldn't, her heart would break all over again every day she wasn't with Alex.

Traffic slowed again as she made her way into town. Bradford Street was bumper-to-bumper cars, all trying to avoid the sea of pedestrians on Commercial. Realizing she wouldn't find street parking anywhere near the bakery, Lia pulled into a municipal lot a few blocks away.

She checked her reflection in the rear-view mirror. Even with the makeup she'd put on, there were noticeable dark circles under her eyes. Her hair was still protesting its time in Louisiana and was more frizz than curl. Even pulling it back into a twist hadn't managed to tame it entirely. Although part of her wanted to check into a hotel and freshen up, she couldn't bear to put this off any longer.

Lia climbed out of her car and stretched her stiff muscles. She smoothed the fabric of her dress, grateful that it wasn't too terribly wrinkled. She locked her car and walked in the direction of The Flour Pot.

❖

Alex peeked out of the kitchen. The flow of customers was steady. She was glad she'd brought on some of her seasonal help early. In addition to keeping the front of house running smoothly, it allowed her to spend most of her time in the back.

She was glad to spend most of her time baking. Working with her hands was good for her mind and her spirit. It also required enough physical exertion that she was able to tumble into bed and fall asleep, despite the emptiness next to her. There was the added relief of being able to avoid glancing over at Lia's table, only to find it empty or occupied by strangers, or looking at the door every time it opened, hoping to see Lia walk through.

Alex was certain those feelings, those tendencies, would fade over time. It had been only a week, so it was natural that everything was still so fresh. She'd broken her policy against falling in love, but it wasn't the end of the world. Time, along with the company of some pretty and uncomplicated women, would heal all wounds. At least, that was what she kept telling herself.

Annoyed that she was giving herself yet another pep talk, Alex squared her shoulders and went back to work. Since Lia's departure, she'd decided to take up chocolate work again. In addition to having some pretty additions to the display case, the work required a fairly intense level of concentration. Tempering was a precise task and it kept her mind from other things.

As she began the process of dipping the truffles she'd rolled the night before, Alex's mind began to wander. She imagined having a bowl of perfectly tempered chocolate and Lia naked in her bed. She would drizzle the warm liquid over Lia's belly, her breasts. She would slowly lick the chocolate from Lia's nipples, then work her way down. Lia's scent would mingle with the aroma of the chocolate. Alex imagined having the tastes mingling in her mouth.

Jeff pushed through the swinging door, snapping Alex back to reality. She realized that she was gripping the edge of the table, practically panting with want. It took a fair amount of restraint not to throw the bowl of chocolate across the room.

"Whoa, Chef. You okay?"

Alex shook her head to chase away the images that had invaded her mind. "Yeah, sorry. I was lost in thought for a moment."

"I didn't mean to interrupt you." Jeff seemed unusually hesitant. "There's, uh, someone here to see you."

Alex scowled. She couldn't think of anyone she wanted to see, much less talk to. "Okay. Give me a minute to clean up and I'll be out. Who is it?"

The question was posed to a swinging door. Alex shook her head, stripped off her gloves, and washed her hands. She set her chocolate on a heating pad to stay warm and headed out to see who was asking for her in the middle of the lunch rush.

She looked around. There were plenty of familiar faces, but none of them were looking at her expectantly. She was about to holler for Jeff when she turned and saw Lia standing down at the end of the bar with her hands clasped and a look of nervous anticipation on her face.

It took everything she had not to close the distance between them and sweep Lia into a long and lingering kiss. Instead, she walked toward her slowly. Feelings of hurt and of hope warred for dominance. "Lia."

"I'm sorry to show up in the middle of the afternoon rush. Between the drive and the traffic, my timing is all off."

"Did you drive all the way to Louisiana? And back?"

Lia blushed. It seemed downright daft when Alex said it out loud. "I did."

"Let's go outside so we can talk."

Alex was willing to talk. That was encouraging. Lia nodded, allowing Alex to lead the way through the kitchen and out back. Once they were outside, essentially in Alex's backyard, Alex leaned against the back of one of a pair of Adirondack chairs. It was obvious she was waiting for Lia to do the talking.

Lia took a deep breath. This was it. Alex was looking at her so intently, it was impossible to concentrate. She opened her mouth and the entire speech she'd prepared during her twenty plus hours in the car vanished. Undeterred, she launched in.

"I'm sorry. I was scared and I was stupid and I hurt you. I cannot express how sorry I am for that."

"Okay."

"Okay." Breathe. "Second, Dani is nothing to me. Everything that happened has nothing to do with me wanting to be with her. I let her manipulate me. I let her talk me into doubting myself, doubting you. She knows every button to push, and when there is something she wants, she doesn't give a fuck about the collateral damage of pushing them. That ability comes from the length of our relationship and my own insecurities, not my feelings for her, or my feelings for you, for that matter."

"Okay."

"Okay." Lia paused, wondering if literally flinging herself at Alex's feet would be moving or pathetic. She looked at Alex, whose expression gave nothing away.

"Okay. Is there a third?"

Lia realized suddenly that, in her desperation to apologize and explain, she'd neglected the most important part. "Yes, there is a third. Third, I love you. I am completely, totally, one hundred percent, over-the-moon in love with you. I have been, I think, since those first afternoons in the café when you came to my table and we talked. I'd convinced myself I had no business falling in love, so I convinced myself I wasn't. Or at least I tried to."

Lia stepped forward and took Alex's hands in her own. "I love you Alex McKinnon. I love you and I want to be with you." She freed one hand to swipe away a tear. She grasped the hand again, adding, "If you'll have me."

It was, essentially, the moment Alex had fantasized about since Lia left. It was the moment she'd begun to convince herself wasn't going to happen. As much as she wanted it, she needed more. She needed to understand. "So what changed your mind? Why did you come back?"

Lia looked away for a second, then replied sheepishly. "Sally convinced me I was…I believe her phrase of choice was lily-livered ninny."

Alex raised an eyebrow.

"She's got kids. She's gotten rather creative in her use of non-cursing insults."

"Ah." Alex's heart did a little flip inside her chest. Still, maybe she did want Lia to squirm a bit. "It took a trip to Louisiana and a week of nagging to convince you?"

Lia cleared her throat. "No. No, it did not. It took me three days to get to Louisiana, two more to sulk. She effectively convinced me I was an idiot in a single morning. I spent one night with my parents and then got back on the road."

"Well, when you put it that way."

"Look, Alex, I know I'm probably the last person you feel like you can believe right now. I'm not asking to just pick up where we left off. I'm asking for a chance, and we can go as slow as—"

Alex cut her off. "Where are your things?"

"My things?"

"You moved out of your apartment. Where did you put all your stuff?"

The abrupt shift left Lia confused. Alex could see it in her eyes. Rather than offering any clarification, she crossed her arms and waited.

Eventually, Lia half-shrugged. "Everything's still in my car."

"There's a closet and a dresser and half a bookcase cleared out for you upstairs. That should hold most of it for now."

Alex watched realization dawn on Lia's face. It was quickly followed by a look of guilt. "You did that for me?"

"I did, the day I asked you to move in. I guess I was being optimistic."

Lia cringed. "I'm so sorry I freaked out and ran away."

Alex looked at the woman who'd stolen her heart. She was here, in the flesh. Alex reveled in the incredible lightness that filled her chest. She happily shoved aside all of the fears and worries that it might be over, that she might have to figure out a life without Lia. Then she smiled. "I considered posting a want ad for a lesbian with a U-Haul, but I didn't have the heart."

Lia thrilled at the gleam in Alex's eye. She allowed herself a glimmer of hope before shaking her head. "I really fucked everything up, didn't I?"

Alex took Lia's face in her hands. "Yes, but you're fixing it now. And, it just so happens that I'm still madly in love with you."

Alex leaned in and kissed her. Lia felt her knees go weak and her skin grow warm. Why she ever considered giving this up seemed suddenly absurd. "I can't tell you how happy I am to hear that."

"Good. Now it's your turn to listen. First, don't ever run away again. If we have a problem, we work through it. Together."

Lia smiled, still feeling a little sheepish. "Okay."

"Second. I mean it. Don't ever ever do that again."

"Okay."

"Okay." Alex squeezed her.

Lia leaned back. "Okay. Is there a third?"

Alex kissed her again. "Yeah, there's a third. Welcome home."

About the Author

Aurora Rey grew up in a small town in south Louisiana, daydreaming about New England. She keeps a special place in her heart for the South, especially the food and the ways women are raised to be strong, even if they're taught not to show it. After a brief dalliance with biochemistry, she completed both a B.A. and an M.A. in English.

When she's not writing or at her day job in higher education, she moonlights as a baker and is slightly addicted to Pinterest. She loves to cook and dreams of a big farmhouse in the country with a garden and some goats. She lives in Ithaca, New York, with her partner and two dogs.

Aurora can be contacted at aurorareywrites@gmail.com
Website: www.aurorarey.com

Books Available from Bold Strokes Books

Illicit Artifacts by Stevie Mikayne. Her foster mother's death cracked open a secret world Jil never wanted to see…and now she has to pick up the stolen pieces. (978-1-62639-4-728)

Pathfinder by Gun Brooke. Heading for their new homeworld, Exodus's chief engineer Adina Vantressa and nurse Briar Lindemay carry game-changing secrets that may well cause them to lose everything when disaster strikes. (978-1-62639-4-445)

Prescription for Love by Radclyffe. Dr. Flannery Rivers finds herself attracted to the new ER chief, city girl Abigail Remy, and the incendiary mix of city and country, fire and ice, tradition and change is combustible. (978-1-62639-5-701)

Ready or Not by Melissa Brayden. Uptight Mallory Spencer finds relinquishing control to bartender Hope Sanders too tall an order in fast-paced New York City. (978-1-62639-4-438)

Summer Passion by MJ Williamz. Women loving women is forbidden in 1946 Hollywood, yet Jean and Maggie strive to keep their love alive and away from prying eyes. (978-1-62639-5-404)

The Princess and the Prix by Nell Stark. "Ugly duckling" Princess Alix of Monaco was resigned to loneliness until she met racecar driver Thalia d'Angelis. (978-1-62639-4-742)

Winter's Harbor by Aurora Rey. Lia Brooks isn't looking for love in Provincetown, but when she discovers chocolate croissants and pastry chef Alex McKinnon, her winter retreat quickly starts heating up. (978-1-62639-4-988)

The Time Before Now by Missouri Vaun. Vivian flees a disastrous affair, embarking on an epic, transformative journey to escape her past, until destiny introduces her to Ida, who helps her rediscover trust, love, and hope. (978-1-62639-446-9)

Twisted Whispers by Sheri Lewis Wohl. Betrayal, lies, and secrets—whispers of a friend lost to darkness. Can a reluctant psychic set things right or will an evil soul destroy those she loves? (978-1-62639-439-1)

The Courage to Try by C.A. Popovich. Finding love is worth getting past the fear of trying. (978-1-62639-528-2)

Break Point by Yolanda Wallace. In a world readying for war, can love find a way? (978-1-62639-568-8)

Countdown by Julie Cannon. Can two strong-willed, powerful women overcome their differences to save the lives of seven others and begin a life they never imagined together? (978-1-62639-471-1)

Keep Hold by Michelle Grubb. Claire knew some things should be left alone and some rules should never be broken, but the most forbidden, well, they are the most tempting. (978-1-62639-502-2)

Deadly Medicine by Jaime Maddox. Dr. Ward Thrasher's life is in turmoil. Her partner Jess left her, and her job puts her in the path of a murderous physician who has Jess in his sights. (978-1-62639-424-7)

New Beginnings by KC Richardson. Can the connection and attraction between Jordan Roberts and Kirsten Murphy be enough for Jordan to trust Kirsten with her heart? (978-1-62639-450-6)

Officer Down by Erin Dutton. Can two women who've made careers out of being there for others in crisis find the strength to need each other? (978-1-62639-423-0)

Reasonable Doubt by Carsen Taite. Just when Sarah and Ellery think they've left dangerous careers behind, a new case sets them—and their hearts—on a collision course. (978-1-62639-442-1)

Tarnished Gold by Ann Aptaker. Cantor Gold must outsmart the Law, outrun New York's dockside gangsters, outplay a shady art dealer, his lover, and a beautiful curator, and stay out of a killer's gun sights. (978-1-62639-426-1)

The Renegade by Amy Dunne. Post-apocalyptic survivors Alex and Evelyn secretly find love while held captive by a deranged cult, but when their relationship is discovered, they must fight for their freedom—or die trying. (978-1-62639-427-8)

Thrall by Barbara Ann Wright. Four women in a warrior society must work together to lift an insidious curse while caught between their own desires, the will of their peoples, and an ancient evil. (978-1-62639-437-7)

White Horse in Winter by Franci McMahon. Love between two women collides with the inner poison of a closeted horse trainer in the green hills of Vermont. (978-1-62639-429-2)

Autumn Spring by Shelley Thrasher. Can Bree and Linda, two women in the autumn of their lives, put their hearts first and find the love they've never dared seize? (978-1-62639-365-3)

The Chameleon's Tale by Andrea Bramhall. Two old friends must work through a web of lies and deceit to find themselves again, but in the search they discover far more than they ever went looking for. (978-1-62639-363-9)

Side Effects by VK Powell. Detective Jordan Bishop and Dr. Neela Sahjani must decide if it's easier to trust someone with your heart or your life as they face threatening protestors, corrupt politicians, and their increasing attraction. (978-1-62639-364-6)

Warm November by Kathleen Knowles. What do you do if the one woman you want is the only one you can't have? (978-1-62639-366-0)

In Every Cloud by Tina Michele. When Bree finally leaves her shattered life behind, is she strong enough to salvage the remaining pieces of her heart and find the place where it truly fits? (978-1-62639-413-1)

Rise of the Gorgon by Tanai Walker. When independent Internet journalist Elle Pharell goes to Kuwait to investigate a veteran's mysterious suicide, she hires Cassandra Hunt, an interpreter with a covert agenda. (978-1-62639-367-7)

Crossed by Meredith Doench. Agent Luce Hansen returns home to catch a killer and risks everything to revisit the unsolved murder of her first girlfriend and confront the demons of her youth. (978-1-62639-361-5)

Making a Comeback by Julie Blair. Music and love take center stage when jazz pianist Liz Randall tries to make a comeback with the help of her reclusive, blind neighbor, Jac Winters. (978-1-62639-357-8)

Soul Unique by Gun Brooke. Self-proclaimed cynic Greer Landon falls for Hayden Rowe's paintings and the young woman shortly after, but will Hayden, who lives with Asperger syndrome, trust her and reciprocate her feelings? (978-1-62639-358-5)

The Price of Honor by Radclyffe. Honor and duty are not always black and white—and when self-styled patriots take up arms against the government, the price of honor may be a life. (978-1-62639-359-2)

Mounting Evidence by Karis Walsh. Lieutenant Abigail Hargrove and her mounted police unit need to solve a murder and protect wetland biologist Kira Lovell during the Washington State Fair. (978-1-62639-343-1)

Threads of the Heart by Jeannie Levig. Maggie and Addison Rae-McInnis share a love and a life, but are the threads that bind them together strong enough to withstand Addison's restlessness and the seductive Victoria Fontaine? (978-1-62639-410-0)

Sheltered Love by MJ Williamz. Boone Fairway and Grey Dawson—two women touched by abuse—overcome their pasts to find happiness in each other. (978-1-62639-362-2)

Death's Doorway by Crin Claxton. Helping the dead can be deadly: Tony may be listening to the dead, but she needs to learn to listen to the living. (978-1-62639-354-7)

Searching for Celia by Elizabeth Ridley. As American spy novelist Dayle Salvesen investigates the mysterious disappearance of her ex-lover, Celia, in London, she begins questioning how well she knew Celia—and how well she knows herself. (978-1-62639-356-1).

Hardwired by C.P. Rowlands. Award-winning teacher Clary Stone and Leefe Ellis, manager of the homeless shelter for small children, stand together in a part of Clary's hometown that she never knew existed. (978-1-62639-351-6)

The Muse by Meghan O'Brien. Erotica author Kate McMannis struggles with writer's block until a gorgeous muse entices her into a world of fantasy sex and inadvertent romance. (978-1-62639-223-6)

No Good Reason by Cari Hunter. A violent kidnapping in a Peak District village pushes Detective Sanne Jensen and lifelong friend Dr. Meg Fielding closer, just as it threatens to tear everything apart. (978-1-62639-352-3)

The 45th Parallel by Lisa Girolami. Burying her mother isn't the worst thing that can happen to Val Montague when she returns to the woodsy but peculiar town of Hemlock, Oregon. (978-1-62639-342-4)

Romance by the Book by Jo Victor. If Cam didn't keep disrupting her life, maybe Alex could uncover the secret of a century-old love story, and solve the greatest mystery of all—her own heart. (978-1-62639-353-0)

A Royal Romance by Jenny Frame. In a country where class still divides, can love topple the last social taboo and allow Queen Georgina and Beatrice Elliot, a working-class girl, their happy ever after? (978-1-62639-360-8)

Bouncing by Jaime Maddox. Basketball coach Alex Dalton has been bouncing from woman to woman because no one ever held her interest, until she meets her new assistant, Britain Dodge. (978-1-62639-344-8)

All Things Rise by Missouri Vaun. Cole rescues a striking pilot who crash-lands near her family's farm, setting in motion a chain of events that will forever alter the course of her life. (978-1-62639-346-2)

CPSIA information can be obtained
at www.ICGtesting.com
Printed in the USA
JSHW012123021019
1749JS00001B/10